M000005050

ALSO BY MARY TANNEN

Second Sight

Juveniles

The Wizard Children of Finn

The Lost Legend of Finn

Huntley Nutley and the Missing Link

AFTER ROY

AFTER ROY

Mary Tannen

ALFRED A. KNOPF

NEW YORK

1989

THIS IS A BORZOI BOOK
PUBLISHED BY ALFRED A. KNOPF, INC.

Published in the United States by Alfred A. Knopf, Inc.,
New York, and simultaneously in Canada by Random
House of Canada Limited, Toronto. Distributed by Random
House, Inc., New York.

Library of Congress Cataloging-in-Publication Data
Tannen, Mary.
After Roy / by Mary Tannen.—1st ed.
p. cm.
ISBN 0-394-58024-9
I. Title.
PS3570.A54A69   1989
813′.54—dc20   89-45281
CIP

Manufactured in the United States of America
First Edition

To Nancy and Michael for making the journey

AFTER ROY

1

Hilda drops clumsily out of an acacia tree, recovers her balance, and skitters across the clearing, hair bristling, lips drawn back, teeth a white scar of warning on a black face. She leaps onto the concrete ledge, Maggie's narrow porch. She signs too fast. If she could speak it would be slurred into one word.

"HurryMaggieopenhurry."

"What? What is it?" Maggie's lips mimic Hilda's grin of fear.

"Maggiehurryopenplease." Hilda jiggles the latch, whimpers, standing on two legs, clutching at the grid of heavy steel wire, Maggie's fourth wall. Here the human lives in a cage and the chimpanzees roam free.

Hilda looks all right, that is, no wounds or broken limbs, although as always she's a fairly pathetic sight, bald in patches from a fungus cured years ago where the hair never grew back. She's perfectly healthy yet looks sickly, demoralized, like a prisoner in an internment camp.

"Maggie please."

"What is it? What?"

What frightened her? The clearing looks innocent, empty, the grass clipped, the paths that lead nowhere raked just yesterday by Emanuel who complains that it's too much lawn for just one house, one woman. Why not let it grow up around where the dining hall used to be, the other houses? Why keep the paths when they don't go anywhere except to concrete slabs already broken up and grown over? But unclipped grass turns to bush. She wouldn't be able to get to the forest except with a machete. The effort would sap her energy. The disorder would depress her. She needs it this way, the forest coming to the edge of the grass, like a dark wall around a park.

"Hurry open."

Maggie forces herself to sit down again at the table, keeping the BB gun beside her just in case. She makes clucking noises to calm Hilda. Anything could have frightened her. She would panic as much over a dead mouse as a band of poachers.

"Hoo-ah-hoo-ah-hoo-ah-hoo-hoo!" Hilda's mobile lips push forward in an O. Her rib cage pumps like a bellows.

Papers on the table stir. There it is, rain, coming from the west, sounding more like a freight train than a storm, a squadron of helicopters, some ominous machine hovering unseen above the trees. Monkeys scream, desperately clutching to perches high in branches that writhe and crack beneath them.

Maggie joins in Hilda's storm song. G.P. answers from the forest. If the chimps are anywhere near, they'll come running. They hate rain, will never get used to being out in it, which is one reason Maggie had the other buildings torn down. Every time it rained they would break into one of them, sleep there, use it for shelter. It was impossible to keep repairing and cleaning the houses. The university doesn't realize what the station would look like after a year of no maintenance. If it hadn't been chimps squatting in the houses, it would have been locals, just as bad. And yet the university blames Maggie for not taking care of the place, when all she's had to work with are the Friends of Hilda funds. The university doesn't understand how rapidly things deteriorate in the tropics.

The station was built fifteen years ago, but if measured in terms of rate of decay, it's now ancient history. An archeologist would have trouble reconstructing it from the present ruins. If Maggie didn't have photographs, she wouldn't remember it herself, the graceful arrangement of white stucco houses, the thatched, open-sided dining pavilion, which had room for thirty researchers to dine and afterward lounge on sturdy mission-style couches and chairs. There were end tables and reading lamps kept glowing until ten p.m. by a gasoline-powered generator. Maggie still has light fixtures in her house but the generator broke down years ago.

She has running water. She and Emanuel have managed to keep the pipes to the house repaired by cannibalizing the rest of the system. It's gravity fed, one of the few concessions to reality the architects of the station made. The rest of the design was completely impractical, with no provision made for catastrophic changes in government or prolonged shortages of materials. The architects had not taken Africa into account.

She regrets that the ornamental trees and shrubs had to go, but there was no way to prevent it. The oleander bushes were poisonous. She had to dig them out before the chimps started eating them. They quickly destroyed the rest. Now termite bells stand like tombstones marking where trees once stood.

The rain comes all at once, obliterating the yard. Katie and the little ones burst through. G.P. appears among them, stamping, slapping the ground with his hands, charging, knocking Biff onto his back, barreling onto the porch. He makes a screaming spread-eagle leap onto the grid. Maggie notes that his scrotum has grown since she's had this intimate a look at him. G.P. slams the door hinge with the heel of his palm. He kicks the latch.

Maggie bends over her papers. Hilda crouches down, her back to G.P. He came to them from a Belgian circus—his full name is Georges Pompidou—where he was a star act until he bit someone in the face. The circus was going to have G.P. destroyed but his trainer read a translation of Maggie's first *Science America* piece in *Journée* and offered to send the chimp to her. Maggie didn't really want him but she knew the group needed a young male who could develop into a leader to defend them against wild chimps.

So far G.P. isn't showing much leadership ability. He bullies the little ones and is sneaky around Maggie and Hilda. Soon he'll be able to father a child but Hilda refuses to let him practice on her. Who can blame her? His eyes are too close-set. His hair parts in the middle, low on his forehead, so he looks like he's wearing a bad wig. "I've given Hilda a clown for a lover," she wrote to Richard. "You're anthropomorphizing," he wrote back.

G.P. grunts and slides to the floor. He finds a small stick and begins quietly working on the lower hinge. If he were ever to get hold of a screwdriver she'd be in trouble.

He stops to glance over his shoulder at Danny, who is running toward the house, turning his pale face nervously from side to side. He nearly collides with the other three. He fakes a charge but Katie stands her ground. Although they're the same age, Katie is sturdier. Danny backs off and scampers past. He half hides behind G.P., who tolerates him better than anyone else, Maggie included. Anita, Maggie's editor at *Science America*, sent Danny from the States. No one knows his early history, only that he was raised in a laboratory and was used to test hepatitis B vaccine. Like Katie, he still has the white tail tuft and pale face of a juvenile.

Katie clambers onto the porch and reaches to give Poppy a hand up. She is the one who should be the dominant chimp because she is the least corrupted by human contact. Raised in the wild until she was three, she was captured by poachers and confiscated at the border, then turned over to Maggie for rehabilitation. But Katie is too young to be accepted as leader by anyone but Poppy and Biff.

For the present, Maggie is the leader of this band of chimps. On good days she sees herself as someone conducting a valuable experiment, trying to discover how tame chimps can be rehabilitated to the wild. On bad days she thinks she's thrown away her life to squat in the rain forest with a bunch of chimpanzee misfits. On bad days she looks around the deserted station and thinks, This wasn't the plan.

The plan was to free Hilda. Practically from birth, Hilda had been participating in a language-learning experiment at the university. She had been raised as a human child, in a house with toys, books, TV. The object was to see if a chimpanzee brought up in a human environment would learn language more easily, more rapidly, than a chimp kept in a cage. She did. Hilda became the star of the language-learning chimps. She went on CBS and NBC, was written up in *Time*.

When Maggie first went to work as her trainer, teacher, babysitter, Hilda had an official vocabulary of one hundred and fifty words but she knew more than that. And her vocabulary was inventive. An onion was "cry-food." Maggie became her "heart-friend."

Maggie applied for the job because she needed to finance her studies in psychology at the university. She had always gotten along well with animals and she thought working with a chimp might be fun.

Townsend introduced them. When he opened the door to Hilda's playroom, Maggie saw a chimpanzee dressed in jeans, a flannel shirt, and, incongruously, a dog collar, sitting on the floor watching TV. Hilda ran to Townsend and hugged him. (She called him Daddy and gave him hugs, this man who later would try to sell her to a lab, but Hilda carries no grudge.) The trainer on duty moved in with a cattle prod in case Hilda decided she didn't like Maggie.

Maggie squatted beside the chimp, as if she were greeting a child. But Hilda was no child. She laid a hand on Maggie's shoulder, her deep-set eyes fixed on Maggie with a searching look like a wise old woman who had something to say that went beyond the one hundred and fifty words she had been taught, that went beyond all words.

Townsend said Hilda didn't usually take to strangers like that. Strangers? Maggie felt they'd known each other forever.

Those were happy times, the eighteen months Maggie spent with Hilda, safe in Hilda's house near the university campus. They talked. Maggie was responsible for adding fifty-three words to Hilda's vocabulary, more than any other trainer had been able to teach her, including Townsend. Maggie carefully transcribed all their conversations. (Townsend never published them. He said they were not credible, and Maggie was never able to get Hilda to perform nearly as well in front of witnesses.)

The talking-chimp experiments went out of favor. Funds were hard to come by. Project Hilda was especially costly— a whole house, full-time keepers, all for one jabbering chimpanzee. Townsend was considering selling Hilda to a lab or a zoo. It was Maggie who came up with the idea of taking her to Africa and releasing her into the wild.

When Maggie and Hilda first came to D'jarkoume, a small and, at the time, peaceful country on the west coast of Africa, Maggie planned to stay six months, long enough to teach Hilda what plants to eat, which ones to stay away from, how to make a nest in a tree for the night. At the end, Maggie would wait until Hilda came into estrus and release her into a group of wild chimpanzees.

The group Maggie had chosen roamed an area west of the station and was already under observation by a team from the university headed by Dr. Richard Davis of the paleoanthropology department. He was going to teach Maggie which foods chimps eat and how they gather them. It wasn't easy to win Richard over to the project—he said from the beginning it wouldn't work—but when Maggie sets her mind to something she can be very persuasive.

She'd set her heart, her soul, on freeing Hilda.

The main obstacle to this, something Maggie hadn't counted on, was that Hilda didn't want to be free. The forest terrified her. She didn't like the sour figs that chimpanzees thrived on, wouldn't learn to peel a palm frond, to crack a nut.

Hilda's graduation was put off indefinitely. Maggie and Richard couldn't agree on the rules. Richard said he wouldn't let Maggie protect Hilda if the wild chimps decided to attack and Maggie wasn't willing to risk Hilda's life.

This is the reason Maggie came to take on the other chimpanzees. The idea was to form a band of chimps in which Hilda would be safe, a band that would protect her against hostile wild chimpanzees. But a project like this takes time. Maggie has to wait until her males grow older, bigger. She must decontaminate her once captive chimps from their human ways and teach them how to be chimpanzees.

She records all her data in journals. Once a month (approximately) she sends out a newsletter to the thousands of individuals who fund her project, the Friends of Hilda. Maggie also gets money for articles, most of them published in *Science America*. Anita is very helpful and encouraging.

There was a coup, years ago, which was frightening at the time—Hilda left on her own at the station while Maggie was dragged off to jail—but it turned out to be to Maggie's advantage. The democratic government, controlled by the Ilido, the majority tribe, was overturned by the army, which was controlled by the minority tribe, the Moro. As a protest against atrocities committed by the army, the university pulled out and hasn't returned. Only Maggie stayed, by special arrangement. If the university were still using the station, Maggie would have had to move elsewhere. G.P., Danny, and even Hilda, like most older chimps who've been raised by humans, are too dangerous to be let loose around people. A wild chimp is afraid of humans, but a tame chimp knows he is stronger than a human being. G.P., although still an adolescent, could attack and kill a human—Maggie—if he wanted to.

The reason G.P. doesn't attack Maggie or Emanuel is that Maggie and Emanuel have dominance. G.P. respects them. Still, Maggie keeps her BB gun handy, to shake it threateningly when G.P. gets out of hand.

Maggie tries to strip herself of human behavior when she's with her chimps, tries not to speak in words or sign language, but gestures creep in, habits, and the others imitate them. For instance, Maggie's chimps point at things, something chimps in the wild never do. They take cover from the rain like humans.

If Richard were here right now, he'd have her scare everyone off the porch with her BB gun, force them into the rain, back to the forest. No, that's not it. If Richard were here he'd have her ship everyone off to a zoo and call the whole thing a failure. He would have had her do it years ago at the time of the coup. But Maggie doesn't give up that easily, not while they are still making progress.

Some days they don't even come into the clearing, except for Hilda, of course, who still nests in the same nearby tree where Maggie originally built her a sleeping platform.

Was it so bad having them here where she could see them clearly? Was it so bad to feel relief at not having to slog hours through the forest to check up on them? Did it mean Maggie was a hopelessly unscientific sentimentalist if she enjoyed the feeling of having them close, curtained off from the outside by the rain? When the storm lets up they'll wander out looking for food. The tehetou are ripe. After this wind there will be plenty lying on the ground.

Maggie's storeroom is full. Didier came yesterday, wanting to get to her before the rain. He hates mud, splattering up on his yellow jeep, oozing onto his polished boots. For Didier, the greatest gift of Western civilization is the macadam road. He brought supplies for three months, in case a bridge washes out, but he'll come sooner than that if he can. She made him promise. After all, she needs her mail, and the newsletter has to go out every month. And now the piece for *Science America* needs revision. Of course Anita understands how difficult it is, relying on Didier to take the mail. She hasn't given Maggie a deadline. She even—where is it in the letter?—hinted that she might be able to get money for a jeep. Maggie needs one desperately. There used to be two jeeps and a truck at the station, but they were confiscated along with the two-way radio at the time of the coup. They would let her keep a vehicle now. Didier would help her get permission.

Anita wants the article to contain more material on Danny. She wants the point to come across more forcefully that a laboratory chimp is making the transition to life in the wild.

Maggie leans forward to see Danny huddled alone at the end of the porch. He jerks his head down to avoid her gaze. He never looks any of them in the eye, not even G.P., whom he follows everywhere, but always at a distance. At least Danny follows G.P., accepts another chimp as a model. At least he's able to find his own food. There are many positive things to say about Danny. Anita encourages positive thoughts, unlike Richard, who is negative, who wants to hear how it isn't working.

He calls it being objective, accuses Maggie of being emotionally involved. If she weren't emotionally involved, would she have been able to live here for eight years? He pretends that scientists are devoted to some abstract truth, that they don't care what the outcome of the experiment is. That's the scientific myth. Richard is as passionately devoted to his group of wild chimpanzees as she is to her own group. It makes him bitter that he can't get to his chimps anymore.

If Maggie had a jeep she could drive out and check on

Richard's group. There used to be nearly eighty of them scattered over an area ten to twenty kilometers away. Richard could help her get the money for a jeep. He could help her out instead of writing critical letters when she needs encouragement.

Didier brought the mail in a canvas sack. She began reading it last night by the light of the kerosene lantern, but after Anita's suggestion for a rewrite and Richard's letter, and with the usual hideous insects divebombing the lantern, Maggie gave up and put the rest away for morning.

Maggie's mother, Marion, has sent a letter and a copy of last month's *Vogue*. The perfume samples have been torn out, by a girlfriend of Didier's, no doubt. As usual, all the letters have been neatly slit open. Maggie once asked Didier who read them. "Les fonctionnaires," he answered. For all she knows, it's Didier himself. He claims he doesn't speak English but Maggie suspects this isn't so. Before the coup, Didier was a driver attached to the station. Now he is paid by the government. Shortly after he took over his new post, he showed up wearing a heavy gold Rolex watch. Neither he nor Maggie has ever mentioned it.

Didier treats her well, always has a smile, showing his remarkable even white teeth. He brings presents, this time Belgian chocolates in a tin box. She ate several last night after everyone had gone to sleep.

They're quiet now, sitting with their backs to her, contemplating the rain. They can sit for long periods of time doing nothing.

"Don't you wish you knew what they were thinking when they get like this?" she asked Richard once.

Richard said they weren't thinking anything. "They can't think like we do because they don't have language."

"But they store information. They remember from one year to another where a particular fig tree is."

"But they don't think it in words. They just go there at the right time."

"It must feel like being in a trance, like something is leading you . . ."

Richard accused her of romanticizing.

Hilda coughs and looks at her, hoping for cough medicine, but if Maggie gives it to her now in front of the others, there will be pandemonium. Later, if the coughing continues, if it's genuine, she'll sneak Hilda some medicine to keep the phlegm from settling into her lungs. Hilda had pneumonia once and the vet in D'jar says she'll get it again if Maggie isn't careful.

It came so suddenly last time. One day Hilda had a cough but seemed healthy, and the next she was shivering on the porch, gasping for air. Maggie took her in, wrapped her in a sleeping bag, forced hot broth down her throat. Emanuel, who was young then, maybe fifteen, walked all the way to Dobo to get Mfui to come with the truck.

She still doesn't know what Emanuel told Mfui in order to get him to come. It wasn't the truth, because when Mfui saw her staggering out with Hilda wrapped in the sleeping bag, Mfui threw the truck into reverse. He wasn't going to let a sick animal into the cab of his truck. Emanuel had to argue with him, offered all kinds of money to make the trip. Maggie was paying it off for months afterward.

She knows the locals think she's crazy for living with chimpanzees, and Maggie wasn't acting entirely sane that day, with Hilda shaking and wheezing in her arms. Mfui made Emanuel come too, as if the boy could protect him from the crazy *blanche*.

Actually, she gets along with the locals, with Mfui, who charged her much less when she had malaria and had to go into the hospital in D'jar. He saved her life that time, he and Emanuel. Mfui has the only transportation in Dobo. He collects old automobiles and trucks—they seem to come to his yard to die—and uses their parts to keep his own wrecks on the road.

Now Maggie keeps syringes and antibiotics in case Hilda comes down with pneumonia again.

Hilda coughs. "Hurry Maggie medicine please."

"I don't think you realize how backward Hilda is," Richard said when Maggie first went to see him about her plan to free Hilda.

How could he call Hilda backward when she knew more words in sign language than any other chimp? She would look at picture books or television by the hour (had her favorite programs). She made her bed and washed dishes. She knew when Maggie was sad, could read her moods better than any human.

Backward in chimp behavior, Richard said. Her body language and vocalizations were all wrong.

Maggie's face went hard. She'd thought Richard was a friend. Hilda had liked him, the few times he'd come to observe. She'd responded to his sturdy, slightly pudgy build, to the way he sat with one ankle resting on his knee, waiting for Hilda to make the first move.

But then, Maggie didn't understand academic politics. She was only a naive graduate student who assumed everyone there was pursuing lofty ideals, searching for Truth instead of scrambling after funds. It wasn't any different from the music business, except the money wasn't as good. Richard thought the money being spent teaching chimps to use sign language was a waste. To him, Hilda, the star performer of the psychology department, was a pathetic mutant, neither human nor chimp.

"Maggie give Hilda look-book. Hurry please." Hilda signs rapidly, stretching her arm through the grid. She's spotted the *Vogue*. Maggie covers it with the mailbag.

"Maggie give Hilda look-book." Hilda bangs on the grid.

Maggie bares her teeth.

Hilda screams, which rouses G.P. He hoots, circles the yard, leaps on the grid. Soon the group of them are screaming and hooting. Maggie jumps on the table and hoots back at them. She waves her BB gun, stamps her feet.

They lope off across the soaked yard, steaming now in the sun. Hilda stops at the edge of the trees and coughs pointedly in Maggie's direction. Maggie has to duck to hide a smile. Impossible not to smile at Hilda's tricks, at her attempts to get Maggie's attention. Maggie gave up long ago trying to explain to Hilda why it had to change, why Hilda couldn't have cocoa and TV anymore, why Maggie wouldn't speak to her in anything but chimp sounds. How do you explain freedom to someone whose happiest days have been spent in captivity?

2

Whenever Sparks is in New York City, he feels like he's being kept inside a box. He misses sky, clouds, and stars. In this city only the rich and powerful see sky. Krusky gets sky because he is the head of the record company and his office is on the thirtieth floor, with a river view. Sparks is trying to see past Krusky to the white clouds scudding by.

If he looks at Krusky, he is tempted to place his hands on either side of Krusky's head and move it firmly to the beat. Krusky is just off it slightly—gets it, then loses it. Sparks and Roy used to laugh about it years ago when Krusky was a minor drone in the legal department, running around to the clubs, learning what was in, what was out, parroting the latest phrases. Now he's the goddamn head of the record company. He's the one who tells Sparks if something's good or not. He calls Sparks in when he signs one of those groups who look great on stage, on video, but can't get it together in the studio. He brings Sparks in to give the kids a crash course on song writing.

"It's better," Krusky says. "These kids are going right up onto the charts with this one." Krusky used to have big, hungry eyes. Now that his face has grown around them, they look small, sunk into pillows of fat, but still greedy.

"It wasn't a song before," Sparks says. "Just a melody and a bass line. I put it together for them. They're nice kids. They're going to give me co-writer on it."

"Who says?"

"Andy, Wilbur—"

"That's very nice, but wait till you try to get a contract on it. I know their lawyer. He'll never give it to you. And even if he does, I'm not putting you on the jacket as co-writer."

"This time—"

"It's not the way it works, you know that. You're not in the group, not in the video. It's not your image. It wouldn't do either of you any good."

"I think I know enough about image . . ."

Krusky's eyes are down to slits. If Sparks knows so much about image, how come he's let himself get into *People* and *Star* as Mr. Hollywood, escort to the stars? How does he expect Krusky to give him credit on the *Satan's Children* album when his picture is in *People* sitting in Chasen's with Janet Lind?

Janet is an old friend, a very decent person, as a matter of fact.

Look, Krusky says, he doesn't want to get into an argument. He doesn't want to insult Sparks's lady friends. Sparks should go out with whomever he wants. Sparks is too old—he's got too much dignity—to worry over his image and that shit. What Sparks should do is think of himself as a consultant, a highly paid consultant. Up until now he's been a pleasure to do business with. He knows how to get things done, not like most artists.

Krusky puts a cushiony hand on Sparks's shoulder as he sees him out of his office. Krusky gets along great with artists, but it's like dealing with aliens, does Sparks know what he means? But with Sparks, Krusky has always felt comfortable, as if Sparks belongs to the same tribe. He's more a business-man than an artist.

Sparks can still feel the fat fingers on his back even after Krusky has retreated behind his door. On the way out he stops to see Connie, like Krusky someone who has risen in the company over the years. Unlike Krusky, Connie knows some-thing about music, has some sensitivity, which is possibly why she is director of publicity and Krusky is president.

There's a commotion in the outer office when she sees him, kisses on both cheeks, an arm entwined in his as she draws him into her office.

"I was just looking at you last night, in my *People*."

"Oh, that."

"Is she as gorgeous in real life as in her pictures? Tell me it's all done with makeup and lights." Connie closes the door and seats Sparks on the sofa beside her. She crosses her legs, displaying nice calves, and pushes her hair back from her face.

How long has it been? she asks. It seems like ages since he's been in New York. He's too comfortable, no doubt, at home, with his pool, all that sun, beautiful women . . .

Connie says Krusky is out of his mind not giving Sparks co-writer credit. There are still a lot of Light fans out there who would buy any album that had Sparks's name on it—in fact, there are new fans every day. Her son plays the *Sweet Mercy* album all the time. He loves it—likes it better than the new stuff Roy puts out.

Connie wants to know how many years it's been since the last album. Sparks has to think. Sometimes it seems like a lifetime ago, and sometimes as if it were yesterday. He still hears cuts from it on the radio, usually when Roy has a new solo album out. It must bug Roy. He'll never have hits like he used to when they were together.

Ten years, that's how long it's been, and almost twenty years since the first one.

"Twenty years. That was the first album I worked on, re- member? That's when I met you. God, I can't believe I'm that old."

Everyone's old, Sparks says, everyone who knows how to write music.

Connie says Sparks should do an anniversary album with Roy, get as many of the original members of Abiding Light as they can find—

Whoever's still alive, says Sparks.

Why not? Connie thinks it's a brilliant idea. Why doesn't he stop up and see Roy right now?

Roy has an office in this building, something that's news to Sparks, although Roy has had it a while, according to Connie. Roy wanted to set up an office way back when they were the Light. Sparks wouldn't do it. Offices were something you went to only when you couldn't avoid it, when you had to sign something at your lawyer's or when you had to see someone at the record company. You always stood around feeling out of place and ill at ease and you couldn't wait to get out. As soon as the Light broke up, Roy got his office, called Haven Enterprises, Sparks heard. He has never been there, first be- cause he doesn't like offices, and second because Roy got bigger than Sparks and it is up to Roy to come to Sparks, not the other way around.

Sparks doesn't explain this to Connie. He thanks her for the idea, worth looking into, steps into the elevator and goes up instead of down. Connie, in her enthusiasm, must have put him on the Up elevator. He follows a messenger out at the first stop and presses the Down button. While he is waiting, he sees that the first door down the hall has HAVEN ENTERPRISES neatly painted in gold on the frosted glass door, like a goddamn dentist office or something.

He pushes the buzzer, smiles at the video camera, and walks in.

He is expecting a beat-up leather sofa, the kind of coffee table people put out in the street for the garbage men to take away, covered with dust and back issues of *Rolling Stone* and young long-haired women in blue jeans talking to friends on the phone, offering natural sodas and herb tea from a kitchen in the back. He sees deep pile carpeting with Chinese rugs laid over, light oozing out from behind panels, and cabinetry that matches exactly the honey-colored hair of the receptionist.

"Looks like the office of the president of Exxon or something."

"You're not the delivery boy from Pasta Presto."

"You thought I was?"

"I thought you were my lunch. That's why I buzzed you in." Her hand is on the phone. She's half out of her chair. He alarmed her, coming in like that, commenting on interior decoration.

"Sorry. I dropped in to see Roy. Is he in the back somewhere?"

"If you were close enough to Roy to be able to come in unannounced, you'd know that he's never in the office." She has the kind of nose that looks like it's been pinched together at the end. Reminds him of someone—Maggie. Maybe Roy hired her because she looks like Maggie.

"Why's he paying the rent? What's he keep here, if he's never in?"

"His people."

"Oh yeah. His people. Any of them around? Who's his key guy, his manager? . . . Away? All of them? Where are they?"

"Wait a minute, shouldn't *I* be asking *you* questions? All I know is that you're not the boy with my lunch, who should be coming soon. Any minute. Could you give me your name at least?"

Sparks leans over the desk so she can see his face at eye

level. It has changed, certainly. His hair, for instance, is re-treating and has turned almost white, but he hasn't altered beyond recognition. Besides, he's in the public eye often enough. Maybe this one isn't a big reader of gossip columns.

She smiles back at him. They have a little chemistry going but she still hasn't caught on.

Then the light goes on in her eyes. Synapses connecting.

"Weren't you somebody once?"

". . . !"

"Oh God, I'm sorry."

"That's all right. It will make a good story, in about ten years, when I've come to terms with it."

"I can't believe I said that. It's the job, this job. I'm *becoming* a receptionist. What I meant was you were famous, weren't you? Or are. I should know you, shouldn't I? Why do I feel I'm just getting deeper and deeper into trouble here?"

It's funny because he was the one they always used to go for. When he came out on stage, you'd hear twenty "Sparks!" for every "Roy!" Sometimes it got on Roy's nerves, the way, walking on the street, everyone noticed Sparks first.

"Samuel Parker King. Known to those who know him as Sparks. Played lead guitar in the Light, Abiding Light, the group—"

"This is embarrassing."

"You're young."

"But I walk right by you—I mean the gold records. They're in the hall. Every time I go to the john. I'm not really a music person. I'm just trying to get enough money for graduate school."

"Are they really away, all of them?"

"Paris. Recording."

Sparks had heard that Roy did this. He would get interested in something and take a whole group with him for months at a time.

"I'm not really involved. They don't tell me—don't want me to know that much. I'm supposed to be bland and polite, guard the door and not give anything away. I'm not in the inner circle."

Sparks used to be part of the inner circle, but he didn't think of it as Roy's, or anyone's in particular.

"Let me write your name so I can tell him you came by. I know he'll be sorry he missed you." She opens a black book.

Sparks sits on the corner of her desk and looks down at the book. She smooths a lock of hair behind her ear and giggles.

"You definitely have to find another job. That was very receptionist. Don't forget, I know Roy. He's not going to call me back. Don't write it down."

She tells him that her name is June, and that she lives alone not far from here. She walks to work.

"We're going to have to break up Women's Studies for the holiday table. Put the psychological stuff in Psychology and personal growth in the—growing things." Yolanda makes growing gestures over her head.

"You mean Personal Awareness / Self-Help?" Roger asks.

"That's right." Yolanda swings off in an arc to right some disorder on the paperback table and to investigate a young man in a bulky down coat who's getting suspiciously close to the racks.

"Yolanda, why are you still in your coat?" Roger is saying this for his boys, the two attractive graduate students he hired to work part time during the holiday season. He presents her as a character. It's part of the gay male bonding ritual, she supposes.

"Because I haven't had time to take it off."

The man in the down coat, seeing her looking at him, backs away from the racks and ambles toward the door. Yolanda makes a sign behind his back, meaning that Roger is to file his face in his memory of customers-who-bear-watching.

Yolanda locks her bag in her desk drawer in the back of the store where they have their offices, she and Roger, not offices exactly, but desks in a room filled with cartons of books coming and going and a computer that can find a book by author, title, or subject and tell if it is in stock or not, but everyone usually asks Yolanda first before bothering with the computer.

In this windowless room, Yolanda has lunch and often dinner (wheat-free, yeast-free salads and casseroles from Ethan's New Age Take-Out Kitchen around the corner).

The Constant Reader isn't one of those bookstores that feature recessed lighting and quiet browsing spaces. Roger and Yolanda often say they'd die of boredom in such a place. The Constant Reader is jammed with paperbacks—along the walls, on free-standing carousels, in racks five feet high where patrons brush up against one another, not always apologizing—all lit with fluorescent lights which Roger says make his skin look ghastly, but which throw clear images onto convex mirrors hanging in the corners of the ceiling, letting the staff tell at a glance who is slipping a thin volume into the inside pocket of his overcoat. For some reason, people who would never steal anything else think they have the right to take books.

Yolanda does not put her coat on the bentwood rack in the corner. Instead she takes a large pushbroom outside to give the sidewalk its morning sweep. She can feel Roger and the assistants smiling in her wake as she marches through the store, broom in hand. When Yolanda can't do it, Roger gives this job to the most recently hired employee, as an initiation rite, she supposes, but Yolanda enjoys sweeping. She likes the regulation that storekeepers are responsible for keeping the sidewalk clean in front of their shops, likes the homey, small-town feel of it. She welcomes the exercise of pushing the broom in the open air, and the opportunity to greet her neighbors passing by.

"They're magnificent. Like a forest has come to town," she says to Pete, who has finished setting up his Christmas trees along the curb. He and Yolanda had a chat when he pulled in this morning. She recognized his accent. "I'm from Geneva," she told him, no need to qualify it as Geneva, New York, not Geneva, Switzerland, as she did for most people. He said his family had a farm on Route 245. Yolanda thought she knew the one.

"Where did your friends go?" Earlier there were two young men with him. They rushed off to see the sights, Pete said. He doesn't expect a great deal from either one, just someone to watch over the trees for a few hours at night while he sleeps in the truck.

"Here, I should be doing that." He reaches for the broom. He's wearing a heavy wool shirt, no jacket. Back home they don't consider forty degrees jacket weather.

"I don't mind. It's nice to sweep pine needles instead of used condoms for a change."

She blushes when she realizes what she's said. He laughs. "I like your window display."

The theme is "Wrap up an adventure for the holiday," her first holiday window of the year. It features Dorothy outfitted for a safari. She would have preferred something like what Hepburn wore in *The African Queen*, but made do with what she could borrow for Dorothy from the Banana Republic up the street. Swags of mosquito netting festoon the corners of the window. Dorothy stalks through tall piles of adventure novels and travel books.

"That's really an interesting dummy."

"I call her Dorothy." Yolanda doesn't like to hear Dorothy referred to as a dummy. She found her in the basement, wrapped in sheets and lying in her original wooden crate. She was made in France in the thirties and has a finely chiseled Modigliani nose and almond eyes. Despite her slender proportions, she weighs two hundred pounds with her iron stand, and once placed in the window, she has remained there. She's extremely rare. The Museum of Decorative Arts wants her passionately but Yolanda can't bear to let her go.

Dorothy has another admirer, Yolanda notices, a man in a down jacket with the hood up, sweatpants, and running shoes. He is pressed up against a corner of the window, his back to the street. Discreetly, Yolanda moves to where she can see him better, to make certain he isn't relieving himself against the front of the store, which sometimes happens. But his hands are harmlessly hidden away in the pockets of his jacket. He is looking at the books, first with one eye then the other, in a way that reminds Yolanda of a bird. His nose, short and pointed, also makes Yolanda think of birds, the seed-eating kind, finches. His face is familiar. Yolanda is certain he is a customer, one of the regular but quiet ones who come in to browse but never ask for a specific title. It takes Yolanda several minutes more to realize he is the author of one of the books on display. Didn't she just put a pile of them in the window yesterday, every one of them with his face staring out at her? But in her imagination she had attached the face to a larger, more imposing body.

"You're Gordon Crews, aren't you?"

"What?"

"The book in the window. *Mombatu*. You wrote it."

"I did?"

"Your picture's on the jacket."

"I guess it is."

She introduces him to Pete. Hasn't she seen him many times in the store? He admits that he comes in every now and then, that he lives only blocks away.

She loves his work, only wishes she'd known that he lived in the neighborhood. Why didn't he tell her? Every year she does that window—has he ever seen it?—of neighborhood authors? But he was probably away a lot, traveling.

"I hate to travel."

"I mean for your books. This one set in the rain forest—"

"Never went. I won't fly. I'm afraid of boats."

Now that Yolanda reexamines the picture on the cover, which she assumed had been taken in Africa, she can see that it could just as easily be Riverside Park in the background. Probably is.

He's sorry to disappoint her, he says, but Yolanda, although disappointed, says not at all, that the book is wonderful and she certainly *believed* it. His other books have been adventures as well, one set in the Himalayas, the other in the Yucatán. She doesn't have the heart to ask about those.

The Constant Reader is one of the few stores in town that carry his books, he says. Yolanda says they sell very well, which isn't exactly true because she remembers sending quite a few back last time. She overordered because she liked it so much.

"What were you doing talking to Gordon Crews all that time, Yolanda?" Roger asks when she comes in.

"You knew who he was? I didn't, even with his books staring me in the face."

Oh, but he's always wandering through the store, didn't Yolanda know? He lives on Riverside Drive, in a big place he inherited from his grandmother. He rents out the rest of the rooms, which must be how he keeps alive. It's certainly not from his royalties.

One of the new assistants, a tall, slender blond with gray eyes, comes by. "I don't know, Yolanda," Roger raises his voice, "I think you just use that broom as an excuse to flirt with the boys. Who was that other young man?"

"Who? Oh, a home-town boy. He's selling trees."

Yolanda hangs up her coat in the office and rakes her fingers through her hair in front of the mirror, trying to arrange it in a better way. Roger's tone reminded her of how her brothers used to tease Aunt Frances about having a boyfriend, as if it were the most preposterous idea. How old had Aunt Frances been then? Fortyish probably, like she is now.

"Yolanda?" Roger sticks his head in the office. "What was that book that got a good review in the *Times* about three weeks ago, about how the brain works?"

"*Layers of the Mind*. Terrance Mosely."

"Do we have it?"

"On the nonfiction shelves. Middle one, second in from the corner. Green cover."

"Thanks."

3

NOVEMBER
VOLUME VI, NO. 11

FRIENDS OF HILDA

While you are enjoying your Thanksgiving dinners, think of us here at the station who have also been feasting on nature's bounty, in this case, *Macrotermes bellicosus* (that's termites to you). This is the time when they sprout wings, leave the mound they call home, and come out to party.

I first became aware that, once again, the harvest was upon us when I woke in the middle of the night to find several thousand squashy little insects in bed with me. They had come in searching for a warm place to spend their first homeless night. I emitted a fair amount of shrieking and screaming noises, leapt around, squashing bodies wherever I stepped, and wiped myself down with kerosene. This certainly kept the horrid beasties off, but I couldn't stand the smell. I went to shower and the floor was covered with them. They kept dropping on me from the ceiling.

In the morning our clearing was sparkling with discarded silver wings. Hilda was picking termites out of her hair, wiping them nervously off her hands. Katie, however, was acting as we would if we woke up starving one morning and found a plate of pancakes on the bedside table. She was murmuring soft little grunts as she popped termites, squirmy fresh, into her mouth. Poppy and Biff, following Katie's example, were also picking up a quick snack. Danny and G.P. were experiencing conflicting emotions. Hunger encouraged them to copy Katie and dig in, but Hilda, because of her special relationship to me, has higher status than Katie. If Hilda wasn't eating them, it must not be socially acceptable.

I know that termites are rich in amino acids, something that's in short supply in the chimp diet. For years, I've been trying to get Hilda and the rest to chow down on them but I have always stopped short of *demonstrating* how yummy they are. If you take the job of alpha-chimp seriously, however, there are some things you just have to do. I picked off a termite that was conveniently crawling across my forearm and held it up for all to see, announcing that I was only going to do this once so they'd better all watch. I

transported the insect to my mouth, all the
while making ecstatic feeding sounds.

Hilda looked at me suspiciously, sauntered
over, opened my mouth and inspected my
back molars, which still held squashed
Macrotermes bellicosus. You can bet I hadn't
swallowed it, although the locals relish them,
fried, usually, with onions and curry.

The upshot is that Danny and G.P. have
added termites to their diet. Hilda, however,
is having none of it. I haven't demonstrated
my love of termites again, but even if I
scooped them up by the plateful, I have a
feeling Hilda wouldn't go for them. At least
the others are feeding madly on them. I even
let Katie into my house to clean out the ones
living there. I'm wearing bug repellent to
discourage them from cuddling up too close
tonight.

Oops! There's mail call. Must go. I'll try
not to mash any *Macrotermes bellicosus* in
with this letter. Enjoy your turkey and
stuffing!

Maggie Russell

Sparks has this newsletter folded in the pocket of his jacket.
He is wearing what he always wears when it's cold—dunga-
rees, boots, flannel shirt, shearling jacket, and stetson—no
matter where he is, LA, Lubbock, Paris (although he hasn't
been to Paris in a long time), or New York City. He walks
up Broadway, his hands in his pockets, the only one in quasi-
cowboy garb, but not feeling out of place because anything
goes on Broadway. He passes a tall black man in purple robes

and a pillbox hat, a woman shopping in bright blue spandex tights, and an elderly man with roller skates and a headset. Santa Claus is handing out leaflets in front of a cut-rate drugstore. Koreans stand guard over forests of Christmas trees on the sidewalk. Sparks is taking the letter to Olly.

He found it on the kitchen counter when he was flipping through June's mail, waiting for his oatmeal to boil. When he saw Maggie's name at the bottom, he turned back to the photo on the front, a murky reproduction of a woman sitting on the ground with chimpanzees. It could be Maggie, or it could be any number of women he's known, including June, who looks so much like Maggie that Sparks can't call up Maggie's face without its turning into June's.

The letter sounded like Maggie, at least on the second reading. Last time he'd heard from her she'd been going to take up psychology at a university in the Northwest. How that would have led her to an African jungle, Sparks doesn't know, but Maggie specialized in abrupt transitions.

Finding the letter like this was a surprising coincidence, something which might have kept Sparks musing and amused through breakfast, but nothing more. What made him act, what caused him to burn the oatmeal and call June at the office to confess that he had been looking through her mail, was the label on the outside of the letter. It had been addressed, automatically by mailing machine, to Haven Enterprises.

"They're old friends," he said to June when he'd gotten through the awkwardness of explaining about the mail. "Don't you see? He's a contributor. It all connects."

But June, who is very linear, very East Coast, insisted the connections were circumstantial. Haven Enterprises contributes to a lot of causes. June is the one who brought "Friends of Hilda" in to the accountant, and he OK'd the donation. She doubts Roy even knows about it.

And what about the new album, the one that's just coming out. Doesn't that have an African theme? Sparks hasn't heard it, but it's hard to avoid. Tower Records did a whole window on it. It has African back-up musicians, June said, but that has nothing to do with "Friends of Hilda." The album was recorded in Paris.

Sparks is taking the letter to Olly to see what she knows about Maggie and Roy. He's glad to have the letter as an excuse. It would be awkward, just walking in off the street after all these years, when he should have been to see her long before, when Roy first set her up in business. "Olly's going to take a break from the road," Roy told Sparks. "She's tired of traveling." It was going to be Roy's business when he retired, so he wouldn't have to support himself by performing in Las Vegas, playing in smaller and smaller rooms to aging, dwindling audiences.

Sparks has an idea of what Olly's store looks like, but he doesn't know if he's imagined it or if someone once pointed it out to him from a car going by. It's located on upper Broadway, far from the theater district, a place an out-of-towner wouldn't get to unless he was visiting someone who lived in the neighborhood. At first the area looks seedy because of the panhandlers begging with paper cups, peddlers selling used magazines on the street, a young longhair speaking quietly and earnestly to a blank wall, but then Sparks sees some upscale mothers pushing single and double strollers, going in and out of shops with freshly washed windows, buying French pastries and Italian cheeses.

Olly's store is fairly big and looks just as he remembers or imagined it. Olly, however, has changed so much that Sparks nearly turns around and walks out. She used to be slender in a gangly, adolescent sort of way, but now she's skinny. Her hair, which was straight and long and made her look like a New England poetess, is cropped short and sticks up, leaving miles of naked neck. She looks plucked. She's wearing a jump-suit which hangs from her shoulders with no hint of a body underneath, no breasts, no hips. It's as if the flesh has been burned away. If he didn't know Olly, he'd say cocaine. If she didn't look so healthy and energetic, he'd guess she was the victim of a wasting disease.

Olly doesn't see him. Her gray eyes sweep right past in favor of a pile of books that need straightening on a display table. Sparks follows and places his chin directly on the stack of books.

And then they are laughing and hugging. Her neck goes blotchy and her cheeks are red. She has that same wide, artless smile that makes you want to please her just to see her smile again.

How typical of Sparks to come popping into her life after all these years and expect to be greeted with hugs and kisses. When she first saw him, her heart speeded up and she walked by, pretending not to know who he was, hoping he'd get confused and go away, but Sparks counts on being welcomed like the long-lost brother, no questions asked, and before you know it that's exactly what you're doing.

She is genuinely glad to see him—the same Sparks, but even better-looking now that his hair has turned silver and he has acquired some manly parentheses down his cheeks.

She leads him around to her office in the back, which suddenly strikes her as airless and cluttered.

Does she see much of Roy? he asks.

No, never. When she first opened the store, she used to call him whenever he came into town, to invite him over to see how she was getting on. He always said he would but something invariably came up.

"Roy never was a reader," Sparks says.

"No."

"That can't be our Maggie," Olly says when Sparks shows

her the "Friends of Hilda" newsletter, with the picture of the woman and the chimps picking fleas off each other.

"I don't know. It looks like her to me, the shape of the head? And the letter sounds like her. Read the letter."

Olly squints, then perches her glasses on her nose. Yes, she has to agree that she can hear Maggie's voice in there, but think about it, Sparks, Maggie used to complain if there wasn't a paper strip over the toilet seat in the motel, remember? Maggie liked clothes, money, good food. She was so pretty. Why would a pretty woman go hide herself in the jungle? Olly examines the picture again. The face is just a blur, could be anyone. And Maggie Russell isn't an uncommon name.

Sparks shows her the address on the letter: Haven Enterprises, which means Roy is contributing.

That doesn't mean anything, Olly says quickly. He owns half the bookstore, yet he's never been to see it.

Sparks looks around at the boxes, at the mess of papers on Olly's desk. "Why do you think he's still holding on to it?"

Olly blushes. "It can't be because of the fantastic return on his investment, although it does all right, for a bookstore. I wonder about it sometimes and I figure he still wants the connection—"

"With you."

"Either that, or he's forgotten he's still in it with me. Maybe that's more likely. I don't ask, just send in the statements every month, to the accountant, of course, not to Roy."

It's been too long since Sparks has seen Olly. He's missed her. "Olly, how about lunch? Is there a place around here we could grab a hamburger and a beer?"

"Oh! I—sure. Let me go ask if they need me. We have all this new help and extra customers, for Christmas and stuff."

Yolanda stands near Roger who is toting up a credit card sale. She can't go out with Sparks without explaining about allergies. She'll end up eating bad things anyway and have an attack (gasping in the taxi while Sparks races with her to the emergency ward). Just talking to Sparks has made her all blotchy. She can feel it.

"Isn't that Sparks from the Light?" Roger asks, not looking up from the register.

"Yes. An old friend. He stopped in to look at the store."

"I didn't know you were in with the glitterati, Yolanda. His picture was on the cover of *Star* last week, taking some actress—no, it was a singer, Cina Wong—to some fabulous do."

Yolanda goes back to Sparks to say, as she had feared, that it isn't possible to leave the store right now. But maybe he will be free tonight, after the store closes at eleven.

Sparks says he'll call if he is, but he doesn't think so. He's heading back home soon. His gig is up here, and he finds if he stays away too long his life gets complicated. But he'll call soon. It's been too long.

After Yolanda has seen him out the door, she realizes that they forgot to exchange phone numbers.

"Yolanda," Roger asks, "what was that novel, came out about six months ago, about the researcher who falls in love with a bushman?"

"It was a year ago. *Tropical Longings*, Letitia Marshall, but unless they want it for a gift they should wait a month for the paperback."

Smoky curls of mist coming from the forest are pulling Maggie back to a time she'd rather forget, Stockholm, world tour, sitting in bed with Roy in a cloud of marijuana smoke.

"Do you believe in destiny?" she asked.

He snorted clouds of smoke and let his too heavy head fall against the pillows, the forehead a massive dome and under that pale eyes lurking, rimmed in red because of the marijuana and with sparse lashes, then a long slender nose from which smoke was still faintly curling and a thin red mouth, too red. Stubble on the chin.

What kind of destiny? If she was talking about a pattern of outside events, no. If she meant the destiny of personality, he might be able to get behind that.

Oh. She wanted a cigarette, which he provided but didn't offer to light. She pulled the sheet up primly to cover her breasts. She wanted to tell him that she believed in destiny, that the moment she saw him in concert she knew that she was meant to follow him, that without him she would never be able to arrange her life into coherence.

She left everything—school, her friends—for him. She never would have stepped out of her life like that for Sparks, who was a crowd pleaser, the one everyone fell for, the way he strutted around the stage jamming with the drummer, the bass, making eye contact with the audience. He, Roy, was the one who drew her, because of the way he hid behind the keyboards, lost in the music. His complete absorption in what he was doing attracted her.

"When I went backstage"—she tried again, her knees chastely draped in white sheet, her unlit cigarette held between pale fingers—"I came into that room full of people and you looked at me right away and I—"

"We looked at all of them."

She lit the cigarette herself. He was feeling guilty and taking it out on her. He would have only cut her down if she had gone on to describe certain immediate changes her body had undergone when he fastened his eyes on her—and he did. He had stared. If it hadn't been for Olly, as usual glued to his side, Maggie would have been his right away. Now she wanted him to tell her that he had felt it too from the beginning.

Roy put his joint, still lit, in the ashtray between them and let his eyes sink back into the shadow of his brow. There was no use talking to him when he was in this mood. Maggie turned her profile to him, hoping he would watch her and speculate, invent more interesting thoughts for her than she could herself. She was wrong, as it turned out. Instead of enlarging her, he had reduced her.

It's unlike Maggie to allow her mind to get snared in the past, because she has to be present at all times, active, alert. It was the fingers of smoky mist reaching out from the forest, humid vegetable breath that drew her back. The rains have been tapering off all week and this morning the sun is beating down on the clearing. Poppy and Biff splash through a puddle by her door but they don't stop. They're going to join the others, who are hammering away at the panda nuts. It's an industrious sound. That and the sun returning are giving Maggie hope and energy. She scrubs at the sheets in the sink. They'll never be white again, no matter how hard she tries. Everything here turns reddish brown, but at least she'll know they're clean.

With everyone out of the way, she can risk hanging the sheets outside in the sun. She strings a rope from the porch to a nearby acacia, whose thorns have protected it from hungry chimps, automatically checking for snakes before reaching in among the branches. Once a branch turned into a green mamba and slid out from under her hand. She didn't leave the house for days.

God, that sun feels good. She straightens the sheets on the line, feeling guilty for enjoying the sun when rain was needed. If this is the end of the rainy season, it's too soon, too soon for the last three years in a row. Before the rains this time the forest floor, which should be like a wet sponge, dried so it crackled when she walked and the river was reduced to puddles.

Richard wrote that it could be part of a natural wet–dry

cycle, but he's afraid it might be a permanent change caused by the destruction of the rain forest. He always asks for information. Is the new government committed to protecting the park? She can only report what she has seen: several acres burned at the edge of the park in the buffer zone and rows of coffee bushes planted in the ashes. Emanuel says arrests have been made, but someone is cultivating the bushes. In the south, beside the river, she came across a patch of blinding light. Gold miners had dug around the roots of every large tree, all of which had died, leaving the upper canopy a wasteland of bare branches. Another time, on the road from Dobo, she saw trucks hauling mammoth logs strapped to flatbeds, but no one would say where they were coming from.

When she first came with Richard, they used to see elephants in the forest, twenty or thirty at a time. Shortly after the coup, poachers got in and slaughtered numbers of them for ivory. No one has seen an elephant since.

Sometimes Maggie wonders if the forest is still out there, or if she is sitting in the middle of an ever dwindling patch of trees. Have Richard's chimps gone the way of the elephants? Sad as it might seem, it would remove a threat that has been hanging over Maggie from the start.

There used to be around eighty of the chimps roaming the forest west of here. Richard had them all named, had even figured out many of their relationships. When Maggie went with him on his "follows," they usually saw only a few at a time, a small band of males, some mothers and children. Chimps gather in large numbers only when there's a tree full of ripe fruit, or a female or two whose red swollen bottoms announce that they are in estrus, fertile, ready for mating.

It was several weeks before Maggie and Richard came upon a mating party. Richard said Maggie would be especially interested because the female was a stranger. Usually chimps chase a stranger away, but if it is a female in estrus, the males may mate with her and later protect her from hostile chimps. Maggie's plan was for Hilda's bright blossoming posterior to be her badge of admittance. Among the males, Maggie recognized Boris for his mangled ear, Jacques for his prize-fighter nose, and Popo, who carried one shoulder higher than the other.

The female was young and nervous. She would present her bottom, but when a male approached, she would scream and run away. The three males, who were generally friends—Richard thought they might be brothers—were beginning to fight among themselves in their frustration. Meanwhile, the female was trying to make friends with some of the juveniles hanging around on the outside, but the mothers would snatch their children away from her. Maggie's own palms were sweating, her heart was pounding, watching this little female darting around, seeking allies, spiraling into hysteria. Maggie looked at Richard, but he was busy watching through his binoculars and jotting down notes.

"Oh God, I can't stand this. Let's just walk in there and scatter them."

"Shh!" Richard put a hand on her shoulder and forced her down again behind a log.

It was quiet now. The chimps stood still, as if Maggie's appearance had made them forget their lines. Then the silence turned inside out, into a cacophony of screams and roars, a drumming on the earth, crashing in the trees. Through the binoculars, Maggie could see only a blur of bodies. Richard was watching and marking quick symbols in his book.

Maggie saw the red spot in the middle of the fray, and the little female escaping, only to be caught up in Boris's arms and slammed to the ground.

"Stop them! Stop them!" Maggie tore at Richard's notebook and beat his back to keep him from taking notes while murder was being committed. "Stop them! Stop!"

Richard pinned her to the ground, a knee on one shoulder, a hand on the other. She could only hear the screams, feel the pounding in the ground beneath her. A small chimp ran by without even seeing them.

When it was over, they found the female lying on the ground with her arms and legs bent at unnatural angles. Her nose was mangled and bleeding. Her eyelids fluttered when they approached. Richard bent down beside her. Maggie took off her poncho to carry her back with them. Only after Richard stood up and Maggie saw the red gash in the chimpanzee's throat did she realize what he'd done.

Why? Why? How could he be so cruel, so coldblooded? The other chimpanzees would have come back, he said, to finish their work. She was too far gone to save. He wouldn't have, anyway—he was there to observe, to interfere as little as possible.

Later, when tempers had cooled, Richard said that it was just as well Maggie had seen what can happen to a strange chimp, even a female in estrus, when she enters the group. Sometimes they don't accept such a female. It would prepare Maggie for what could happen to Hilda.

"But we wouldn't let it happen," Maggie said.

"How would we prevent it?"

"We'll have a gun, guns, with us."

"And kill the wild chimpanzees?"

"If we have to . . ."

What made Hilda's life worth the taking of the lives of wild chimpanzees? Richard asked. Because she was a trained chimp, because she had been contaminated with human ways? If Maggie was committed to freeing Hilda, she had to be committed all the way, even if it meant letting Hilda die. The lone chimpanzee did not exist in nature. If she couldn't live as part of the group, then let her die. Either that or give her to a zoo, a lab.

That was the choice Richard offered for Hilda, either the quick brutal death in the wild or the slow humiliating one in captivity. Maggie invented a third option.

Hilda comes toward her now, picking her way among the puddles. She is carrying something in the crook of one arm. Panda nuts. Hilda drops them on the porch.

"Maggie open please."

"Absolutely not."

"Hurry. Hilda hungry."

It takes strength and skill to open a panda nut, strength to crack the outer shell and skill not to crush the buttery almonds inside. The others, except for Poppy and Biff, have mastered it more or less, but Hilda is too lazy. Perhaps Maggie made a mistake in the beginning, cracking the nuts for her, and now Hilda considers it a point of honor to refuse to crack her own. Or maybe she's too weak. She never eats enough during the rains, spends too much time huddled on the porch.

Hilda picks up a nut and thrusts it into Maggie's hand.

"No, goddamn it. You think I want to spend the rest of my life in this snaky place feeding you nuts?"

Hilda screams and runs after the nuts Maggie has flung on the grass. Maggie retreats into her house. No, no, she will not come out until Hilda opens the nuts herself.

Later, Hilda is lying on the edge of the puddle, which has dried to a wet, reddish-brown patch of mud. Hilda lifts her head and looks at the nutmeats Maggie is offering. She reaches out with an attenuated arm and accepts reluctantly, as if she is doing Maggie a favor.

4

"I don't understand. She was in the Light?" June, still wrapped in her chenille robe even though it's a work day and she'd ordinarily be out the door by this time, is sitting in the unmade bed, propped by pillows, holding a mug of coffee in both hands.

Sparks folds his extra pair of jeans into his duffle bag. "She did some singing on one album. And on stage, the last tour, she joined in on a few numbers. Roy taught her one or two things on the harmonica. Mostly she tossed her hair around and looked good."

June sips her coffee. It must be her third cup this morning. "Was she talented? Was she any good?"

"She was OK. Not bad."

"And before that, she managed—"

"She tried to be road manager but the club owners took advantage of her. You have to have some larceny in your soul to be able to deal with those guys."

"I guess what I'm trying to get at is, what was the connection, what was the basis of her relationship with the group?"

"She was one of the girls—the women—who lived with us on the road."

"Someone's girlfriend?"

"Yeah."

"Whose? Yours? It doesn't matter. I'm not jealous or anything."

"Well, mine, yeah. But we were more like a family, everyone helping out. Maggie, this woman Olly, they did a lot of unofficial things. They started out, Olly was Roy's girlfriend, Maggie mine, but the whole thing developed. The women weren't into being exclusive. You know, Maggie had a thing for Fry—Steve Fry the drummer?—for a while, and that was cool, and Roy or I might get it on with someone for a night, or a month. It didn't matter."

June says it sounds ideal, for the men.

Sparks goes to the bathroom to collect his things. He's looking pale. Time to get back to his own place. It was the times, he explains to June, talking to her from the bathroom as he finds his shaving cream, his shampoo. Things were easier then, less complicated. People didn't talk about commitment and relationships. The world was younger then.

June says she wonders if Sparks isn't still living in the sixties. Oh Christ, he tells his reflection, here we go again, just as he had been congratulating himself on how smoothly the thing with June was working out.

"Hey, you'll come out, stay at my place for a while." He comes back into the room. "We'll drive down to Mexico. I've got a bed in my car. It's a Bronco. You know what those are? Ugly mother, all black. Looks like a hearse." Her back, under the soft furrows of her robe, trembles like the beginning of an earthquake. He rubs across her shoulder blades.

June is still in her robe, watching from her door, when Sparks leaves with his duffle bag over his shoulder.

"You have a dinner date, Yolanda?"

"I guess you could call it that, Roger."

"What is it with you and Gordon Crews lately, Yolanda?

Every time I look around he's lurking over by Cookbooks and Travel."

Roger's little joke. Is she so impossibly old that it is a joke to have a date? Could what she and Gordon are doing be called dating?

The store is crowded for ten o'clock on a Thursday night and the shoppers more purposeful than the usual after-dinner browsers. They are thick around the holiday table, where they can find copies of books on display already gift-wrapped. Gordon, disguised by a lumpy hand-knit scarf which covers his mouth and chin, is keeping a watchful eye on his own small stack of ready-wrapped books.

"You sold a copy of *Mombatu* today," he observes, trailing after Yolanda as she goes for her coat.

"I sent it to a friend." She hates to tell him that, but she can't lie because the next question would be who bought it. Yolanda sent it to Roy, on impulse. She read a review of his album in the *Times*, the one for which he used African music and musicians. "Heard you were interested in Africa," she wrote. "Thought you might like this. Olly." No "love" or anything, no invitation to stop by or call. Still, she feels she went too far, that sending the book to Roy was a mistake.

Gordon pulls his scarf closer, preparing to face the icy blast. It's colder than it has been, going down to the teens tonight.

"Why don't you go in the store, get warm," Yolanda says to Pete, who, she's glad to see, has relented and put on a down jacket at least. "You can stand in the window and watch your trees from there."

"I'm afraid I'll start reading and forget to look out."

Yolanda buries her face in the branches and inhales deeply. Upstate pines. If she brought one home she'd probably cry for days.

Down the block the Kims are selling trees too, outside their all-night produce stand, so the sidewalk is nearly walled in from the street with pines and spruce. Late on a cold night when people are scarce, the trees, dark and fragrant, are more present than ever, bristling ranks of them chained together, an army of slaves from the barbaric north country.

Gordon is picking out spareribs and fried dumplings from the Kims' hot-food bar. Yolanda has a nice casserole that Ethan made fresh today, but Gordon finds Ethan's cooking too wholesome for him. He claims he is fighting a family tendency toward longevity. He hopes that by eating the wrong things he will die at a reasonable age and be spared the inconvenience of living into his nineties.

At the check-out, Mrs. Kim shows Yolanda pictures of the new baby. Gordon picks up some chocolate-covered cherries. "For dessert," he explains. "It's fruit."

Yolanda lives in what used to be the master bedroom of a townhouse built at the turn of the century. Her apartment is short on closets but it has the original marble fireplace and a plaster rosette in the center of the ceiling where the chandelier used to hang. In the back there is a rudimentary kitchen behind a waist-high counter. She has hung bookshelves on either side of the fireplace, the kind that hook into metal brackets. Something about them isn't quite right. They look temporary, a little unstable, but they've been holding up fine, for however many years it's been.

She and Gordon put their dinners on the table by the window. Yolanda says she might have a bottle of white wine in the refrigerator. She knows she does because she ran out this morning to buy it, even though she can't drink wine because of her allergies.

"You have a great view." Gordon is looking at the lighted windows across the street.

"Don't I? They could watch me too, I guess, but they're always occupied with each other. No one has time to sit by the window and speculate on who lives over here. On floor four, the parents go out and leave the boys a lot. When they do, the boys tend to throw things out the window, and on floor three, they're both lawyers, I think. Anyway, they both leave with briefcases in the morning. They have a baby and a live-in nanny who watches TV in the daytime."

"I like people who don't have curtains. It's a generous gesture, I think. Do you watch while you eat?"

"Sometimes. Or I read. There's a lot to keep up with. What are you doing Christmas?"

"Nothing."

"Oh. Is that by choice?"

"It's not like I'm a mailman, see, or a stockbroker. My work has its own timetable. I don't stop everything because it's Sunday, or because it's Christmas or something."

"That makes sense."

"It does, doesn't it? I had the hardest time convincing my parents, who thought because I was their only child, I should stop everything and present myself at their doorstep every time alternate-side-of-the-street parking was suspended. I mean, it's no big deal, a forty-five-minute bus ride to New Jersey, but I resented the expectation that I would be there just because it was Christmas, or Saint Swithin's Day, or whatever. Then they decided to take trips so they wouldn't notice if I wasn't home for the holidays. They go on tours to places you wouldn't consider going: Tibet, Patagonia, Borneo. They wear running shoes and hats with brims. They read up on it before they go and show slides to their friends when they come back." Gordon chases a fried dumpling around in the clear plastic container. "It's all very sad and empty."

The dumpling jumps the edge of the container and lands on the floor. Yolanda scoops it up with a napkin and puts it in the garbage. She brings back a knife and some extra napkins.

Yolanda thinks it sounds nice, the way his parents travel together. Her mother would have loved it, but by the time her parents were financially able to travel, her father had heart trouble and they couldn't. After her father died, Yolanda had hoped that she and her mother could travel together, but it turned out her mother had a brain tumor, poor thing, and never got farther than New York City, one time.

Gordon watches her with one eye. He is sucking on a sparerib, emitting small babyish eating sounds. The talk of holidays and families is making her melancholy and she is regretting having sent the book to Roy. She pours some more wine in Gordon's glass, which is empty although she can't remember seeing him drink from it.

Gordon, having abandoned his struggles with the spareribs, is wiping his hands and face on the extra napkins, leaving a crumpled pile of them at his place. His back is turned to the windows across the street, where the boys on floor four are sending little balls of white stuff, wet toilet paper maybe, to the sidewalk below, and the lawyers on floor three are enjoying a candlelit dinner. (Perhaps Yolanda should buy candles?)

Gordon lifts his wineglass by the stem and then seems to forget it is in his hand as he examines the room. Most of the furniture has come from home except for the parrot-green Chinese rug, which Roger made her buy because it was a bargain and which doesn't go with the rest of the furniture, and the king-size bed. "What do you need such a big bed for?" her mother asked when she visited. Yolanda said she liked plenty of room to stretch out. Her mother didn't say that Yolanda was in fact a quiet sleeper, a spare figure who took up only a quarter of the bed.

"Nice room," says Gordon. "I like your things." The wine just makes it over the edge of the glass and dribbles on Gordon's leg. Yolanda hands him her napkin.

Didier is inspecting splashes of red mud on the side of his yellow jeep. He doesn't see Hilda until she is beside him presenting her bright swollen bottom and peering coyly over her shoulder. Didier jumps back. Don't worry, Maggie tries to tell him, Hilda's in estrus; she's inviting you to mount her. Maggie is never sure how anything is going to come out when she says it in French. Didier looks revolted. Maggie feels she's betrayed Hilda, that she's failed to convey Hilda's feelings properly.

She doesn't see G.P. until he is galloping across the clearing, stamping his feet and hands.

"Va t'en!" she screams to Didier, which isn't the right thing to say either. Luckily the BB gun is near and she can fire into the air, making G.P. hesitate just long enough for Didier to get into the house.

G.P. gets worse every time Hilda comes into season. You can't blame him. To male chimps, the swollen bottom is a sign, an invitation they find irresistible. Hilda won't have anything to do with G.P. She screams when he comes near. G.P. is stronger and could force himself on her but Hilda has dominance—that is, Hilda backed by Maggie—and in this group, as Maggie explained in her letter to the Friends of Hilda, when a lady says no, she means no.

Maggie calls Emanuel to bring the supplies in from the jeep. He comes, sullen and already sweating, his tattered shirt open, his khaki shorts held up by a rope. Hilda, crouching in a corner of the porch, clutching the wire grid, watches him carry in the canvas sack of mail, the cartons of groceries. She's in love with Emanuel, but too intimidated by G.P. to do anything about it now. G.P. has broken off a palm frond and is waving it over his head, screaming, pacing the clearing, but he won't come near. He's afraid of Emanuel.

Emanuel sets the boxes down in the storeroom. *Emanuel, be careful*, she calls, or rather *wise and nice* because she can't think of the French for "careful." Emanuel slaps bare feet on the cement floor. He doesn't look at Didier, who is sitting at the table making marks on paper with Maggie's pen.

Watching Didier sitting with studied ease, his military-looking khakis starched and pressed, his gold Rolex glittering on his narrow, velvet-black wrist while Emanuel trudges back and forth with supplies, Maggie finds it hard to believe that both are natives of the same small country. They could belong to different races entirely. Didier is leggy, tall and slender. Emanuel is short, with short thick legs. Didier's head is an ellipse, set at an angle to his neck, so his forehead slopes back to a high domed crown. His lips are thin, his slender nose aquiline. Emanuel's head is round with a heavy overhanging brow, low-set ears, a bridgeless nose, and everted lips. You could use them as textbook examples of the two tribes of D'jarkoume, the Moro and the Ilido.

Richard blames the French for the coup because, although they turned the government over to the Ilido, who make up ninety percent of the population, they had formed an army that was ninety-five percent Moro. He claims the French chose the Moro for the army because they were tall and elegant and looked good in uniform. Didier says the Moro are fighters, that the Ilido are cowardly and don't like to fight and that's why there weren't any Ilido officers at the time of the coup.

Didier taps the pen on the table, waiting for Emanuel to finish. He consults his watch. Emanuel slams the door going out. Didier keeps his eye on his jeep until Emanuel has passed it.

"*Crétin*," Didier mutters under his breath.

Maggie brings him a Coke, then shakes the mail out on the table. Once again the check from Richard is larger than usual. Richard can't figure out why donations are coming through so strongly. His letter sounds critical, as if she's to blame for the donations. She'll read it again later when she has more time. She signs the check over to Didier for deposit. He gives her the cash for the check she wrote last time. It isn't much, only what she needs to pay Emanuel and buy fresh produce from the locals.

"Leave the money there," Maggie tells Didier. She hates to touch it. It's so old, damp, and dirty, and has a sweetish smell, as if it's been hoarded in small quantities, wrapped up in garments, and kept close to the skin. Don't they ever print new money? Didier reminds her that D'jarkoume is a developing country, his excuse for everything.

What is that sound, Didier wants to know. It's the chimpanzees cracking nuts in the forest. Only Hilda remains. Go, go. Maggie waves the broom at her. Hilda leaves, suggestively wagging her bottom at Didier. He stretches, looks for Emanuel, but Emanuel always disappears after unloading the jeep. Didier goes to the bathroom, where Maggie can hear him washing up, and then to the bedroom.

She follows him in. He is already laying his starched khakis neatly over a chair. Africans are matter-of-fact about sex. They handle it like a business transaction. Maggie doesn't know why, but this detachment excites her more than warmer, more sentimental approaches.

Moro wives get paid by their husbands for sexual services. Maggie does not get paid. That would be absurd. She pays Didier for bringing her mail and doing her errands in town. Although she enjoys the sex as much as Didier, Maggie has the feeling that everything she does with Didier is building up a credit and that some day he will honor her account and come through with a favor when she needs it.

"Qu'as-tu?" she asks. He's not himself, not at ease.

"Qu'est-ce que c'est?"

It's only Emanuel, that idiot, raking the path under her window, although he did it yesterday. She can't call out to him to stop, can she? Anyway, the shutters are closed, the door is shut. They are alone with stripes of light lying across their legs.

When Maggie wakes, the stripes have widened to bands and have moved off the bed to the wall. Outside Hilda is screaming and banging on the grid.

G.P., his penis red and erect, is trying to force Hilda down.

Maggie screams, grabs the BB gun off the table. "Get away from her, you clown!" G.P. bares his teeth at her, but he backs off. Hilda groans and sinks to the concrete, still clutching the grid. G.P. throws himself on the ground and ejaculates into the grass.

It is only when Didier comes out in his briefs that Maggie realizes she has played this whole drama out in the nude. She hands the gun to Didier and goes back for her clothes. As she is getting dressed she hears the dry scratch of the rake. She peers between the slats of the shutter and sees Emanuel calmly moving the rake across the gravel, his face immobile.

Maggie shivers and pulls on her T-shirt.

5

"You're driving to Lubbock?" Joy asked, lightly mocking. Hadn't he heard about the miracle of flight?

Yes, he knew about airplanes, how he could struggle into a crowded terminal, surrender his baggage—two duffles full of presents for nephews, sisters, brothers-in-law, parents—at the counter and hope he'd see it again at the other end, wait hours for a plane that had been snowed in at Denver, and feel grateful when he was finally herded through passageways reeking of diesel fuel to sit too close to people he didn't know.

In his Bronco, which is black with tinted windows, he is singular, discrete and in command. He will drive for hours, spinning through the desert in the night, and then will pull over to the side of the road and bed down on his own futon mattress. He is protected by an alarm system that could crumble concrete and a .45 Colt Commander on the floor beside him.

Joy would have come if he'd asked. She hinted that it sounded like fun, listening to tapes, driving through the desert all night, and he feels a little guilty leaving her alone, but she's been staying with him over a week while she gets over Willie and she's got to learn eventually to make it on her own. Besides, if Sparks brought a woman home for Christmas it would give everyone the wrong idea. The time Maggie came, his mother had the baby pictures out to show her the next day. They all liked Maggie because she was beautiful and helped with the dishes. His mother said it gave her goose bumps to see the way he and Maggie looked standing together.

Sparks met Maggie's mother once. Marion, her name was. She had frosted blond hair, good legs, kind of a husky voice. She flirted with him. What amazed Sparks at the time was how little she had. His parents had accrued layers of possessions, children, grandchildren, and all Marion had was a small apartment in Westwood furnished with a couple of asparagus ferns. And she had Maggie, of course.

A Porsche overtakes him and, almost before he is aware of its passage, speeds beyond reach of his headlights. Christ, he's doing fifty-five miles an hour. Are we reaching senility or what, Sparks, driving fifty-five and reminiscing about the old days. Reminiscing. Whenever anyone asks him about those days he rolls his eyes, feigns amnesia. The trouble is, he doesn't have enough going right now. The mind slips into the past when there isn't enough to hold it in the present. That, and the letter, that newsletter Maggie sent out addressed to Haven Enterprises. It started his idle brain buzzing over past events.

Then again, why not? Who's to know? He's out here in the desert, rolling along at—seventy-five now, sealed up in his Bronco. He can do whatever the hell he wants. He could even play Roy's new album. Connie gave him the tape, though he never listens to Roy unless he hears him over the radio and even then he turns him off half the time. This one is different, Connie said. It's really brilliant and you should know what he's doing, in case you two get together again for an anniversary album. You never know.

Connie assumed he didn't listen to Roy because of envy, but that isn't it. He's embarrassed for Roy, the way he picks up other people's music, their rhythm, their instrumentation, and then runs his melodies and rambling monologues over the top. It's how he began with Sparks and the Light, taking their Texas music, theirs by inheritance, and changing it just enough to appeal to middle-class suburban kids. Roy pasteurized them, homogenized their music. After he did it with them, he went Latin, or was it R&B? It's all mixed up, but anyway, that's what Roy does. His career has been a smorgasbord of musical traditions, all smoothed into something a fifteen-year-old from Encino can digest.

This time it's African music. There's an odd rolling beat to it, so the melody is just ahead of the bass line. You can see Roy working on it until he gets it, that little skip in there. It would intrigue him. The background voices are singing gibberish, growls and hoots, primitive, although the music is sophisticated. Roy's words as usual make no sense. They're words Roy likes the sound of, that match or complement the music. Roy once overheard a phrase while he was waiting in line at a deli and put it in a song because he liked the way it fit.

The Light would get letters from earnest high school students, college English majors. One guy even wrote his doctoral thesis on the meaning of the lyrics. Roy would read the best letters out loud and they'd all laugh, except for Olly, who would get upset to think that people were puzzling out meanings that Roy never put in. She wanted to answer them and set them straight, but Roy only allowed her to thank them for their interest and congratulate them on their insight.

Sometimes the lyrics meant something, but they were very personal—in-jokes, communications to close friends. In the *Sweet Mercy* album, the last one, Roy left a message for Sparks so subtle that Sparks didn't even hear it until after the group broke up. It was a piece of background noise, a snippet of studio conversation that had been recorded by mistake, Roy saying "So long Sparks." He must have sneaked it into the final mix.

Now the messages, if they exist, are for others, Roy's people, whoever they are. Roy doesn't dwell in the past, has no taste for nostalgia. Sparks knows this, and yet he is playing the same song for the third time, thinking he's having auditory hallucinations.

"Humbabubba humbabubba," it sounds like. "Eden is a state in the mind." More humbabubba. Something about frogs chiming like bells in the night. Frangipani days—or daze? What is frangipani? Sugary, he thinks, a sweet dessert, like burnt sugar. Or is it flowers, a tropical vine. Something tropical. Maggie days or daze. Later he thought magpie, but he played it over and it is definitely Maggie. Something about stars falling to ground and sparks flying to sky in fiery constellations. OK sparks. You could talk about sparks in a song and not mean Sparks. But the end. This is what knocks him out. In the fade-out, you hear someone calling, "Olly Olly in come free!" Which is how he used to call her, all the time.

A Shell station is coming up on the right where Sparks usually fills his tank because the gas is cheap. The shiny pumps, the emblematic yellow sign, stand out in the black desert night. In the burning glare of sodium vapor lights, a phone booth looks hyper-real, like a phone booth in a dream. He sees himself inside calling Olly. He can hear her nasal western New York tones, her careful polite skepticism. Sparks fills the tank at the self-service island, scrapes bugs off the windshield.

Back on the road, he plays the song one more time. The Shell station vanishes in the rearview mirror. There is no one behind him and nothing in front except the twin beams of his headlights. He tries calling up Maggie's face but it is lost, confused with the face of that girl in New York—June.

Sparks takes the tape out and tosses it in the side pocket. He puts in an old Al Green he hasn't heard in a while.

When his mind has wandered on to other things, the vision of Maggie comes, barefoot and tangle-haired, wearing a summer dress above the knee, walking toward him through squares of colorless light in the corridor of a hotel in Stockholm. Her face is smooth as stone.

What Sparks had forgotten about Maggie is how her face never gave anything away. Not that Sparks needed it spelled out for him. He said something crude, then regretted it because it implied he cared more than he did, but her face, smooth planes in the pale light, did not flinch.

Pete is holding out a short, fat Scotch pine. Yolanda can't believe he didn't sell it; it's the perfect shape.

"I was kind of keeping it for you, actually."

"But I don't—"

"No, take it. It's a present. You gotta have a tree—or drive back with me tonight and I'll drop you at your folks' house. Unless you have plans . . ."

"There's a party—" Yolanda stops herself. She was going to tell him about the party on floor four. It's their annual bash. They've been preparing for days. She actually had been looking forward to it, had put some sparkling apple juice in the refrigerator in anticipation, but she's afraid it wouldn't sound good to Pete. It could sound pathetic, even. It's the tree. Without Pete's tree standing in her living room with a couple of make-do ornaments—Christmas cards and the like—it would have been a perfectly OK night, with the apple juice, a book, and a party to watch on floor four, but the tree could wreck everything.

She explains to Pete that her parents are deceased and that her brothers, their wives, and babies have moved into the old house on Main Street. Not that they wouldn't love to have her, and have asked her repeatedly, but she isn't used to the changes they've made. She feels displaced when she's there.

Then come home with him, says Pete. Try Christmas with a whole new family.

Dorothy has quite a large family, although, of course, only evidence of them appears in the window. Tonight she looks up from the presents she's wrapping (books) and raises her glass in a toast to an unseen person, undoubtedly Dorothy's husband, because she is attired in a peignoir from the fancy new lingerie store in the next block. There is real champagne in her glass, thanks to Roger.

Roger bought half Roy's share in the store. Yolanda thought she should offer him part, although she easily could have come up with the entire sum. Roy sold it to her for the same price he paid for it, a gift practically. Yolanda told Roy's lawyer to thank him for her, as Roy was out of the country. Roger said it was cause for celebration and brought in champagne for everyone.

Mombatu is right beside Dorothy, set off invitingly by red tartan wrapping paper. Roger had the inevitable comments on how Gordon's book kept cropping up every time there was a new window, no matter what the theme, but Yolanda didn't give him the satisfaction of hearing her defend herself. The fact is that Gordon's book makes an excellent gift. It has nothing to do with her friendship with Gordon, who is working through Christmas Eve, treating it as he would any other night. Yolanda respects that. Either you should go all out for a holiday or ignore it completely—although Gordon isn't ignoring it exactly because if he were truly treating it like any other night, he would be here waiting to go over to the Kims' to buy dinner.

Pete's very kind, she says, but he shouldn't worry about her. It's not the first time she's had Christmas alone and it won't be the last. She's developed a talent for solitude, really she has. She kisses him on both cheeks and watches his pickup rattle off into the night on the long journey home. She stands holding the tree at arm's length, not wanting to take it but

not willing to abandon it to the street either. Floppy bits of
snow are twirling past the street lights. Down the block she
sees Gordon, his face tucked into his scarf and his shoulders
drawn up around his ears.

"I thought you'd be gone by now," he says through his
scarf.

"I was trying to decide what to do with this tree."

Gordon doesn't mind carrying the tree ten blocks down to
the all-night grocery store. When Yolanda comes out with the
Cornish hens, the cranberries, the butternut squash, and
mincemeat, he looks like a patient elf, standing quietly while
the snow settles on the tree and his stocking cap.

They don't eat until after midnight, but the party on
floor four is still going strong. Yolanda has never stayed up
to watch it this late. It's a pretty sight—the women in strap-
less formals, the men in black tie. Their movements from a
distance seem choreographed, as if they are performing a
mime show in a lighted box, separated from their audience
(Gordon and Yolanda) by a diaphanous flowing curtain of
snow.

Across the table, Gordon, his eyes reflecting candlelight,
his chin shining from the grease of the Cornish hen, says he
has never seen her eat so much.

It's true. For some reason she is ravenous tonight and reckless. Drinking wine! It's her second glass—or third? Pete's
tree, standing in a bucket, leans rakishly against the bookcase.
Yolanda didn't have time to invent any decorations for it. But
it's beautiful without them and much bigger than it seemed
on the street.

"Look how lovely the tree is, Gordon! Do you think people
decorate them to tame them, so they don't look so savage and
wild? Maybe the old Celts used to bring a tree into the house
at the winter solstice, as a charm or something to pull the light
back, and later generations found the naked tree too unsettling

so they began dressing it up, making it look like another piece of furniture."

"Is this what they always do at the end of their party?" Gordon is looking out through the snow to floor four, where all the guests have departed and the host and hostess are slowly undressing each other.

"No! I don't know." Yolanda tugs at the cord on the Venetian blinds and brings down the curtain on floor four's Christmas pageant.

"Yolanda!"

She has to laugh at his face, like a disappointed baby's when his toy is taken away. But it's not right. It's voyeurism, peeping Tomism.

"If they didn't want us to watch, they'd turn off the lights, or go into another room."

"Oh no, they have no idea we're watching. They don't know anyone lives over here. They don't think about me."

"If we can see them, they must see us."

"No, no. They don't see us. Those kinds of people don't look out at other windows. Because they're so involved where they are."

"Insiders, not outsiders. Participants instead of observers." Gordon's hand finds its way past the serving bowls, the candles, to Yolanda's hand.

With the window blocked and Pete's tree looming to her right, Yolanda feels closed in and her apartment absurdly tiny, too small for two people to act out any drama at all. She pats his hand and clears the plates off the table.

While she is washing dishes, Gordon comes up behind her.

"They've gone to bed. I think we hurt their feelings by putting the blind down."

He places his hands on her hip bones. "You're so thin."

She hands him a plate to dry. "I feel fat, like a stuffed goose."

Outside, the snow is just beginning to stay on the sidewalk. Floor four is dark and silent. "I should be going," Gordon says, "before the snow reaches the tops of my sneakers and I'm trapped here for days."

"Snowbound."

"Exactly."

"Well, why don't you stay here, since the conditions are so perilous out there? I'd feel terrible if you froze to death walking that block on Riverside Drive—"

"If I became snow-blind, disoriented—"

"Attacked by wolves."

Yolanda insists he use the bathroom first, finds him towels— does he want a shower?—no toothbrush, sorry about that, but he says his finger will do fine.

While Gordon undresses, Yolanda goes into the bathroom. Her face is all blotchy and there are hives coming out on her chest. All that sugar, the wine. She applies an ointment to them, then brushes her teeth. A little makeup, foundation if she can find some, will hide the red splotches. She doctors them up the best she can. In her medicine cabinet is a diaphragm, never worn, in a pink pearlized case. She got it from her doctor a couple of years ago when she went for her checkup. It comes with a sample spermicide, thank goodness, because she never would have thought to go out and buy a tube. It's amazing what sudden unexpected changes a life can undergo, even one as seemingly placid and orderly as her own.

In with the towels, wrapped in lavender tissue paper, is a negligee the owner of the new lingerie store, Vicki, persuaded her, or pressured her, to buy when she went begging a peignoir for Dorothy. It's black with pink trim. It doesn't look as good on her as it did in the dressing room with Vicki fussing over how Yolanda, with her height and slim figure, could "carry it off."

"I've never had a negligee before," Yolanda said.

"Well, honey, what are you waiting for?"

Gordon's sweatshirt and sweatpants are on the back of Grandma B.'s rocker. He is quietly sleeping on the far side of the bed in his T-shirt and his shorts, probably. She imagines Gordon wears boxer shorts. Yolanda is hugging her ribs, shivering next to Pete's tree, all dressed up in the wrong costume.

She opens her dresser drawer carefully so as not to wake Gordon and feels around for her flannel pajamas. She changes into them and shoves the negligee into the back of the drawer.

Yolanda would have expected Gordon to sleep the way he eats, with his arms and legs going off on independent journeys, but he sleeps with quiet focused intent, as if his restless mind at last finds peace in one damped-down brain wave, a delta wave rocking him into a dreamless calm. He stays on his side of the big bed while Yolanda, her mind buzzing from sugar and wine, lies light and bony on the other.

Yolanda and Roy used to sleep all tangled together—in his broken-down bed at college those nights when Yolanda, who lived at home with her parents, would tell them she was staying in the dorm with a friend studying late; in borrowed beds in the first year when they lived in New York; in motel beds, thousands of them when they were on tour; in a white iron bed the time they rented the cottage in New Hampshire—so many beds, but they never actually owned one bed in common.

Hilda, on the porch, leaning to one side to avoid sitting on her red swollen bottom, watches Maggie pull on tall rubber boots. It looks as if it must hurt female chimps to be in estrus, and yet they want sex. Townsend did an experiment once when Hilda was in season, showed her a porno magazine of men with erections. She put it on the floor, turned the pages solemnly until she came to a particularly graphic close-up, squatted over it, and rubbed her bottom up and down. Another time, she blatantly propositioned Townsend and some of the male assistants by backing up to them, her red posterior held in an invitingly ready position.

In the wild, a female chimp is very accommodating, allowing the young males to practice on her when she's coming into and going out of estrus. Unless she is closely guarded by a dominant male, she'll mate with several partners when she's most fertile. It's in her interest to form alliances with as many males as possible, because she'll have that many more protectors for herself and her offspring.

Although G.P., Danny, and even little Biff are interested in Hilda's swollen bottom, she'll have nothing to do with them. She did proposition Emanuel this morning when he was raking the paths. He shooed her off with his rake, calling her names in his language. Richard says Hilda prefers Emanuel over G.P. because she doesn't realize she is a chimp. Maggie thinks it's because Emanuel is dominant. G.P. is a clown, a buffoon. This morning he joined his hands over his head, thrust his erect penis out—the poor thing is erect almost all the time now—and hopped toward Hilda like somebody doing the limbo. Hilda screamed and ran up on the porch. Maggie laughed so hard she almost dropped the gun.

Maggie is taking the gun, a canteen of water, and a knapsack with two oranges, binoculars, compass, her notebook, and serum for snakebite.

"Come on, old girl."

Hilda looks at her dubiously from the porch.

"You gotta eat. Come on. Look, I have the gun." Maggie crosses the clearing, keeping an eye out for G.P., who could come bursting upon them at any minute. She hears only the peaceful, industrious sound of chimps cracking panda nuts with sticks held in both hands. Katie is teaching the little ones. Maggie took Polaroids. They're a little dark, but one is good enough for "Friends of Hilda."

Hilda, seeing that Maggie is going through with it, finally

gets up and scampers after her, keeping her face turned toward the sound of the nut-cracking. Even if Hilda could or would crack nuts, G.P. wouldn't let her alone long enough to feed. Maggie has to take her several kilometers away to where she thinks there might be figs ripe enough to have fallen off a tree. The easiest thing would be to take Hilda into the house and feed her until she's past estrus, but that would be a betrayal, not only of the Friends of Hilda, but of Hilda and of Maggie herself.

"Want to go home. Please," Hilda signs from the edge of the clearing.

"This is home, goddamn it," Maggie snaps. "The forest is your home. Now get in here."

Hilda follows, reluctantly but easily. Where Maggie stumbles over vines and roots, Hilda picks her way nimbly. She doesn't look as pathetic here as she does hanging around the house, partly because her bald patches don't show up as much in the fractured light of the forest.

"She's home," Maggie said, the first time Hilda let go of her hand and walked alone in the forest, and Maggie's heart opened with pride for what she and Hilda had accomplished.

If home is where the heart is, Richard said, then her home is halfway around the world on a sofa in front of a color TV.

Why did he have to be so negative? Was it so terrible to save an animal, to restore her to the life that was hers by right?

It wasn't what Maggie was saving that Richard objected to, he said. He was concerned with what she might destroy in the process.

His chimps, his precious wild chimps. Well, eight years and she hadn't even seen them. She wasn't hurting them. And she was helping. Anita says the success of this project will break ground for more rehabilitation projects.

Hilda wants a rest. Maggie finds a convenient log to sit on and takes out her canteen. Hilda reaches for it but Maggie yanks it away and threatens with her gun. Use the stream. Chimps don't drink out of canteens. Hilda's hair rises. She rocks back on her heels. Shush. If there's one thing they don't need it's a tantrum. G.P. will be on their trail in minutes. Maggie takes the oranges out of her sack and tosses one to Hilda.

"That's it. That's all I have, so you'll have to find your own food from here on out."

So far they haven't come across much to eat. The new leaves are all too high in the trees. Hilda's afraid to climb that far. Anyway, it would make Maggie nervous to watch her.

The sharp scent of citrus slices the heavy air. Maggie rubs some peel on her wrist. Hilda does the same. Something bright floats down. Maggie leans back on the log and searches the canopy with her binoculars. Red colobus monkeys are feeding on orchids growing high in a fork of a tree. There's a rush of wings and the sound of trumpets, a heavenly host of not angels but hornbills, the fantastically huge birds who accompany colobus, feasting on the clouds of insects the monkeys stir up in their tumultuous passage.

"My God! It's Christmas Day!"

Hilda wants a hug. Whenever Maggie shows emotion, Hilda needs reassurance. Maggie drops the gun.

"There there. It's OK. I'm happy, see?"

If she could have a picture of this—Hilda and Maggie, their arms around each other sitting on a log while high above them, red monkeys feast on lavender orchids—she would send it to Roy as a Christmas card and she would say—No, she wouldn't say anything, just let him see that now she is happy.

Are you happy? was Roy's eternal question, not because he was interested in *you*, were *you* happy, but because he wanted to know what it looked like.

Once they took a house in Jamaica, Olly's plan. She would periodically arrange vacations for the four of them together.

The house was whitewashed stucco rooms, each one a separate building with its own thatched palm roof, connected by covered walkways. There were ceiling fans, a swimming pool, the turquoise sea, palm trees, and homemade banana bread for breakfast. They drove to a village in the mountains and bought a bag of marijuana. Sparks and Maggie found horses and rode on the beach. They came back and dove naked into the pool.

"You look like one of those ads on television." Roy was sitting in the shade, smoking a joint. His eyes were rimmed in red. What a talent they had, Roy said, to be able to call forth happiness in the appropriate setting. Just give them some beach and sun and they had a normal healthy animal reaction. Happiness, simple as that.

Roy and Maggie talked about happiness in Paris. They had gone for a walk, just the two of them. It had started to rain and they had ducked into a teashop run by Englishwomen, to have some café au lait and share a piece of cake. A tape of Baroque music was playing in the background—Rameau, Roy said. The tables were covered in red paisley and there were old books lying around that anyone could read. The china was unmatched.

Roy said the best thing about the place was that it had appeared at exactly the right time out of nowhere when they most wanted it and least expected it, but if Maggie continued going on rapturously cataloguing its charms, she would ruin it completely for him. She reminded him of his mother, who used to start encouraging him to eat the minute she set the plate in front of him, thereby turning what had probably been a reasonably appetizing meal into something he could barely gag down.

Maggie laughed, ran her fingers through her hair, fanned it out to dry. She lit his cigarette and her own, watched drops of rain making quick curling tracks down the window. She knew how she looked to him.

This is happiness, she wanted to say. See my face? This is happiness. She knew his talk, his banter, was mere noise to cover up what they both were feeling when after years of waiting, they were alone together for the first time and happiness was only moments away.

Hilda groans with pleasure and slings an arm across Maggie's lap so she can groom it. Maggie smacks her lips, removing bits of leaf. Love. A chimpanzee can accept it, return it, but Roy could wear you out with loving him. You could bombard him with love and not an atom would make it through.

The monkeys and hornbills have gone screaming and trumpeting on their way. Maggie takes a compass reading and sets off again with Hilda. They walk by shafts of light, where the equatorial sun has managed to drive through holes in the canopy roof. Sometimes there's a pygmy tree, so called because the roots grow high off the ground, making a tentlike shelter in which pygmies supposedly hid from buffalos and elephants. Pygmies disappeared from this forest way before the elephants. Richard said their last recorded presence was in the 1920s. It was the Ilido who, one way or another, drove them out. The Ilido, in turn, had been forced into the forest region by the Moro, who invaded the savannah from the drier north country.

The Ilido are farmers who hate the forest and burn it to plant their crops. They tried to force the pygmies to live in the clearings where the Ilido could watch and control them. The pygmies, who had a social system hardly more structured than that of chimpanzees, refused to be organized. They simply melted away. Richard thinks most of them died or intermarried with the Ilido. Some may have migrated into central Africa. The locals believe that pygmies still live in the forest but that they use magic to make themselves invisible.

It's easy to be invisible in the forest, where massive trunks with buttresses can span twenty feet, where the forest floor drops and rises abruptly, where termite bells are higher than men and lianas hang in confusing tangles. More than that, it's the shadows that press in and constrict the space, destroy perspective, so that you only see what is immediately ahead.

Sometimes Hilda gets lost from sight and then she or Maggie will hoot softly until they find each other. This is how they go together, sometimes side by side and sometimes apart. Maggie hears her now but can't see her. It sounds as if she's feeding, maybe on figs. Maggie is moving toward her when Hilda screams.

"Hilda?" Maggie has to control her own fear.

Hilda crashes over a fallen log and clutches Maggie around the waist. She is trembling. Maggie can smell the fear on her. She strokes the back of Hilda's neck where the hair stands straight up. What is it?

"Ugly," Hilda signs.

"Snake?"

"No snake."

"Man?"

"No man."

"Show me."

Maggie lets Hilda lead her over the log, down through a swampy place and up the other side. Hilda stops and pushes Maggie forward.

Ants are on it so that it is a seething mass of brownish red bodies. From what she can tell—she doesn't dare get closer because the ants will climb right up her rubber boots, will burrow into her clothes—it's a colobus monkey, perhaps one of the ones she saw earlier. She pokes the body with a stick and then drops it fast before the ants can swarm up her arm. Something has bitten off the top of the head and eaten out the brain.

If it's a young monkey with a soft skull, a chimp will eat the brain first, Richard said. They watched Richard's band go after colobus. She and Richard had been following Boris. He had teamed up with two other males, Jacques and Popo, and had accidentally or purposefully come upon a family of colobus feeding high in the trees. The chimps circled on the ground, quietly, almost casually, feigning indifference. Without any evident signal between them, they settled on a lone young female feeding peacefully on some leaves. One chimp staked out her tree while the others began climbing two neighboring trees. The monkey, seeing the chimp climbing stealthily toward her, screamed and leaped to the other tree, into the arms of her captor.

"Why don't they at least kill the poor thing before they eat it?"

Richard shushed her, although God knows Maggie's screams wouldn't be noticed with all the other screaming going on. Chimps don't understand death, he said, have no empathy for the pain of a monkey.

The captor ripped an arm off the living monkey and gave it to the one who had originally chased the prey, then thumped the bleeding animal against a branch to stop its thrashing and screaming. Maggie put her field glasses down and looked away.

Her group wouldn't be hunters. They could get all the protein they needed from nuts, seeds, insects. Hunting fills a social function, Richard said: cooperation in the chase, food-sharing with females and infants. Maggie didn't want her group bound together by killing another creature. You can't change the nature of the beast, Richard said, but kindly. That was when he still liked her, before their friendship fell apart.

Maggie holds the BB gun in readiness. It suddenly seems unforgivably reckless to have taken Hilda this far west when she's in season. They could be watching right now, close by. It isn't like chimpanzees to leave a kill only half eaten. There would be a group of them. They would share the meat.

Maggie scans the branches overhead with her binoculars. Nothing that she can see. She motions to Hilda and carefully, quietly, they withdraw from this place. Maggie has the sensation of being watched by many eyes, but she doesn't try again to find them in her glasses.

In the night Maggie sits up in bed. Her watch says midnight, but it's bright outside. She hurries to the day room. A moon looms over the clearing, an unusual and disturbing sight here, where even in the dry season the night sky is covered with clouds. Christmas Day, which began with a rush of wings and monkeys eating orchids, has ended with a licked-out skull and a death's head moon. She hugs herself and strains to hear— what? A leopard padding through the grass, a human crunching gravel outside her door, but the only sound is of peeper frogs like wind chimes all around.

6

Sparks, sipping papaya juice while he makes his calls, is enjoying the February sun on his terrace. Connie sounds appropriately envious, says it's snowing in New York. Sparks grins. She should come out. Maybe she just will, leave the family, the publicity department to muddle on without her and she'll come out for a week. "Except that my face will probably be all over the cover of *Star*. That's what happens to women who stay with you."

Only the ones who *want* to be on the cover of *Star*. Sparks can be very discreet. For instance, she would be shocked to know who just spent two weeks with him, who left only yesterday.

"Oh Sparks, who?"

He can't say. Later, maybe. Not now. Someone who's trying to get her head together, who needs time away to think things out.

He's cruel, Connie says. Sparks knows she's a gossip hound. It's like leading a man dying of thirst to water and not letting him drink. She makes a few guesses, not even close, and then comes to the point: she likes the tape and is sending it on to Krusky. Are they working on more songs?

The thing is, Sparks has to go back to Steamboat. Eddie won't come into Los Angeles. He lives on a sheep farm and is afraid that the excitement of Los Angeles, the whole music–drug scene, would put him over the edge. Not that Eddie was doing so great in Steamboat, but Sparks doesn't tell Connie this.

When Sparks drove up to Steamboat after Lubbock, it was lambing season. Wanda was up in the night with the sheep and then working all day. Eddie was nodding out in front of the TV. He smelled. He always gets out of hand this time of year, said Wanda, because she can't watch him every moment.

"Take him out for walks. Let him know you're around. He'll ease off in a few days. Thank God you've come. It's not so bad when he's spacey, but he gets abusive too."

Eddie looked too strung-out to abuse anyone, let alone Wanda, who has increased in size as Eddie has shrunk. If Eddie hadn't started to come around immediately, Sparks would have left, but Eddie was glad to see him. He cleaned up his act and in a few days he was able to start working. Eddie has a nice little studio in a barn he remodeled. Sparks was amazed at the equipment—electronic keyboards, drum machine, all hooked up to a Macintosh computer. But Sparks didn't want to use any of it. They recorded just guitars, pure and simple. At the end of three weeks they'd taped four new songs. "It's like the original Abiding Light sound," Connie says. Sparks probably should have stayed until they finished a whole album. Wanda was doing everything she could to make him feel at home.

"If you could just hang out here a couple more weeks—" She laid her hand on his. "I haven't seen him this good in the longest time." Sparks looked at her hand, which had grown thick and hard, so he wouldn't see her eyes going watery. He wondered if it had been a good or a bad thing that Eddie had had Wanda to take care of him.

Eddie wasn't interested in whether Maggie and Roy were in some kind of contact again. He doubted it and even if it were true, he said, it wouldn't have anything to do with Sparks. "They're out of your sphere. They're in your past."

On the deck of the house, Eddie had set up his telescope under a star-crowded sky. His hand shook slightly as he adjusted the lens.

Sparks told him about the song, how all their names appeared in the lyrics.

"Take a look," Eddie said.

Sparks saw a marbled planet with a red eye. Four silvery moons hung suspended around it. It didn't look real.

"What do you think about the names, I mean he doesn't— my name is just the word, *sparks*, something about sparks in the sky—"

"Come on, man, you know the words never meant anything. He'd throw in what he had for breakfast if it fit the beat. You're wasting your time."

"He used to write messages into his songs sometimes, remember?"

Some messages, Eddie said. *So long Sparks*, to tell Sparks he was breaking up the group, and that song he wrote about Maggie. Why would Maggie even want to see Roy again? Why would any of them?

"Hey, you know what constellation that is? It's Taurus, man. You see the horns and the bright red eye? The stars make a picture for us but it's only the way we see them. That eye, for instance, is much closer to us than the stars in the face. We draw in the connecting lines but they don't exist in fact, you see what I'm getting at, man?"

Sparks said he didn't think the metaphor was too obscure for him.

"So you think circumstances are pulling you back to Roy, but the pull is probably coming from inside you. Maybe you want to be twenty-five again, you see what I mean?"

The philosopher-astronomer of Steamboat Springs. He said he liked looking at stars because it was looking into the past. "The stars in the bull's face, that's how they looked a hundred and forty years ago. The light from those stars we're seeing now started coming to us before we were born. Kind of puts it into perspective, doesn't it?"

Sparks doesn't relate any of this to Connie. He only tells her that it was as if he and Eddie had found something they'd lost, that writing those songs together was like being back in little clubs in Texas, the ones they started in, before they even heard of Roy McCleod.

Among the papers Sparks has brought out to the terrace this morning is the "Friends of Hilda" letter he found at June's house. He unfolds it as he talks to Connie, and when he hangs up, he writes a letter to the address on the back, a post office box in Oregon. He puts a stamp on the envelope and goes out, still barefoot and in his robe, to the mailbox at the end of the driveway. The mimosa is in blossom and its peppery scent mingles with the sweet wild fennel.

"Oh Chip, hurry out there with the shovel and the bag of salt—you know, it's in the office by my desk. If this stuff freezes we're going to have to rent a jackhammer to get it off the sidewalk."

Chip, one of Roger's newest recruits, shrinks inside his black turtleneck. Yolanda wishes she had asked one of the hardier assistants, but it's too late now. "Bundle up," she says. "There are all sizes of rubber boots in the closet in the back, if you don't have any. But hurry. If it gets trampled and then freezes . . ."

He'll probably catch pneumonia and it will be all her fault. Yolanda would do it herself, but there are two customers-who-bear-watching in the store. It's a good day for shoplifters. Because of the weather, everyone is required to wear the kind of large voluminous coat that is the shoplifter's uniform. Yolanda sends Rick to watch over the thirteen-year-old sticky-fingered science fiction enthusiast, while she supervises the mouse-haired woman in the trench coat. She's over on the side where all the paperback fiction is arranged alphabetically according to author. It's the only section she goes to. It took Yolanda a while to get on to her, to realize she browsed but never bought. Yolanda finds if she stands nearby, the woman leaves after a few minutes.

The pale hand weaves like a butterfly, up and down the shelves, lighting here and there. Yolanda approves of her taste, but not her methods.

"Excuse me. Do you have *Mombatu*?" a voice asks.

She's a pretty young woman whose face reminds Yolanda of someone, but she can't think who. The stylish purple coat looks as if it had hardly got wet and the leather boots wouldn't last a block in this weather. She must have come by cab.

"I called and they said you had it. I called all over town and no one else has heard of it."

"What a shame. It's a wonderful book. You might have seen it in the display window? It's a perfect Valentine's Day gift."

"My boss sent me after it. He wants three copies. Do you have that many?"

"I think I might have three left." Yolanda bends to look under the Valentine's Day gift table where she in fact knows there are twenty copies of *Mombatu* stored.

"Who is your boss, by the way?"

"Roy McCleod?"

She says it as the younger people do, with a questioning inflection. Yolanda wonders why they do it like that. It's kind of endearing. It gives you permission in advance to say, "No, I never heard of him," or "You'll have to excuse me. I'm completely apolitical. He's a state representative, isn't he?"

Yolanda does neither. Instead she gives a vague nod, as if she thinks she knows who he is but she isn't sure.

Too late, she sees the mouse-haired fiction enthusiast walking empty-handed through the door right between Roger and the architect who, ironically enough, are planning where the anti-shoplifting scanner will go. Yolanda raises her hand toward Roger and then lets it drop. After all, she didn't actually see the theft occur and she doesn't want to embarrass the woman in the doorway in front of everyone.

It was Roger's idea to put in the anti-shoplifting device. Yolanda thinks it looks dreadful, and what if it misfires and buzzes someone completely innocent? But Roger said he couldn't be bothered memorizing every shoplifter who comes in, as Yolanda does, and besides, for all her vigilance, they still lose books. He's also planning a cafe upstairs where they can have readings. Yolanda is insisting on red paisley table covers and unmatched china cups. "Yolanda, since when have you been getting decorating ideas?" Roger was amused, but he's going along with her suggestion.

"You sold three of my books today," Gordon says. She hadn't expected him to show up in this weather. He told her that last year he didn't go out at all from January twenty-second to February eighteenth, but here he is again, waiting for her to close so they can have dinner together. He's going to the Kims' for some ribs. She already has a casserole from Ethan.

"Someone lifted a copy of Alice Munro's stories. Now I'm afraid she'll be back for the new hardcover when it comes in."

"Alice Munro?"

"No, the shoplifter."

"Who bought them? I figured today, of all days, no one would be out. Was it a particularly busy day?"

"What? Oh. All to the same person. Roy McCleod."

"Who's that? The name sounds familiar."

"A singer?" Yolanda tries the inflection the young woman used. She likes the effect.

They walk back to Yolanda's. The footing is treacherous because some brownstone owners shovel the walk in front of their houses and others don't. If you're not out there shoveling your walk the minute the snow hits, you get an icy track down the middle that's nearly impossible to remove. Yolanda slips on a bit of ice and falls into Gordon, who surprises her by catching her and holding on to her a moment longer than is necessary.

"Are you all right?"

"Yes, thanks." But her heart is jumping around. She looks at her savior in his down coat with hood up, lumpy scarf wrapped twice around his face. She imagines Roger sardonically smiling over her maidenly heart tremor.

She and Gordon have never repeated their sleepover experiment. Sometimes she thinks Gordon is gay, that Roger knows this, and that they are all laughing at her. Most of the time she's convinced it's something in her that makes Gordon take her as a friend but nothing more. If someone like the young woman in the purple coat came along, would Gordon be stimulated to carry on more than a just-friends relationship?

"You're hungry tonight," Yolanda observes. Gordon is gnawing away at his fourth sparerib.

"Mmmm." He sucks on the end of the bone.

Floor three is also enjoying a candlelit dinner. Floor-four adults are out for the evening. A basketball, or volleyball, is sailing through the living room.

Was *Mombatu* completely imaginary, or was it based on fact? Yolanda asks.

Gordon takes a paper napkin from the clean stack, wipes his hands on it, and leaves it with the wad of used ones on the other side of his plate. It was kind of a composite, he says, based on reading and research he did at the library.

"The political situation, the tribal thing?"

All the African nations have the same problem, more or less, of trying to work with the national boundaries left to them by the European colonists, boundaries that have nothing to do with tribal separations, so that very different, historically antagonistic peoples find themselves bound up together into one nation.

Gordon looks helplessly after a rib bone that has escaped and landed on the parrot-green rug. Never mind, she says. The tribe in *Mombatu*, the one that was so gifted musically, the one whose history and traditions were all in song—

It could fit many tribes, Gordon says. The one he was thinking of in particular was the Ilido of D'jarkoume.

D'jarkoume. She's heard of it.

There was a terrible massacre, does she remember? The ruling elite was wiped out in a matter of days. The minority tribe took over.

"I think an old friend of mine might live there, in the jungle."

"He's got to be crazy."

"She. She's involved in an experiment with apes. Living with chimpanzees, I think."

Well, that explains it. Women do things like that, go off to live with the animals. Does Yolanda know what the rain forest is like? There are rats as big as terriers, ants that can devour a human baby. Poisonous snakes. And there's the political situation. They could have a revolution at any time.

"But there must be something that's good, something that keeps her there. It can't be as terrible as you say."

There are attractions, Gordon admits. Certain people like the feeling of danger. Then too, it's an escape, isn't it? Some people find ordinary life more threatening than the exotic.

Would he ever want to visit, to go there? Yolanda takes Gordon's plate and retrieves the bone on her way to the kitchen.

"But why would I go now? The book is written. If I were

to go anywhere, it would have to be the Arctic, because that's
what I'm working on, but I'd be crazy to go there. If you travel
on the ground, besides the danger of frostbite, you risk getting
caught on a patch of ice that breaks off from the mainland
and gets swept out to sea. I'd have to rent a private plane to
take me around, which is just as dangerous and it's expensive . . ."

It isn't a basketball or a volleyball. It's a balloon. Yolanda
knows because one of the boys on floor four has opened the
window and shoved the balloon out. It dips and then catches
an updraft and soars up over the street and out of sight. Gordon, you can't just live in the imagination, she tells him. Sometimes you have to come out of this rut of a life you've set up
for yourself and venture forth, get involved, dare to experience
something, anything, firsthand.

Gordon is looking at her as she stands in the middle of her
studio apartment, lecturing him on life. Sauce from the spareribs lingers in the corners of his mouth. Behind him a ghostly
shape presses against the window pane. It is the balloon, captured by the wind.

"Let it in," she says.

"What?"

"The balloon. Let it in."

Gordon opens the window. The balloon flies in on a gust
of air. Gordon slams the window shut and the balloon bobbles
to the floor. Yolanda goes to wash the dishes.

When the university built the station, this tropical fantasy, this
Disneyland research center, they were in a high state of op-
timism. They did not provide for certain contingencies—gasoline shortages, unavailability of parts, military takeovers.
They did not see how easy it would be for the army to line
up the president and most of his cabinet on the dusty parade
grounds of Koume and shoot them all in the head.

The designers of the station planned for rain, for the sixty or so inches that fell each year. They put wide gutters on the houses and crisscrossed the green with raised gravel paths, but they did not make any provision for drought. They assumed that the spring behind the station would continue indefinitely to provide thirty researchers with showers and toilet flushes, and therefore did not put bulky, unsightly cisterns on the roofs, did not devise ways to catch and save the rain.

Maggie can hardly blame them. For three years she has seen the spring get low in the dry season. She has had plenty of time to come up with a plan that is better than this one of carting buckets up from the river. Each time she hasn't wanted to face it.

When she turned on the tap the other morning and it rattled and spit out a trickle of muddy water, her heart caught in her throat and she thought, This is it, as if much more was involved than the inconvenience of having no running water, as if this was a signal that it was time for her to—what? Shut the door behind her for the last time, go somewhere, do the next thing.

"Emanuel!"

He came running, which was good to see, considering how surly he's been lately. He agreed to walk to Dobo to find Mfui and try to get a truck from him and, if possible, some empty oil drums to store water in. With Mfui's truck, they will be able to haul enough from the river to take care of her needs for a while, if she's careful.

Maggie pours the plastic buckets she filled at the river into the drum beside the house. What good is all this effort if she only needs a shower afterward? She strips off her rubber boots, her forest clothes, and throws a basinful of precious water over her body. It must be over a hundred degrees and it's not even ten o'clock. She expected them back yesterday, thought that by now she'd have several drums of water, but something must have held them up. Maybe Mfui didn't have a truck that was working.

It's quiet in the clearing. The panda nuts are gone and everyone has to travel farther for food. Yesterday Katie came in with Poppy and Biff. They looked so thin, Maggie gave them a handout of eggs and bananas. They were on the porch with Hilda this morning, begging for more. She took them all down to the river where there were some sweet-leaved min-ninyo vines growing low. They all fed contentedly, even Hilda, but when Maggie left they tried to follow. She had to scream and threaten with the gun to get them to stay.

It's unnerving, this quiet. Even the monkeys are gone. There is usually a party of them coming through bellowing and screeching, with hornbills trumpeting their accompaniment, but now all she hears is a dry chittering sound, termites working their jaws. It's always in the background but other sounds generally cover it.

If Emanuel were here he'd be singing. It often annoys her because in addition to singing in French and in his own peculiar tribal language he also sings American songs in English, which he doesn't understand and so gets the words all wrong. But she would like singing now. It would drown out the relentless insect sound. Maybe that's why the locals are so obsessed with making music all the time, so they don't have to hear the dry rattle of insects gnawing at everything that is planted or built.

Maggie puts on a T-shirt and wraps a length of African cloth around her waist, a lappa. Her Western-style clothes rotted long ago. Marion once sent her new ones but Maggie never received them. It broke Marion's heart because she had put a lot of time into choosing them. Marion now contents herself with sending *Vogue*, presumably so that Maggie can keep up with the latest styles. It's as if Marion has a learning disability; she can't seem to grasp what Maggie's life is like here in the rain forest. She longs to see Maggie again, writes that she will buy clothes for Maggie, have them waiting for her when she gets off the plane in Los Angeles, if Maggie will only tell her what she wants. Anita Gerson is encouraging Maggie to come present a paper for a primate conference in Los Angeles in May. She says it's important to establish her credibility. Most animal researchers are constantly being visited and evaluated, but Maggie's case is special because she has chimps who have tested their strength against humans and who could attack a visitor. Not only that, the very purpose of Maggie's work, to de-acclimate her chimps to humans, would be jeopardized by having visitors. Anita says just the fact that Maggie could leave her chimps for an extended period of time would prove that the project was successful.

Maggie turns the pages of *Vogue*, a little more noisily than necessary, to cover the whisper of insects. She tries to picture herself talking, with slides, before an audience of primate people. As a group they are skeptical, envious. After all, there are only so many grants, limited funds for research. There are complex rivalries in the field that Maggie doesn't even know about, but which impinge upon her. They won't go easy on her, especially now, when her funds are mysteriously growing.

Does Anita actually believe that Maggie would abandon her chimps to show slides to a roomful of primatologists? She doesn't understand, she couldn't, even if Maggie sent long letters and Polaroids every day for a year. She'd have to live here, live this life, in order to know.

This is the hottest time of the day, when the sun is right over the clearing. Maggie dozes at the table, then gives up the struggle and lies on her bed. She falls asleep composing letters in her head to Anita and Richard about how dry it is, and how she needs a jeep so she can get out and cover more area.

She is not aware of falling asleep until something wakes her and propels her to the day room where she sees G.P. and Danny on the porch, screaming and clinging to the grid.

The smell of their shit hits her in the face. It's the smell of fear. They've defecated on the porch, something they would do only in fright or anger. Her own bowels loosen in empathy. She makes clucking calming sounds although she knows her wide eyes betray her, looking past them at the forest. She expects to see anything, poachers, elephants even. Calm down, calm down, won't you, for God's sake! Shhh!

They whimper, crouched down, trembling, hugging each other. Maggie strains her eyes, her ears, then it comes, almost sensed as a vibration rather than heard, a thumping, a fierce rapid drumming. It's a sound she hasn't heard in years, not since she went with Richard into the forest to watch his chimpanzees. When the band is on the move, the males find trees with wide spreading roots that stand like flying buttresses on a gothic cathedral. They rock back and forth on the edge of the buttresses and then leap and rapidly drum on the sides. The sound reverberates for miles. When the band is on the move.

Hilda is down by the river with Katie and the little ones. Maggie left them there, forced them to stay when they wanted to come back; perhaps they sensed even then that the wild chimpanzees were approaching. Maggie grabs her gun and then realizes she is wearing her skirt and sandals. She pushes G.P. and Danny aside to get to her muddy forest clothes which she left in a heap on the porch. She pulls them on, yanks at her boots.

"Hilda! Katie!" she shouts. As she plunges into the forest she hears G.P. and Danny screaming—the males she's been bringing up to defend her little band from wild chimps, the future leaders and protectors. They haven't even moved off the porch.

7

"Do we have spring fever or what?" Roger, coming in at ten minutes to one, stands for a moment surveying the window display that Yolanda has been working on all morning. She has taken seed packets and taped them up to make a frame for the scene within: Dorothy in a gardening apron and straw hat, watering can dangling from her fingers, surveying neat rows of books on gardening, cooking from the garden, decorating country houses, living off the land, memories of childhoods spent in the country. The books are meant to seem as if they've just pushed up out of the ground.

"A lot of people in the neighborhood have country homes or dreams of country homes. I thought we'd capitalize on it."

Floor three is gone every weekend now. Gordon is sure they've bought a place in Connecticut. Yolanda wonders if her display will draw them into the store.

For the first time since last October, it's warm enough to leave the door open. People are coming and going through the shoplifting detector. No one seems the least bit leery of it, but Yolanda still fears that the alarm will go off by accident. She does have to admit that it's nice not to have to scrutinize every customer who comes into the store.

Up the block, a small man swaddled in bulky gray warm-up clothes is being borne along in a sea of mothers with strollers. Gordon said that he didn't know if he could get away, that if the work was going well, he would stay with it. He wanted that freedom, didn't want to have to feel he had to be anywhere at a particular time, but here he is, coming to Yolanda at one on the dot. Yolanda puts her hand on his arm to rescue him from the flowing crowd. He looks startled, then smiles.

"Do you think you need that hat?" she asks. "It's supposed to be seventy today."

Gordon puts his hand on his head. "Oh. I must have put it on out of habit. It doesn't matter."

Roger says he never thought he'd see the time when Yolanda would take off two hours in the middle of the day. "It must be nice, to be in love in the spring," he drawls. But it isn't love. It's the combination of spring weather and a lightening of her sense of responsibility. She hadn't realized before what a burden it was having a silent partner. Now that Roy is out of the picture, she is much less anxious about the store, doesn't feel she has to be there twelve hours a day, seven days a week.

"Where are you taking me?"

"To the Conservatory Garden."

"Where's that?"

"About a Hundred and Fifth and Fifth."

"On the East Side?" Gordon stops at the curb.

"It isn't far, really. Do you want me to carry that?" Yolanda means the bag that holds their lunch.

"No, it's OK. It's just that I don't usually go to the East Side. My ex-wife lives there."

"I didn't know you were married."

"A long time ago, to someone who lives on the East Side."

"Do you think we'll run into her, if we don't leave the park?"

"Probably not. She works. In midtown, I think."

The Conservatory Garden is at a peak, with apple trees in full bloom and lilacs just beginning.

"Gordon, are you looking at this?"

"Hmm? Yes, but I don't want to talk about it. What do you say, except 'ooh, hmmm, oh!' In fact, Jean-Jacques Rousseau said that same thing, didn't he? That the only appropriate response before nature was 'Oh!' or the only proper prayer, because he only prayed outdoors—"

"Then say 'Oh!' Anything's better than nattering on about the anxiety center of the brain—"

"The *locus ceruleus*, the blue place."

"When we're surrounded by such beauty—"

"But then you see how you are being reduced to triteness, Yolanda?—'surrounded by beauty'—Isn't it better to see all this and keep up a conversation about some article you read in the *Times* and let the soul take it in, pure, uncontaminated by words?"

"But I'm not sure you're really seeing it."

"I am. I am. Ooh, ah, oh!" He twirls a clumsy circle under the falling blossoms.

Yolanda takes the lunch from the bag and arranges it on a bench in the sun: turkey and lettuce on wheatless, yeast-free bread that Ethan baked, carrot and cucumber sticks, seedless grapes, two small bottles of mineral water.

"A healthy lunch," Gordon remarks, picking up a sandwich in the middle so the filling droops out of either end. Two interested pigeons skid to a halt at his feet.

"Don't worry. One healthy lunch won't prolong your life." She is holding her sandwich particularly carefully, as if to demonstrate the proper way. "It's hard to imagine you ever being married."

"It wasn't my idea. She engineered the whole thing, and then she was the one who decided it wasn't working. That was her phrase, 'It's not working,' as if it were an appliance that couldn't be repaired." Gordon waves his sandwich through the air, attracting more pigeons from the far corners of the garden. "I thought it would be nice, you know, to have someone around who might remember to do things I forgot, like change the sheets, kind of like having a mother you could sleep with. But my wife said I never transferred the way I thought, from me to us. Apparently this marriage thing involved a whole other way of thinking, which I never got. That's why it didn't 'work.' "

Abruptly, the sandwich finds its way to Gordon's mouth. He greets it with small infantile grunts of pleasure.

Yolanda leans back on the bench and takes a sip of her mineral water. "I was never married, but I was very close to someone for a while. We were so close I didn't know where he ended and I began—a boy I met at college, one of those lone genius types who never have any friends, except me. I was his friend. Then he got famous. He was a—you know—a singer."

"Who? Anyone I know?"

"It was a long time ago." Yolanda puts the loose papers in the bag. "I never expected him to be famous. It was the last thing I ever would have expected."

Gordon says he doesn't know singers very well. He is scattering his crusts to the pigeons who are fighting over them in a cloud of dust and feathers. "I often think the reason my wife left me was that I didn't pick up my socks. She walked in after work and my socks were still lying on my side of the bed where I'd left them the night before. That just triggered it. She packed up and left. I often thought if I'd put my socks in the hamper, the thing would have gone on indefinitely. We'd still be married."

"Once you've been close to someone like that it never really ends. I mean, even though I wasn't married to this singer, sometimes I'll hear one of his songs—on the radio of a passing car—and I'll just stop—" And what? Yolanda doesn't know what she means to say, or why she is telling Gordon.

"Look at all these pigeons." Gordon waves his arms. "Let's go before they eat us alive."

Yolanda wants to walk under the wisteria arbor, which is up a steep flight of stairs. Gordon isn't sure it will be worth it, but she persuades him that the view will recompense them for their effort, and the experience of walking under blossoms will be an extra bonus.

Gordon puffs a bit going up the stairs but he doesn't complain. They look down on the tops of the apple trees and on an eddy of pigeons around the bench where they were sitting.

"I don't really know much about the male-female thing. I guess in my work that must come out. Reviewers probably mention that weakness, that failing."

No, not that she can recall, Yolanda says, but of course, the adventures in his books are so dazzling, the places. Now that she thinks of it, in *Mombatu* there are some very good bits of the male-female thing. "Rachel and Hernandez," she says. "Up in the trees, when they're both hanging from ropes . . ."

Gordon smiles. "That was nice. I'd forgotten that part. But it's easy when you're making it up. It's easy to imagine when both parts are you. Getting an 'us' out of two distinct people"—he gestures to the space between them—"seems almost impossible, in real life."

Is the sound of windshield wipers working in the rain intrinsically melancholy, the even funereal beat, the whine in minor key, or is it because we only listen to it in the hollow times, the between times, like when we're sitting on the highway waiting for a wreck we can't see to be cleared away?

Sparks is in his Bronco, watching the students pass, thinking how young they have become since he last played a concert here. Bare legs flash beneath a yellow slicker. Sparks rolls down the window. Can she tell him where the anatomy lab is? She leans in with the trusting manner of girls up north, and gives him precise and intricate directions.

In the laboratory students are picking over bones. Sparks asks for Dr. Davis and averts his eyes from what looks like a desiccated human arm. A young woman pushes her glasses back on her nose and points to an office in the back.

The door is open and the reading lamp is on, as if this Dr. Davis has just stepped out, leaving his work on his desk, presided over by two mounted skulls, one human, one probably ape. Sparks half expects to see Maggie in the photos tacked on the wall, but the shots are of chimpanzees, not humans. There is one wall of bookshelves, the kind found in student rooms: metal strips with holes, the shelves fitted into them. A professor should have permanent bookshelves at least. Among the books are some carved African masks of black monkey faces with mirrors for eyes. There is one crude statue of a man, crusted over with something dark and crackly.

"Dried blood and dung. Mashed entrails. Supposedly, if you touch it your hand falls off."

Sparks pulls his hand back and hides it in his pocket. The man in the doorway is short, slightly pudgy, sturdy. He wears corduroys and a plaid shirt. A dark beard obscures his face so Sparks can't read his expression, but his wide stance tells Sparks that he has invaded this man's territory.

"That's what the guy who sold it to me claimed, anyway. It increases the value of a piece if it's been used in ceremonies. But don't worry. He desanctified it so it couldn't cause any more damage. See, the arm's missing. If it's not whole, it doesn't have power."

Sparks sees now that the idol's arm has been hacked off at the elbow.

"I'm Richard Davis." He thrusts out a hand for Sparks to

shake. It's muscular and warm. "I've always enjoyed your music. I was a follower of the Light, from the beginning."

"The world gets smaller as you get older," Sparks says.

There are only two chairs in the office. Richard has slid into his behind the desk. Sparks takes the other, a straight-back chair without arms, which he turns around and straddles. As he speaks, Richard absentmindedly caresses the top of the human skull. Both skulls are worn smooth, from Richard's hands, no doubt. He is a man who plays with bones.

Maggie never shared her past with Richard, at least, not the part she spent with the Light, probably because she couldn't have been on the road with the group and also assisting in a graduate lab as she claimed. When Richard read Sparks's letter and recognized the name from the Light, he pulled out an old album, and sure enough, Maggie was on the back. "She looked familiar when I first met her. Maybe that's why I warmed to her in the first place. And all the time, it was that face on the record jacket."

It would have been the *Sweet Mercy* album. Maggie talked Roy into letting her sing on it. Sparks was against it because Maggie's voice, small and bland, lacked quality. Roy gave in to her; he always did. Roy liked her desperate energy. "Having Maggie around is like handling dangerous chemicals. She could just go whoom! Go right up!"

Poor Maggie. Sparks always suspected she was dangerous mainly to herself. She fought so hard to be on an album and the only effect it ever had was to discredit her with Richard.

"So what happens now? Are you going to call her back, take her monkeys away? How serious is this?"

Richard smiles. With his beard, his watchful eyes, he looks somewhat apelike himself. Sparks had expected him to be more connected to Maggie. After all, he sends out her newsletter. Instead, he seems to be feeling Sparks out for information about her. What does he think Sparks knows?

Richard asks him about the political situation in D'jarkoume. Sparks doesn't know a thing about it. There was a coup, Richard says. A lot of his friends in the former government were assassinated, which is why he's afraid to go back, why he can't check up on Maggie, what she's doing.

Check up on Maggie? Sparks wonders what she could be doing out there with her chimpanzees. He assures Richard that he hasn't seen Maggie in years. It was just curiosity about an old friend that brought him here.

"It's a long trip to make out of mere curiosity."

Sparks doesn't want to tell him about the words to the song. It wouldn't sound good, that Roy puts a couple of old names in a song and Sparks drops everything to go chasing after—what? Hints, fragments.

"I like to travel. I have a Bronco fixed up with a bed, a sound system . . ."

The lab has emptied out. A faucet drips somewhere, echoing the rain outside.

"Sounds kind of depressing, sleeping in a car in the rain. My house is ten minutes away. Why don't you follow me there? I'll make us dinner, put you up in the guest room. It has a view, when it isn't raining."

Like Sparks, Richard prefers to live in high places. They go for a mile or more up a winding road before Richard pulls off up an even steeper driveway. Through the rain, Sparks makes out a log house with a deck, kind of a Northwest chalet, Paul Bunyan modern, something Richard built himself, no doubt. An old German shepherd comes out from under the porch, wagging her tail.

Sparks likes the inside better than the outside. In fact, he could live in this house, and he doesn't feel that way about most. He likes the open kitchen and living room, big and square with plenty of windows on one side and a stone fireplace with floor-to-ceiling built-in bookshelves on the other. The books have to do with anatomy, anthropology, myths, not the usual. Sparks could hole up here and just read for a month.

Richard pulls out a bottle of decent California burgundy and starts the logs in the fireplace while Sparks inspects his sound system. It's antiquated but still good. Richard would like to play something for Sparks, does he mind? Go ahead. Sparks has music on all the time at home.

Oh, hey, anything but that. He must have heard it ten times on the radio coming up. Besides, this version sounds terrible. Is there something wrong with the speakers?

Richard comes out from behind the kitchen counter, wiping his hands on a towel he has stuck in his belt. "No, don't turn it off yet. Have you listened to the background?"

Those clicks and cries, moans and shudders, that gibberish behind Roy's own senseless mutterings, of course Sparks has heard it, and it disturbs him. "I think it has to do with the beat. It's off by our standards. They stick an extra half measure in."

Richard has rerecorded the tape so that the background track is prominent and Roy's voice recedes.

"I couldn't believe it when I first heard it on the radio," Richard says. "He's got— Do you know where that song comes from?"

"Africa."

"Yeah, but what country?"

"I don't know one of those countries from another. They keep changing the names."

"D'jarkoume."

When Richard says it, it's as if Sparks knew all along. That story June gave him, about Roy picking up an African group in Paris, never sounded right. It's Maggie. Of course. It has to be. "Maggie days . . . Frangipani daze . . ." Sparks checks the lyrics on the back of the album jacket.

"That song they're singing?" Richard is back in the kitchen, putting hamburger into the skillet. "If you played it in D'jarkoume they'd throw you in prison."

"Why?"

Richard breaks up the hamburger with a spatula. It's a long story, but basically the situation in D'jarkoume is that there are two tribes, the talls and the shorts. The shorts are the original inhabitants—going back a thousand years, give or take a hundred. They make up ninety percent of the population and until the coup seven years ago, they were pretty much running the country after the French left.

"The coup—that was the talls?"

"The talls. The army. Although they insist that there are no tribes anymore. Everyone is equal. But all the government officials, all the officers in the army, almost everyone who owns property or has money, is tall. The workers, the peasants, are short."

"So what's it have to do with this song?"

Richard hands him the spatula and begins chopping tomatoes. "The shorts have an artistic tradition. They're skilled carvers of masks, idols. They also have a tradition of song and dance. Every event in tribal history has its song, its dance. That's how they preserve their heritage."

"This song is essentially the Ilido's—the short tribe's—national anthem. If you played it in D'jarkoume today it would be like playing the Marseillaise in Vichy France."

Richard figures that Roy's recording of the song is being heard in D'jarkoume. It's an international hit, and right across the border from D'jarkoume is the most powerful radio station in all of Africa. It's commercially owned, plays popular music, African and American mostly, several hours a day. Richard hasn't heard anything, from Maggie or his other friends in D'jarkoume, but then, their letters have to pass through censors. He has to assume that the record is being heard and that it's having an effect.

Richard takes the spatula from Sparks and stirs in the tomatoes. The tape is over but Richard doesn't put another one on. He covers the pot. How about a soak in the hot tub while the chili is simmering? Chili is better if it cooks awhile.

The rain has changed into a cold mist. They pad naked out to the deck. Sparks holds the wine and glasses while Richard pulls the cover off the barrel, releasing a cloud of steam. The dog sticks a friendly inquisitive nose into Sparks's crotch. Richard growls to her about manners. Sparks lowers himself slowly through the steam.

"How's the temperature?" Richard comes down opposite Sparks.

"Perfect. I have the same arrangement in LA. Only it's a Jacuzzi, and my view is downtown Hollywood."

"There's a pond out there in the daytime, whenever the rain stops." Richard gestures past the porch railing.

The dog groans as she settles on the deck beside them. Sparks smells wet dog, pine needles, and earth.

"Now you know why I lured you up here." Richard's face is partly lost behind the humid exhalations of the tub.

"Lured." An odd choice of words. It reminds Sparks that Richard is a stalker, a watcher of wild animals. What's he looking for? What does he want Sparks to tell him? And why is Sparks here? They are both waiting for the other to tell him something.

When Sparks turns the Bronco around in Richard's driveway the next morning, the rain is coming down as if yesterday had been only a warmup. Folded in the pocket of his jacket is a paper Richard gave him with the phone number and address in New York City of the UN delegation from D'jarkoume, the diseases he should have himself innoculated against, the names of people he can contact once he reaches D'jarkoume.

It was Sparks's idea to go. He came up with it after dinner, as he and Richard took turns, and competed, at tending the burning logs in the fireplace. Richard tried to talk him out of it, telling him about the difficulties, the dangers, but the more Richard talked, the more eager Sparks was to go.

The odd thing is, Sparks doesn't know why, what's driving him. He's after something but he doesn't know what it is, only knows when he is getting closer. He felt it when he picked up the letter at June's house and discovered it was written by Maggie and addressed to Roy, when he heard his name in Roy's song, and last night, when he was talking to Richard about D'jarkoume.

Does he expect to discover Roy with Maggie fomenting revolution in the jungle? Last night Sparks went out to the Bronco and brought in some marijuana—Richard hadn't had any since graduate school—and they got to sharing some, talking more freely, making jokes. Sparks was picturing Roy and Maggie in camouflage fatigues and mirrored sunglasses, leading an army of short oppressed Africans. "And I'll show up at the last minute and save them."

"Maybe you will."

Richard said he tried to rescue Maggie during the coup. He'd had something going with her, even thought about marrying her. "But she was in love with a chimpanzee—no, seriously." He jabbed at the logs with the poker. The fire hissed back at him. "That's why she's dangerous. She'll do anything. It doesn't have to be logical or moral, as long as she thinks it's what Hilda needs, what she needs to survive."

"Oh my God! For Christ's sake, put that thing away. Shit. Didier! Tu m'emmerdes! Ce fusil! Vas! Allez!" What's the meaning of it anyway, a guard with an automatic rifle? He'll kill them all. Didier has brought a soldier with him, a tall jumpy young man who leaped out the moment the jeep pulled in front of the house and trained his gun on the forest. What if some of the animals had been here? He would have killed them.

Maggie can't think of the French for "Put that thing away."

Finally she gets them to understand, she hopes, that the guard is not to shoot the chimpanzees, no matter how much they threaten him, that they are not dangerous, that they merely look frightening, which isn't completely true, unfortunately.

G.P. has become a terror, attacking the little ones for no reason, even challenging Hilda and Maggie. Maggie keeps her BB gun with her at all times. It's the presence of the wild chimps that is making him behave like this. Patrols of them— she has to assume they're Richard's group—have been lurking in the area. Maggie has to take her group out and stand guard while they forage. So far the wild chimps have been too shy to show themselves. She hopes they've gone now. There's been no sign of them for three days. Maggie sent hers out alone today for the first time.

At least the guard can be of some use. He can help unload the supplies. But the guard won't budge from the hood of the jeep, where he sits cradling his gun. And Didier won't carry packages because it would cause him to lose face in front of the guard.

Where is your boy? Call your boy, Didier says.

Emanuel is in town, or at least, Maggie assumes he is. Mfui came a couple of days ago to haul some more water for her and he took Emanuel back with him. Emanuel often goes off for a few days at a time. Maggie suspects he has a wife or a girlfriend in Dobo. When he comes back he takes care of as much work in one day as he used to in three, so Maggie hasn't complained.

She opens the back of the jeep and slides out a carton of canned goods, thinking that if she starts they will be shamed into helping. The guard doesn't even look at her. He's keeping his gun trained on the forest. What does he expect to come out of there? Absurd. Didier remains seated at the table, won't even get up to open the door for her. She remembers that it is normal here for women to carry while the men loll around.

Maggie is dirty and sweating when she finally finishes and joins Didier at the table where he sits immaculate in his pressed khakis. She usually offers Didier a Coke or a beer, refreshment after coming so far, but she'll be damned if she'll offer them anything. She gets down to business, as cold and abrupt as she can manage to be in French, which always forces her into a tentative, childish manner because of her uncertainties in the language.

Why did he bring a guard with him?

It's a new regulation, Didier says softly, as if he's afraid of being overheard. There has been trouble in Koume and all government employees must be protected by armed guard.

What kind of trouble?

Didier lowers his head. In the main market, three tax inspectors were discovered murdered. Their legs had been chopped off at the knee.

Beyond Didier's head is a long shadow on the wall, which Maggie realizes for the first time is mildew. It sickens her, the way the mildew creeps in. It turns her stomach.

Cruel mutilations happen in D'jarkoume, more than Maggie likes to think. It's a primitive culture. A couple of years ago in Dobo, two little boys disappeared. They were later discovered with their hearts and livers cut out. It was assumed the organs were used in a sacrificial ceremony.

But why, if murders took place in Koume, would the army send a guard with Didier to Dobo?

Didier, with his head down, his shoulders hunched, looks frail. He speaks to her in a low urgent voice about a song, an American song that has become a "hit"—he uses the American expression—all over the world. It's forbidden within D'jarkoume, but it comes in on the airwaves from Waza-Balu. People play it everywhere. The English words make no sense, but behind the English words and the American singer, there is another song of the Ilido tribe. Hearing that song is driving the Ilido into a frenzy.

The authorities are confiscating all radios. Didier is going to have to take Maggie's and keep it for a while.

Why? He knows it's not a two-way, just a plain radio. Maggie hardly listens to it, but still, it is some connection to the outside world.

It's for her own good, Didier says. If he doesn't take it, the guerrillas might steal it and kill her to get it. They're savages, wild men.

The guard, sitting on the jeep, transfers his gun to one hand and brushes a fly from his face. Maggie feels as if a terrible and imminent danger has been revealed to her, but then she stops herself. Just as when one of the chimpanzees comes flying to her in fright, she has to remember that Didier's fears are not necessarily her own. Even if a war should break out, she will be a neutral party, not involved.

Still, a war will be inconvenient. It will interfere with her mail, her supplies. If there is a rebellion, she only hopes it's over fast, like the last one was. How irresponsible and typical, somehow, of an American to make a popular song out of a tribal anthem. She would bet it was someone from her generation, somebody left over from the sixties, using politics to squeeze out one more hit, somebody full of uninformed and ultimately selfish idealism, someone who doesn't care to think about the misery he could be bringing on a country he's probably never seen.

Maggie's hand is lying between Didier's two long black ones, which are soft and unpleasantly clammy. He has never held her hand before or spoken to her of love. She strains to hear what he is saying. She bends close and watches his lips. It helps her to understand if she can see the person shaping the words.

She won't forget him, will she? They have been lovers—or loving, she isn't sure what he means. She *owes* him—or she should? If there is a war, he will have to escape. She will take him with her, won't she? She won't forget?

Maggie withdraws her hand. Don't be absurd. There won't be a war.

But if there is, he insists.

His gold Rolex gleams on his dark wrist. The whites of his eyes are gold too, at least in this light, but his teeth are incredibly white. He isn't showing her his teeth now. He is imploring her with his eyes.

Yes, yes, as he is saying, he did rescue her from jail in D'jar after the coup. They probably would have let her out in a few days anyway, but she was wildly grateful at the time. It wasn't pleasant, the jail in D'jar. But what does she know about him, really? A man who wears a gold Rolex watch in a country where the average yearly income is six hundred dollars. A man who drives a Mercedes jeep, when his countrymen travel on foot, or if they're fortunate, packed into broken-down minibuses. You have to ask yourself, how does he get his money? What did he do to get that watch? Just because he's always been good to Maggie doesn't mean that Didier couldn't be guilty of crimes she couldn't imagine.

The guard shifts his gun. Didier rises. Sitting, he and Maggie are about on the same level, but when he stands he towers over her. It's his legs. All the Moro have long legs. For an instant, Maggie sees the legs, in their pressed khakis, cut off at the knee. She looks away. He turns her face toward him. They were lovers, he reminds her.

He takes a cloth from his pocket and wipes the dust from the driver's seat. Cautiously, the guard moves from the hood to the passenger's side. The jeep leaves fast in a cloud of red dust. If there is a war, Didier will never make it this far into Ilido territory to claim the rescue he says she owes him.

She must get herself a jeep, a truck, some transportation. She cannot afford to be dependent upon anyone in times like these.

8

JUNE

VOLUME VII, NO. 6

FRIENDS OF HILDA

At last! A break in the drought. We had our
first real downpour last evening, heralded by
black and white colobus monkeys bellowing
and screaming, hornbills blasting like a bunch
of drunkards with party horns, and finally
and most dramatically by our own little band.
Once so spoiled by civilization, so cut off
from their instincts that they used to run for
cover at the first sign of rain, they have
evolved into creatures of the forest who
understand that their well-being depends
upon rain, that rain is to be celebrated, not
feared.

I was on the porch wondering, with my
poor dense denatured human consciousness,
what was causing the monkeys and birds to

raise such a racket, when G.P. came tearing
across the clearing waving a palm frond.
Hilda screamed and ran to hug my waist.
(She's coming into estrus and G.P. has been
courting with more than usual vigor.) But
G.P.'s display had to do with rain, not
mating. He galloped in a circle, hitting the
ground with his branch, stamping his feet.
Enter Danny—our skittish lab chimp, who
screamed when his bare feet first stepped on
grass—also waving a palm frond, hair frizzed
with excitement, eyes blazing. Katie and the
little ones were sitting up in the oil-nut palm,
out of harm's way, where they could get a
good view.

G.P. and Danny continued their display for
a full ten minutes until the sky was black and
the rain was crashing down around them. I
stood watching, shivering, feeling for those
ten minutes as if I were back in time with our
prehuman ancestors, witnessing the first rain
dance, the first religious ecstasy.

It rained last night, but not enough to get the spring running
again, just enough to make the paths slick. Emanuel left a
week ago to bring Mfui with his truck to fill the barrels again
and hasn't returned.

Maggie doesn't know what to do about Emanuel. Scolding
is no longer effective. He's changed in the last year, as if he
realizes that Maggie has become more dependent on him than
he is on her. True, she lets him keep the house he lived in
with his father; she gives him a weekly salary, but if Emanuel
were to leave Maggie, she'd be lost. Who does she know
locally? Mfui. Fat Mfui with his sly sideways glances would

put someone else up here to help her, but could she trust him? At least she's known Emanuel since he was a boy. She had his hernia repaired at the hospital in D'jar. The veterinarian did it for him. "You bring your chimpanzee in to the doctor, but you let your boy walk around with a hernia," he accused. The veterinarian was Ilido, one of the few educated ones who stayed on after the coup. A lot of boys had herniated navels, Maggie said. It was quite common. Common among poor boys who don't have anyone who can pay for an operation, the vet countered. He did it himself for fifteen dollars more than what she was already paying for Hilda.

God damn. Maggie's foot slips in the mud and she goes down on one knee. It's going to be harder coming back when her buckets are filled with water. She hangs them from a stick she uses as a yoke across her shoulders, an arrangement that leaves her top-heavy and unable to use her hands for balance. It doesn't help that Hilda keeps stepping in front of her.

"Hilda, go, go, give me some room for God's sake. Shoo."

Hilda scampers ahead, then looks back over her shoulder. Her red bottom blazes like a beacon in the dark forest, but Hilda doesn't want anything to do with G.P. She used to be contemptuous of him. Now she's terrified. Maggie thinks she's exaggerating her fear to get Maggie's sympathy. At every sound she whimpers and runs back to Maggie. She did not want Maggie to leave the house without the gun. "Look, I can't carry two buckets of water and a gun," Maggie said when Hilda tried to drag her back for it. "If you're so afraid of G.P., why don't you carry the gun?" She actually considered, only briefly, letting Hilda take it, until she realized the idea was insane, or close to it.

Water from last night's rain is still dripping down through layers of leaves. Maggie's soaked through, from rain and per-spiration. Her boots are heavy with mud. Hilda, nimble on all fours, forgets for a moment that she is pathetic and afraid and goes on ahead. She even snatches a handful of succulent new leaves. Maggie smiles. Hilda is becoming a chimp in spite of herself.

"Hoo?" Hilda comes whimpering to Maggie.

"For Christ's sake, what is it now?" Maggie reaches for her gun just in case, finding, of course, not the gun but the stick she uses for a yoke.

They are at a place where a tree fell last year. Nothing remains of the giant trunk but the long rectangular clearing marking where it fell. Gkoura berry bushes have taken over the space, at least temporarily. Katie and the little ones are grabbing them by the handful. Hilda is so relieved that G.P. is not with them that she rushes forward and hugs everyone. Then they all have to hug Maggie. Maggie sits on the ground and leans back against a Djahin tree, waiting for Hilda to finish feeding.

The animals spread out, quietly munching on berries, moving in and out of patches of sun. There haven't been enough of these quiet times recently. Whenever G.P. is around, Maggie feels more like a prison warden than a guardian. It was a mistake bringing G.P. into the group. He'll never be a leader and protector. Instead, Maggie has to protect everyone against him.

Maggie must have fallen asleep because she wakes at a tugging on her scalp. Hilda is going through her hair, removing sticks and leaves. Katie and the babies have moved on. Maggie gives Hilda a quick hug, picks up her buckets and stick, and they continue.

The river is dry where Maggie usually finds water. She and Hilda have to walk the muddy bed for quite a way before they come to water that is relatively clear. Maggie steps carefully, on the lookout for snakes that may have come down to drink. She's seen more snakes this year than in all the years before. It's the lack of rain that draws them down from the trees, out from their holes, searching for water. Just two weeks ago she nearly stepped on a gaboon viper, a snake she had seen only in pictures and in her dreams. Always when she dreams of snakes, it is the gaboon viper, biting her arm. She shakes and shakes her arm and it hangs on with its fangs, its hideous short thick body writhing in the air.

This actual viper was in the leaves. Maggie was just about to put her foot down when it moved. All she saw was a portion of its back, but she knew what it was. She didn't have to see its piggy little eyes, its broad head, to recognize the gaboon viper, the one that bites and doesn't let go until its victim expires.

"Hilda?"

The sounds are from the other side of the water, but she didn't see Hilda cross. "Hilda?"

It's G.P., comical with a sprig of green behind one ear, G.P., the clown who would be king.

"Good morning, G.P." Maggie says this louder than necessary, a little theatrically, to give Hilda a chance to start toward home or hide herself in a bush. "I like that wreath you're sporting. Very Roman Empire."

G.P. sidles down the bank until he is at the edge of the water. He is watching her, but when Maggie tries to catch his eye he looks away.

"Well, OK, I guess things haven't been so good between us, have they, G.P.? What with my waving the gun at you every time you try to court Hilda, but it's your method, G.P. You lack finesse." Maggie is filling her buckets.

Damned if he hasn't crossed, farther up where it's dry, and he's coming down her side, fast (they're fast when they want to be, and quiet). His hair is shaggy—makes him look bigger. He's lost his foolish bit of greenery. Maggie is thrilled by how wild he looks.

She puts her buckets down carefully. No use trying to walk

away from G.P. when he's like this. He's liable to barrel right into her and knock her over. She squats down with her back to him, something she's seen Katie do when G.P. comes down on her. It seems to appease him.

She hears him stop, puzzled, because she's never done this. Usually she screams and waves the gun. He pads around in front of her, still not meeting her eyes, stealing little glances. Too late, Maggie realizes she's made a mistake. He can tell she doesn't have her gun with her. The stick she uses for a yoke isn't far away. She tries to calculate how much time it would take to make a lunge for it. As if reading her mind, G.P. grunts and sits down between Maggie and the stick. He presents his back to her. He wants to be groomed!

"OK, you big baby." Maggie grunts and clucks, going over G.P.'s back. This is fine as long as he doesn't decide to return the favor. G.P. is an unmerciful groomer. Any slight imperfection on the skin gets rubbed and worked over.

He relaxes and stretches before her so she can work on his armpit. No wonder Hilda is afraid of him. His arms, the very bones, are so much thicker and heavier than Hilda's. It didn't help that Hilda spent her growing years sitting at nursery tables coloring and doing puzzles while G.P. played on trapezes and trampolines. Maggie thinks he's remarkably agile, even compared to wild chimps.

That's not Hilda—no, it's Danny. Of course Danny would have to be around. No doubt he's been watching all this time. Maggie will never trust Danny. There's something schizzy about him, no matter what Anita says. At least G.P. and Hilda were raised by humans. They may be odd for chimps but they've been socialized by someone. Danny was simply deprived. His responses are all out of whack. They don't relate to what's going on around him.

He's interested in this grooming session. Maggie hopes if she ignores him he'll go away. Instead, Danny sits close and begins tentatively fingering through her hair. Ordinarily, if Maggie were home with her gun within reach, she might feel flattered at this kind of peaceful contact, a first for Danny, but not here, trapped between the two males, with no weapon.

She puts a grunt of finality to her efforts on G.P. and moves toward her buckets. Danny screams. He pulls her hair. G.P. wakes out of his grooming stupor and jumps up. His close-set eyes, like marbles, are bouncing around, assessing the situation. Maggie crouches and whimpers, hoping he'll make Danny let go. G.P. grabs at Maggie's hair too and pulls hard. Maggie doesn't know if he's trying to pull her away from Danny or if he and Danny are ganging up on her.

She screams and one of them or both push her face down in the mud. Mud fills her nose, her mouth. Her head is wrenched up by the hair and jammed back into the mud. Something comes down on her back and her mind goes black.

It seems that she's waited a long time to take a breath, dangerously long. She has to breathe. Her head rolls to one side. She draws in, then whimpers.

There is a soft reluctant suck when her head comes out of the mud, as if the earth had already accepted her into itself. How long has she been like this? Her stick, her overturned buckets are nearby. Her arm reaches for the stick but her chest resists. She scrabbles through the mud, half on her side, before she can get to it.

If her back were broken she wouldn't be able to move her legs. She stands. It's the breathing that hurts and she smells worse than the mud. She's messed her pants.

She can hear them, Danny, G.P., Hilda—Hilda screaming for her—but she can't look for them. Her mind lurches from one plan to another but her body won't stop stumbling away from them, toward home.

She peels off her clothes and leaves them in a stinking heap outside the door. She throws water on her body, all she can reach with a cup, that's what she has the strength to lift, a cup of water, but she's still not clean. She can't stop whimpering or shaking and she can't make herself take the gun and go back for Hilda.

"Yolanda, this is Thomas," Roger says.

Yolanda shakes hands with Thomas: short and slender, black hair, green eyes, Slavic cheekbones. Roger is hiring them younger and more beautiful. How does he find them for $4.50 an hour? Roger is looking splendid this morning, in a blue blazer with, of all things, a silk scarf thrown around his neck, more impresario than part-owner of a bookstore. Ever since he began organizing the readings, Roger has been fancying himself a producer.

"Yolanda and I are co-owners," Roger explains to Thomas. "The readings are my innovation. I do them and the cafe. Yolanda mostly takes care of the nuts and bolts, ordering, keeping track of stock—and, oh, she does the windows."

"The windows are amazing."

"Yes, well, that's Yolanda's art form, you know. Dorothy— that's the mannequin's name. We never call her the dummy—"

"Roger, shh! She'll hear you." Yolanda plays along.

Thomas says he likes the window because everyone else up and down Broadway is doing Father's Day. "It's brilliant doing war. I hadn't realized there were so many titles out on war."

"I know. I said, 'Yolanda, why war?' And she said it was in honor of Flag Day. It's quite unusual, isn't it?"

"For some reason, books come out in clots. This spring is full of war books," Yolanda explains.

"And where did you get the World War I helmet and gas mask?"

"Oh! There's a little store in the East Village—"

"Yolanda comes in, wheezing away, because of course she has terrible allergies and the place was so filthy, but she has her prize, her gas mask. She practically died, going down there." They've moved so they are admiring the window from the back. "But Dorothy wears the mask with aplomb. Nothing fazes her, not even war," Roger continues, "which I guess is why Yolanda loves her. She's able to do all the things Yolanda can't." Roger puts his arm around Yolanda's shoulders. "Oh, here, another foible I should warn you about. See that novel?—*Mombatu*—it's in every window, no matter what the theme. It's got some tribal skirmish woven into the plot; that's her justification this time. The real—"

"Roger!" Yolanda squirms out from under his arm.

"She's got this thing going with the author—"

"Roger!"

Thomas's green eyes study Yolanda.

"—one of these torrid—"

"Roger, stop. You're making me break out in hives. And there's a line at the registers." Yolanda steps up to the check-out counter. "I'll take the next person in line, please."

The tips of her ears are burning. She hates herself for playing into Roger's caricature of her, a dotty old maid who lives vicariously through her store dummy. If anything, Roger is more impossible since he became her partner.

By noon Yolanda really does have a full case of hives. Even though she brought her lunch, some leftovers from last night's dinner, she decides to go around the corner to Ethan's. He might have something for her.

Ethan's New Age Take-Out Kitchen is beneath The Constant Reader with an entrance on the sloping side street. He's taken what was a nasty little half-underground space and done wonders with it: black and white vinyl tiles, white ceramic tiles on the walls, butcher-block counters—all sparkling clean and dust-free, because most of Ethan's customers have allergies. They come from all over the city and the suburbs. Yolanda is fortunate to have Ethan right around the corner.

The first time she went to him was the day after Christmas,

she remembers, two years ago. After her mother died, Yolanda went up to spend Christmas with her brothers and their families, who were living in the old house. Her sisters-in-law cooked with lots of sugar and prepared foods. For dinner they had packaged croissant dough wrapped around frankfurters, store-bought coleslaw, canned fruit cocktail in Jell-O topped with Cool Whip for dessert. Christmas Eve, they left Yolanda with the babies and went off to the bowling alley. Yolanda, to her mortification, came down with hives and terrible asthma.

Her choice was either to call her brothers at the bowling alley or die on the kitchen floor. They came home and drove her to the emergency ward, where she was given some antihistamine for her swelling. The doctor said it was probably something she ate. The next morning, Christmas, Yolanda asked her brothers to drive her to the airport.

Often Ethan's is full of customers, but that day it was empty, as it is today. Ethan was standing, as he is today, behind the counter in his white coat, tall and thin like a stork with his long legs and large nose, which fits him now but which, Yolanda imagines, must have caused him some pain in adolescence. He has the studied calm of someone who's learned to weather the unconsciously cruel teasing people sometimes indulge in.

He has a way of focusing on you, of asking the right questions that get you to think. They had discussed the visit to her brothers. He wrote down on a clean white pad everything Yolanda had had to eat. He asked about other things, but did not write the answers down: when her mother died, how the house had changed (playpens in the living room, her mother's breakfront banished to the basement because Patty said it made the dining room too dark).

He had said he wanted to put her on a preservative- and sugar-free diet for a week and see how it worked. Later, he also took her off yeast, wheat, and cow's milk.

Today he has her sit on a stool by the counter while he touches her hives with his long cool fingers and questions her on what she's been eating.

"I'm going to put you on a cleansing diet for a few days," he says. "Cleansing and healing."

He has just stirred up a pot of oat bran and dried papaya. They sit on stools at the counter and have bowls of it with goat's milk. Yolanda begins to feel better, cleansed and healed.

Does she ever go away on vacation? Ethan asks.

Yolanda says that she traveled a lot for many years after college and hasn't really felt the need since. "Those times were so wonderful. We were all friends, like a family. We were young, and after a few years, rich," she smiles. "One time we rented a lovely house on the beach in Jamaica, with a cook who fed us homemade banana bread every morning. That was pre-allergies. Anyway, it would be hard to go someplace alone, after those times."

Ethan opens a file drawer beneath the counter—he has his place beautifully organized—and comes up with a brochure for a healing center in the Berkshires. Try it, he says. It's a very spiritual place. You're encouraged to interact with the other guests. It's impossible to feel lonely. He goes several times a year, sometimes only for a weekend, and comes back feeling renewed.

"Olly? It's Sparks."

"Sparks?" Yolanda sits up in bed. Sparks calling her in the night. It can only be Roy. Something's happened to Roy.

"Hey, did I wake you up? You sound—"

"No, no. It's OK." The light is on across the street, floor four. Seeing it reassures Yolanda. It's not that late. She went to bed early.

"You sound worried."

"Well, I was. It's unusual, you calling—"

"This wasn't a good idea. I'll call back when—"

"Oh, for heaven sakes, Sparks, I'm awake now. Don't hang up or I'll never get back to sleep, wondering—"

He is calling about Roy. Wants to know if she's listened to Roy's new album, *Night Journey*.

In fact, it's the first of Roy's albums that Yolanda hasn't listened to, but she doesn't tell Sparks this, wouldn't want him to know how she's always rushed to buy each new album, taken it home to listen to it in private, over and over again, sifting through the jumbled words and images, the apparently casual asides, for messages, secret messages for her, Yolanda. And she finds them. Every time Roy has a new album, Yolanda hears in the songs how he is coming back to her. This time she decided to spare herself the agony and forgo listening to Roy's songs. Selling his half of the store was Roy's final message to her.

Now as if to mock her, tease her, subvert the first rational decision she's made in regard to Roy, Sparks is racing on about the album . . . an African song . . . Maggie. It hurts even more if Maggie is involved with Roy. How can Sparks not see that? He used to be more sensitive. Yolanda leans back on her pillows and closes her eyes. She wishes Sparks hadn't called, that he hadn't popped back into her life.

"You're in there, at the end. In the fade-out, a child calls 'Olly Olly in come free!' Remember he used to call you that way?"

" . . . "

"Olly?"

"Well, he, you know, Sparks, he would do that, put in anything to balance it at the end, like the tail on a kite. It doesn't—"

"It doesn't mean anything Olly? Think. Think of all the coincidences, in the same song. It has to mean something."

"But what? What would it mean?"

"I don't know. I've thought about it and all I can figure is he wants us to meet there, to reunite."

"All of us?"

Sparks hadn't thought of Olly going with him, but now that she asks, it seems right. Their names are all in the song.

"Sparks, he—Roy—I got a letter from Haven Enterprises last December offering to sell Roy's share of the store. So I—we, my partner and I—bought it. Now to me, this means Roy is not asking me to meet him anywhere. He doesn't call. I haven't spoken to him in eight years . . ."

Of course, she's hurt. Sparks is usually sensitive to these things but this trip is getting him worked up. He can't help it. It's as if once the idea came to him, it has had a force of its own, almost outside of him. It could be that Roy doesn't want to see him, but Sparks on his own has a compulsion to hunt him down, discover what he and Maggie are up to.

It does sound like an adventure, Olly says. She envies him that.

Why doesn't she come? Isn't she curious? They used to be so close, the four of them. Wouldn't she at least like to know? And if she's afraid, of seeing Roy again, or Maggie, she'll have Sparks with her.

It's odd that when Sparks called he wasn't even thinking of Olly going with him, and now he's talking her into it, as if the trip can't be a success unless she's with him. She'll have to have shots, he tells her, and they both need visas, which she can take care of in New York, since D'jarkoume doesn't have anything like a tourist office or even a consulate. They do however have a mission to the UN. Sparks can take care of the airline tickets.

"Of course I'll pay for mine, Sparks."

They'll split everything fifty-fifty, down the middle. It will probably be cheaper, in the long run, two traveling together.

"Oh wait, oh Sparks, wait. I must be out of my mind. I can't. You did wake me up, Sparks. I was sleeping. Let me think about this, OK? I mean, it seems like a wonderful idea. It seems too good. I don't trust it. Let me think about it, in the morning. You know, the cold light of day and all that."

Sparks hangs up and feels his house silent around him. It's too clean. Lupe always overdoes when a female guest leaves after a long visit. The gleaming floors, the polished furniture, look as if they're waiting for something. The floor echoes when he walks across to the kitchen for a beer. The bright white refrigerator with its meticulously arranged shelves belongs in a model home.

Now Sparks feels that the trip won't work unless Olly comes along, but he can't try to convince her against her own judgment. That would be a mistake.

"Olly Olly in come free" . . . "Sparks fly up" . . . "Maggie days" . . . What does it mean? Anything at all? Even if it does mean something, even if it means Roy is calling them to a reunion in D'jarkoume, of all places, why should they go?

Sparks pulls the tab and the beer can sighs in his hand. He looks back at his living room where the light reflects off the floor. Too damn clean. The place is too damn clean and empty.

9

"This is Toto, this is Isadora, and this is Serena." Marion puts her cigarette between her lips, closing one eye against the smoke, and grabs a white Scotty puppy. She holds it on its back; its short legs wave in the air. "Rub her tummy. She loves that."

Sparks rubs the warm pink belly while the dog sprawls placidly in Marion's arms.

Marion and her current husband live in this small stucco ranch, very neat inside, although it smells like the smoking car on a train. Sparks was a little taken aback at first by the house, because Maggie used to regale them with stories of the places they had lived with previous husbands of Marion—a ranch in Arizona, a penthouse in San Francisco. Maggie wasn't above stretching the truth. And it is possible Marion has been forced to lower her standards. She must be in her mid-sixties now, at least, although it's hard to tell.

Her hair is still streaked blond, her tanned face relatively free of lines. She's wearing stretch pants and a loose shirt to her knees, Indian fabric. Only her voice seems older, a hoarse smoker's voice.

So Sparks is going to see her little girl. She's so envious, she can't tell him. If it weren't for the dogs, and her husband, of course, she would drop everything and go with him. She misses Maggie that much. "Look! I've kept all her letters." Marion dives into a cabinet and comes up with a shoebox tied with blue ribbon. Yes, of course Sparks can take them, but he must promise to bring them back. They're all she has of her only child.

"Is there anything you want me to take her, is there anything she needs?"

Marion looks at him for a moment. "There's so much she needs, but I don't know what. I tried sending clothes once and they were stolen—oh, I know. This month's *Vogue*."

"*Vogue?*"

"I usually send them to her but they're always so late, and sometimes she doesn't get them at all." She hands him the magazine, then pulls it back. "Wait. Watch this." She tears out a perfume ad and opens it on the floor, releasing a musky odor. One of the dogs scampers over and rolls with ecstatic groans on the paper. "Isn't that cute? He adores perfume. Don't you!" She rubs the dog's belly with her bare foot.

Sparks will stay for coffee, won't he? They have to catch up. She hasn't seen him in years. When was it he and Maggie came to visit?

Sparks thinks it must have been fifteen, seventeen years ago.

Marion grinds the coffee beans, uses bottled spring water, which she measures before boiling, and pours the water a little at a time through a Chemex filter, all the while interrupting her task to deal with the dogs and smoke a cigarette. While she is doing this, Sparks opens the box and goes through the letters. There is a Polaroid shot in just about every one. At first Sparks thinks he's seeing a cage for chimps, but then there's a picture of chimps hanging around outside. Marion tells him the metal grid is to keep chimpanzees out, that the cage is Maggie's home.

"How does she look to you?"

She looks the same, Sparks thinks, maybe a little leaner in the face, or more defined. It's remarkable how good she looks. Sitting among her dark beasts, she looks particularly smooth-skinned and fair—and loved. In almost every picture she has small chimpanzees on her lap, bigger ones hugging her. "She looks happy," Sparks says.

Marion puts Sparks's coffee before him along with a pitcher of real cream and a bowl of sugar. She watches him stir his coffee. "You never got married, did you?"

"No, ma'am."

"It's funny. When Maggie brought you home I took one look at you and I said, 'He's the one. He's it.' You looked like a perfect couple, you know?" She lights a cigarette. "What happened, Sparks?"

Sparks shrugs. Marion's coffee is good and strong. "I guess Maggie and I turned out not to be the marrying kind."

"I think it was the age. People weren't getting married then. Even I was single for a year or two, trying to make it on my own, all proud and independent." Marion stubs out her cigarette. "Here's Jack."

Through the kitchen window, Sparks sees a short man in a baseball cap wading toward the door through yipping Scotties. He comes in, an older man than Sparks imagined.

"Who the hell are you?"

"This is Sparks, Jack. He's a friend of Maggie's. He's going to Africa to visit her."

Sparks rises to shake Jack's hand.

Jack walks by him to the stove. "What's that, coffee you're having? Got any left?"

Later Olly laughs when Sparks describes Marion and Jack and the Scotties. He called Olly from a booth when he stopped for gas. He'll call again when he's read the letters. Sparks has been talking to Olly a lot lately, planning the trip. He's missed Olly all these years.

Olly phoned back that same night Sparks called her about going to D'jarkoume. It was hours later but Sparks was still up.

"I know this is a mistake, Sparks, but I can't go to sleep until I tell you. I want to go!" She wasn't expecting anything, she said. "Olly Olly in come free" meant nothing to her. She couldn't figure it out, had to assume there wasn't a meaning, that it had gotten into the song by accident. She wouldn't let Sparks argue with her about this. She didn't know if Maggie would like to see her. Sparks had to write immediately and tell Maggie their plans, give her plenty of room to say no don't come, make it easy for her. When Olly had laid down all her rules, her caveats—had left all her back doors open—she said she was thrilled with the idea of going. "I lead such a careful life, Sparks, you can't imagine. And all of a sudden you call me in the middle of the night and it's as if a ladder came down to me from the sky. I can't resist. I have to take this chance. I've been waiting too long, Sparks. It's time to go out and do something, anything."

Waiting for what? Sparks didn't ask, assumed she meant Roy.

When Sparks first knew him, Roy was always with Olly, always touching her, or if he couldn't have her next to him, he'd keep glancing over to her, or if she were somewhere else he'd have to call her on the phone. She was in his songs, always something about Olly.

Later Roy became more independent. He was, after all, a rock and roll star. They were all stars. Only Eddie stuck with Wanda, married her, but Wanda always kept a firm hand on Eddie as far as other women were concerned. Olly took a more laissez-faire attitude, or maybe she felt she didn't have the right. Anyway, there were other women around Roy. None of them lasted very long, and Olly was always there through it all, part of the group, helping out—sound checks, press conferences, wardrobe, whatever had to be done.

And Olly was still Roy's girl, his lover, his "old lady," as he called her. This is something the short-term women friends never understood, because of course they were all part of a certain set Olly would never be in. Some of them came and went without ever suspecting that Roy's androgynous-looking assistant was his longtime, lasting mate.

In a way, that girl—June was her name—was right. Olly, and Maggie too, got the raw end of the deal. But that happens when you hang out with stars, you get taken advantage of, because if you walk out, there are plenty more willing to take your place.

Back in the Bronco, Sparks puts in the tape of the stuff he did with Eddie in Steamboat. Connie called with the bad news that Krusky didn't like it. He said it wasn't commercial, not that he didn't like it, Connie said. It's just that he wouldn't know how to sell it. It doesn't fit into what's happening now.

"You know what's holding you back? You're too damn good," Roy said. They were at the cottage they had rented one summer on a lake. Roy was slumped on the bench, his back to the upright piano. Sparks was on the sofa with his acoustic guitar. "Your hands are too good. As soon as you pick up a guitar they go into these riffs and the song is already written. Here. Try this." He tossed a harmonica over to him. "Try it as an experiment. See if you do different stuff."

He did. One song. It wasn't very good. They didn't put it on the album. There were a lot of arguments that summer between him and Roy over songs. But three gold records came out of it. You hear them still, all the time. They're classics. Sparks always thought it was because of the battles, that the music was better for the fighting that went into it, the tension between Roy going for something new and Sparks holding on to the old. Maybe Roy would say the hits were in spite of the constant disputes, or (more Roy-like) that hits didn't mean anything. What mattered was to keep changing, moving.

Yolanda unwraps each item from its camouflage-patterned tissue paper and lays it out on her big bed. When she has finished, she steps back, her left arm held slightly away from her body.

"Everything. Down to the hat," Gordon says.

"For the sun. He said I'd need a hat, the man in the store. Did I get too much?"

Gordon looks at the safari hat, the khaki pants, two pair with triple pockets, the long-sleeved khaki shirts, with two sets of flap-closing pockets plus an extra one on the sleeve, the long khaki cotton socks, canteen, bandannas, compass, snakebite kit, khaki canvas shoulder bag with exterior pockets.

"I wonder why they think you need so many pockets."

"You're laughing at me, aren't you."

"No, no I'm not. I'm stunned, that you're actually going. I didn't think you were the type."

Gordon has given up his sweatpants and sweatshirt in honor of the heat wave. He is in a gray T-shirt and baggy maroon running shorts. The shorts do nothing for his legs, which are whiter than anyone's should be, even at the beginning of the summer.

"Gordon, don't you go outside in the summer? Your legs look as if they never see the sun."

If he had known she was the kind of person who liked tan legs, he would have booked time in a tanning studio. He'd always thought she was the sort of person who thought things out before she did them. Suddenly this cowboy comes back into her life, flashes his perfect tan, and she's ready to follow him anywhere. He's the kind of man young girls fall for. That unthinking bravado turns them on. Gordon has nothing against Sparks personally. He's only seen pictures of him, usually on the cover of those newspapers in the supermarket, the ones you read at the check-out counter and then put back, and then Sparks is with one of those actresses who are always breaking up and getting divorces, not Yolanda's type, Gordon would have thought. "You're smiling, Yolanda. I'm amusing you."

Well, yes, he is, but only because he's got it so wrong. About Sparks, who is a friend, nothing more. As to why she is going, she doesn't know. In that way, Gordon's right. It is unlike her to act on impulse. She had a strong urge to do something and this was what presented itself.

If she wants to travel there are hundreds of places she could go, interesting, enjoyable . . .

Yolanda doesn't want to travel somewhere alone, sightseeing just for something to do. This trip will be with friends, someone who lives there. Yolanda will see more than she would as an ordinary tourist.

After Gordon leaves, Yolanda wonders what she is supposed to carry in all those pockets. The young man in Banana Republic never told her what went in the pockets. "I know, you've just come from your therapist," he said when he saw her standing in the middle of all the khaki, the hats, the bags, her left arm held slightly cocked and away from her side.

"I'm going to D'jarkoume," she said, wondering if he ever heard of it.

He showed her the pants with the pockets, with drawstrings at the bottoms to keep things from crawling up.

Sparks called after he read Maggie's letters to her mother. He couldn't tell much from them. They were the kind of cheerful communications one has with one's mother. Nothing about wars or uprisings. Nothing about Roy.

"We can't be going expecting to find Roy," Yolanda cautioned Sparks.

No, of course not. They're going on a vacation, an adventure, to see Maggie, help her out if need be. If they do see Roy, so much the better, or maybe not.

"We're taking a break. Stepping out of our lives. We're going elsewhere." Yolanda laughed.

That's about the size of it, said Sparks.

Maggie is sweating in her bed, sweating like a sponge leaking onto her sheets. Heavy blankets weigh her down. She doesn't know where they came from, can't remember having so many. Gingerly, she peels them off, then sinks back, panting.

She is wearing nothing. Her body looks frail and unfamiliar. Across one side, under her breast to her waist, adhesive tape is strapped. Emanuel did it. Perspiration rolled down his cheek; he thrust his pink tongue to one side of his mouth in concentration.

Maggie sits up, whimpering, a too familiar sound, something she's been hearing for a while. How long? She shuffles out to the bathroom.

God. The whole side of her face is purple and swollen. But she has her teeth, her eyes, her hair. Maggie puts her hands to her head. It felt as if they were scalping her alive, but it's all right, a little tender.

She finds a lappa folded on the chair and wraps it around her. The day room is clean, neat, a little too orderly, as if whoever lives here has been away for some time. How long?

On the table, under a smooth stone that fits nicely into the palm of the hand, is the unfinished "Friends of Hilda" she was working on. When she wrote it, she was exultant at how G.P. had retrieved his instinct, at how authentic he looked. She didn't mention that afterward he and Danny had tried to get into the shelter of her porch and she chased them off, afraid they'd try to mount Hilda.

There is no one on the porch now or in the clearing, which is shining from a recent rain.

"Emanuel?" Her voice comes out a querulous squeak. Her face is too tender to shout. She beats a battered pot with a metal spoon. He still doesn't come, which is a relief in a way because she doesn't know if she could face him right away—the whimpering, the mess in the pants. He fed her manioc with a spoon, okra, and shreds of chicken with his fingers. How many days?

Emanuel washed her forest clothes and dried them. The pants are loose; she has to tie them with rope. The boots go on hard, heavy to lift.

Lizards or snakes flee from the path, leaving narrow wakes in the grass. She's dizzy, a little sick to her stomach, but she continues into the forest, hoping she'll feel better in the cool green shadows.

Water oozes up around her boots with every step. Leftover rain is still making its way down the various levels of foliage with an irregular pat-a-pat. Besides the squish of her boots and the water dropping, there is no other sound.

The local people, even Emanuel, are afraid of the forest, wouldn't think of venturing in with fewer than two companions, armed if not with guns at least with knives or spears. They only go to hunt, to cut lumber, or search for gold. A local wouldn't consider walking through the forest for pleasure, gathering panda nuts or the tehetou fruits that taste like marzipan. It isn't the actual dangers of the forest that frighten them as much as the myths they invent. There are certain trees that can hurt you if you look at them. If a young girl looks at a maloue tree, her breasts won't come. There are demons that live in the forest. Once Mfui saw two of them staring back at him from the edge of the clearing. Maggie was standing right beside him and didn't see the demons, but she might now.

The sense of ease and comfort she had in the forest are

gone. The times she fell asleep against a tree while her chimps fed she recalls with disbelief as if watching scenes from a past life. Stumps and fallen logs threaten, as do shadows. A cracking twig makes her start and grip her gun. All the demons she laughed at have suddenly become real, but there is only one demon she fears: G.P.

At the river, the history of her struggle has been obliterated. The river has come to life, sprouted twisting muddy tongues that lick in logs, leaves and other debris, plastic buckets— Hilda? Maggie can find nothing, not marks in the mud, not broken branches, no bits of hair, spilled blood, bones. If there were bones they would be clean by now. Once Maggie saw a dead frog on the path in the clearing when she left in the morning. When she returned in the afternoon, only the small, delicate, perfect skeleton remained. By the next evening even that was gone.

Things move slowly here and then very fast. Because of the heat, because of the multitude of minor organisms waiting to break everything down to its simple starting point, because of conditions conducive to chaos. For years Maggie is Hilda's protector, watching her slow, nearly imperceptible adjustment to freedom, then in one day, within minutes— She hopes it was swift, although she knows chimpanzees are not efficient killers, that they will leave a victim bleeding and broken and come back later to check on their grim work. If the victim moves, they will beat it again. A mother will carry her dead infant around until the body decomposes. They don't understand where the border lies between life and death.

She should have gone back for Hilda. It does not help Maggie to know that she wasn't capable of it, that her body simply gave out and wouldn't follow basic commands. Hilda saved Maggie's life. She sacrificed herself, presented her glowing red bottom to G.P. and Danny. Why should the instincts of a chimpanzee be heroic and those of a human be cowardly?

It's raining hard now. Maggie pulls out her poncho, puts it on, and tucks the gun under to keep it dry. The path has become a stream. Maggie turns off, heading in the general direction of home.

With her head down against the rain, she doesn't see the men until they're almost upon her. She dives behind a log and almost blacks out from the pain. She recovers in time to see one back, then two, bent low, creeping off as reluctant to see her as she to see them. Hunters, locals who've come to poach small game. Holding her ribs, she stands, then quickly drops down. Many more of them, ten at least, are filing past.

She fishes her binoculars from under her poncho. A face leaps to view, looking right at her, making her heart skip because she knows him from the market, a friend of Emanuel's, who sold her rubber boots. He doesn't see her, or if he does he gives no sign but moves on. Behind him is someone else she recognizes from town. There's a flash of white, the butt of a rifle, the kind soldiers carry in dress parades. One man carries a gun strapped to his back, short and thick, repulsive like a gaboon viper, not a gun for small game.

They move quickly, and unusual for them, no one is singing or talking. The only sound is their boots, soon lost in the crash of wind and rain in the trees. When they have gone, it's as if they have never been there, as if she dreamed it, ten or more men creeping through the forest with a bizarre assortment of arms.

Is this what it looks like then, the uprising Didier feared? They're only locals who probably don't even know how to use the weapons they're carrying. They're too familiar to be threatening, are almost comic, really.

G.P. is the one Maggie fears, the rebel leader she has to contend with. What has he done with the band he wanted to lead? Whom has he killed, whom has he spared?

In this rain, if G.P. and Danny are anywhere near, they

will be taking shelter on her porch. She'll kill them. With a BB gun? Not likely. She'll shoot out their eyes and leave them to die slowly, blind and starving.

Her jaw is clenched, her eyes streaming. She can't see, she can't breathe. A twisting vine snares her foot. Maggie stops to untangle herself. Anger is unbalancing her mind, tipping it into madness. She must restore her equilibrium. She takes out her compass and waits until the needle stops jerking around. She was heading all wrong. This way, ah yes, she isn't far. Faintly, behind the crash of the storm, she might hear chimps calling. She hurries on, calm again. She must stay calm.

When Maggie reaches the clearing the rain has stopped. The ground is flooded except for the termite hills, which stick up like volcanic islands, and one high flat place where the dining hall used to be. The group is there, in a heap, a tangle, a chimpanzee *grand guignol*, a horror farce of hooting, panting. Biff on Katie's back is trying to mate her. Danny leaps in frenzied ballet around G.P. Poppy clings demonlike to G.P.'s back while G.P. works over something on the ground.

Maggie's gut clenches. She's clamped down, can't move. At last, ponderously, her legs begin churning through muddy water. Chimpanzees scatter screaming before her. Only G.P. remains.

"Off her, off her you creep!"

The butt of the gun meets his shoulder. Her boot, aimed at his groin, flies through air, sending her down to the mud.

It is her own howling Maggie hears. She wants to stop but it hurts to try. It is Hilda who is rocking her to and fro, patting her back until the rage subsides to shudders and the only sound is the comforting click a chimpanzee makes deep in its throat.

10

"Roger, it's like Ice Station Zebra in here."

It's seventy-eight, he says. Everyone has been sweating and complaining but it's the best he can do; the setting is on maximum. It only seems cold to her because she's overheated from her trip to midtown. He told her not to go today. There's an air-quality alert, a thermal inversion. She looks terrible.

"It wasn't midtown that did me in. It was the D'jarkoume mission to the UN."

Gordon, in running shorts and sandals, pads out from the hardcover section, wanting to know what happened. Did they refuse her a visa? He blinks in the light like some nocturnal creature untimely flushed from his burrow.

"What are you doing here in the daytime?" Yolanda sounds annoyed, a spillover from her frustrations of the morning.

He couldn't work, he says, because of the heat, even though he had every window in his apartment wide open, so he wandered over and when he heard where she'd gone, he decided to stay and wait for the "horror stories."

"Then you knew what would happen? Why didn't you tell me?"

Gordon's hands flutter before his face. He backs away. He

didn't know anything, specifically, only that D'jarkoume isn't eager for tourists, and that it might not be easy to get a visa.

Roger takes her shoulders in his hands and turns her toward the back of the store. "Yolanda, please, go splash some water on your face, freshen up a bit. You're all in blotches."

"I'm not hot. I'm just angry with the woman in the mission. First she never said I needed four copies of each application until I went to hand it in. I went racing around Forty-second Street looking for a place that made copies, and when I went back with them, she calmly told me that passport photos must be attached to each one. Why couldn't she have told me all that in the beginning, when I went down to get the forms?"

"And when you go back with those," Gordon says, "they'll think of something else. You'd better take copies of your airline tickets and bank statements, just in case."

"But it doesn't say anything about that on the forms. There isn't even a place for a picture."

Gordon says it's like a game to them. This is only a taste of what it will be like when she gets to D'jarkoume. There are internal roadblocks. The army and the customs officials run competing checkpoints. "You might get your visas, get over there, and they won't let you out of the airport."

"Yolanda, believe me, if you could see your face—"

"All right, Roger." Anyway, it's an excuse to get away from Gordon, who is irritatingly smug and cheerful about her difficulties. Her face is a mess, not anything she can do about it other than splash some cold water on it, which makes her mascara run. She's thought about keeping makeup here but it never seemed worth it, since the fluorescent lights make everyone look terrible. Roger is changing the lights. That's his next project. He says they don't need bright lighting, now that the anti-shoplifting device is in place. Yolanda worries that the old people won't be able to read book titles if the lighting is lowered. Aren't bookstores like fish restaurants, aren't bright lights practically a requirement?

She'll call Sparks about the passport photos while she's back here, and maybe when she goes out front again Gordon will have wandered off.

It's cold and gray outside. Sparks is having cinnamon toast and coffee in front of the fire, postponing his swim until the afternoon when he comes back from seeing his lawyer about a will. Sparks has never had a will, but he would like to leave his money to his nephews for their education. Who would want his books? Histories mainly and old books about Texas—he collects them. Maybe his lawyer will suggest a library some-where. His guitars and sound equipment are easy. Plenty of friends to distribute them to. Lupe can take the rest, furniture and clothes, filter it down through a network of deserving Mexicans. Some people when they go leave others wandering dazed, unable to continue. If Sparks dies, all that will mark his passage is a small redistribution of goods, a shifting of material things.

"Did I wake you? Your voice sounds funny."

Olly! Not at all. He's been up an hour at least, just hasn't spoken to anyone yet.

Yolanda tells the story of the D'jarkoume mission, but this time, telling it to Sparks, it comes out like an adventure, slightly mysterious and dangerous—the double-locked doors outside the small reception room, the portrait of the president hung high on the wall so that it dominated the space, the bulletproof glass protecting the receptionist, her implacable face and arrogant, taciturn manner.

Sparks says the passport photos are no problem. He'll take care of it when he's downtown seeing his lawyer about his will.

"A will? You don't expect to die, do you?"

"It's just good to have one, you know, Olly, in case. You mean you don't have a will?"

"Well, I wasn't intending to die." Terry, one of Roger's young men, looks up at her from the computer where he's working on inventory. "Anyway, I have nothing to leave."

"Your store."

"Oh, well, I guess whatever I have goes to my brothers, next of kin. It's automatic, isn't it? How did we get on this topic, anyway? Are you thinking you'd rather not go?"

"No. I'm just putting things in order, that's all. Going away is a good excuse to put things in order . . ."

"Yolanda?"

Yolanda gathers up some loose papers on her desk, but she's afraid Gordon caught her daydreaming, her hand still resting on the receiver after hanging up from her call. What had she been thinking about? She can't remember. Her mind had gone off on a journey somewhere.

"It's nice back here," Gordon says.

"It is kind of, isn't it? I don't usually like it because there aren't any windows, but on a day like this it's a blessing."

Gordon takes a chair from another desk, lifts it awkwardly over a pile of boxes, and sets it down opposite Yolanda. "Now that you've seen, now that you've been down there and gotten the reality, you'll change your mind, won't you?"

"Gordon—"

"I know, I know." Gordon waves his hands in front of his face. "I know I'm bugging you and I hate to do it, because in theory I believe one person shouldn't prevent another person—no matter what he feels about a person—I'm a big believer in that. But when you see a person, a friend, going off—becoming deluded."

"Deluded?"

"Yes. Yolanda, you have been charmed by your own imagination, and maybe even by my imagination, my book. You're not looking at it in a realistic way. It's been colored by all the junk—well, not junk, good things and bad things—you've read about Africa, by movies, TV, and so you're not seeing clearly what it's going to be like."

Gordon's nose and the space between his eyes has gone pink. His hair is flying around as if every wisp had a will of its own.

"Gordon, I'm kind of tired. Let's not continue this conversation."

Gordon turns to look at her with one eye, then tries it with the other. "I'm not going to let up. Maybe for today, I might give you a rest, but time is running out. I'll never forgive myself. Yolanda, I'll never forgive myself if something happens to you. This is real." He brings his hands down parallel on her desk top. "Yolanda, this is real, what's happening in this room. We have to get a grasp of what's happening now . . ."

But it seems unreal to Yolanda, as if they are playing parts. This is not how Gordon talks and it is not how Gordon acts. It's as if he's decided to be someone else and is doing a poor job of it.

"Gordon, it's not good for you to be away from your desk in the daytime."

"Maybe I could work here. There seems to be enough room. It's nice and cool—"

"No."

"Why not?"

"There are people running in and out all day. It's chaotic. You couldn't work here."

"I could try, just during the heat wave, until it cools off." He's standing now, leaning over the desk.

"Why are you doing this?"

"Annoying you?"

"Yes."

"Because I don't want you to go to D'jarkoume."

"Why?"

"Because it's dangerous."

"I've never been to a psychiatrist, but I know you have—"

"Only in my youth, for seven years, until my parents figured out I wasn't sick, it was just my personality they didn't like."

"Isn't it true, or don't psychiatrists say, that often when you have strong feelings about something it's because of an underlying reason, something you might not even realize?"

"That's not the main—"

"Anyway, something like that. And maybe what you're doing now, what's disturbing you so about my going to D'jarkoume, is that it is something you didn't dare to do, and maybe something you secretly feel you should have—"

"I never intended to go to D'jarkoume or anyplace else in Africa, first because it's too expensive, and second because I can get better information from the New York Public Library than I could dragging around an incomprehensible tropical country I knew I couldn't really understand. Going there for a couple of weeks—even twenty years—isn't enough. I used D'jarkoume as a vehicle for my imagination."

"Imagination."

"Yeah."

"Maybe imagination is the key word, the thing we're talking about here. You seem to be content to live in your imagination, while I—I can't anymore. I'm tired of living vicariously through a store dummy. It's not enough for me to lie next to a man and imagine sex—"

The entire store is eerily silent and Yolanda can hear her words ringing out. Terry is still at the computer, his back eloquently turned.

"Yolanda," Gordon says in a low voice, "you must never hurt a man's pride. Even a man who looks like me, who isn't like your tall friend with the silver hair—even short, balding men have masculine pride. We all have it. We just do."

Terry does not turn as Gordon leaves the room, does not

look up, even when Gordon trips over a box of books. What power he has at this moment, this inert and unwilling witness. If Terry weren't here, Yolanda could run after Gordon and tell him those weren't her words, not her thoughts. They're Roger's, but she wouldn't tell Gordon that, she'd just say she's tired and nervous; it's all the fault of that woman at the D'jarkoume mission to the UN.

JULY
VOLUME VII, NO. 7

FRIENDS OF HILDA

The atmosphere at the station is tense—with anticipation! Nuptials finally took place between Hilda and G.P. Now everyone is nervously awaiting signs that conception occurred and that an heir is expected. G.P. is a little young to have viable sperm, but if strong sexual drive is any indication of fertility, I'd put my money on G.P. As for Hilda, a chimpanzee will menstruate about nine days after detumescence. We have about seven days to go, so here's hoping!

I witnessed the last of many encounters right here at the station, with everyone in attendance, and, as is usual with chimpanzees, trying to get in on the act— Poppy trying to pull the loving couple apart, Danny cheering them on, and Biff practicing on Katie. A regular bacchanal!

The other good news is that the drought has been broken by a series of downpours, unusual for this time of year. The bad news is

that my supplier can't get in with mail,
medicine, and food because the roads have
turned into rivers. Luckily I have plenty of
food in storage and the locals have been
providing me with produce. I'm going to try
to send this letter out by foot, if you can
believe it, a sort of relay where various
people will carry it and pass it on until it
reaches the airport in D'jar.

It is the little wife of Emanuel who will carry the letter on its
initial leg (at least, Maggie thinks she is his wife. She looks
about sixteen, and about seven months pregnant). She and
her two sisters came into the clearing around noon yesterday,
having walked all the way from Dobo with big bundles on
their heads. G.P. heard them first and came screaming out,
teeth bared. Maggie shooed him off with her gun and gave
the poor frightened girls an armed escort into the house. The
little one screamed when she saw Hilda coming out of the
bathroom. Maggie had to explain, by gestures, that Hilda was
friendly and wouldn't hurt them. The girls don't even speak
French, or are too shy to.

They unwrapped their bundles of vegetables, eggs, and
some of those revolting smoked fish they're so fond of, which
were full of worms (Maggie threw them to Katie and the little
ones after the girls left), and oranges. The girls giggled when
Maggie and Hilda fell on the oranges and started eating them
right away. Maggie had been dreaming of oranges. She served
the girls canned sardines and orange drink made from a powdered mix, which they found wonderfully exotic. They also
ate up most of the bread they'd brought, but that's OK because
it gets moldy in minutes in this weather. They spent the night
in Emanuel's house and are coming back to take her letter to
Dobo. They couldn't tell her where Emanuel is, although
Maggie gathered he is all right, not ill or anything. He's prob-

ably tramping around the forest with his cronies, carrying borrowed or stolen firearms. Maggie would like to know who they expect to come after them when the roads are rivers of mud and probably most of the bridges are out.

G.P. came by early this morning. Maggie chased him away with the BB gun, before he could frighten the girls again. He forced Katie and the little ones to go off with him. Maggie hates to see him bully them all the time, but she can't go with them anymore on their trips into the forest. Even with her gun, she doesn't feel safe with G.P. He comes sometimes and sits on her porch and stares at her. Maggie can't meet his eyes.

He hadn't hurt Hilda as badly as Maggie had feared. When Maggie got Hilda into the house and washed her off, there were only some superficial scratches on her rump and a bite on the ear. She was traumatized, of course, and disoriented. For the first couple of days she would whimper to be let out and when G.P. came near, she would press her backside to the grid.

Now she's used to living with Maggie, has adjusted remarkably after living outside for so many years. She is pathetically eager to take up the skills she learned in childhood— using the toilet, brushing her teeth. She loves the magazines, will sit and go through them for hours.

As long as Hilda was living inside, Maggie thought it was useless and impossible to deny her these little comforts. This is only a temporary arrangement, after all, until Maggie can see if Hilda is pregnant. What happens then isn't clear. If Hilda is pregnant, it would seem unnecessarily risky to let her out where G.P. might attack her. If she isn't pregnant, in two more weeks she'll be in estrus and G.P. will attack her again.

If only she could confide in Richard or Anita, get some advice, but if she put it all down the way it is now, it would look as if the whole thing isn't working, which isn't true, of course. It *is* working. It will work. It's just that right now they're going through a hard time.

11

The air, sharp and cool, smelling of eucalyptus, cuts across Sparks's shins. Lupe shuts the door behind her. "Leave it open, Lupe."

He'll catch cold, she warns, sitting in his bathrobe, still wet from his swim. She's wearing two sweaters, the top one a short fluffy crimson. With her tight jeans, she looks like a small female toreador. It's cold out today, a bad day, evil. It's not an evil day, Lupe. It's clear and beautiful. You can see the mountains. Lupe thinks it's disturbing to see the mountains. It's not a good omen, but she opens the door anyway, a little too much, to prove her point.

Sparks is playing a tape he made off the TV of Roy's video, the one made to promote his hit song, not that it needs promoting. How many more times a day could they play it on the radio?

Unlike most videos, which are lush productions, casts of thousands, Roy's are always spare. This one is no exception, set in an unfurnished beach house on a tropical shore. Roy is half hidden by an upright piano. A line of men, shuffling in step, enter from a door on the right. They are all very black, short, with round heads, and long arms which move in precise gestures, telling a story, it looks like. Here's a boat, possibly a sea voyage. Their song is full of clicks and moans, bird trills.

Now the camera comes in on Roy's face. Sparks has recovered from the first shock of seeing him older, how the flesh on his face has slipped to his jowls. Is the piano hiding a potbelly, is that why Roy never comes out from behind it, or is the concept of the video to keep Roy stationary while the men perform their sedate and eloquent dance?

Sparks shivers and draws his bare feet up under his robe. If this song is a call to revolution, it is oddly ingenuous. Although Sparks can't understand the words, he can tell from the gestures and tone that the men are simply recounting a story. But according to Richard, the mere telling of the story is tantamount to a declaration of war.

Yes, of course, Lupe, you're right. He is not only making himself cold, he is also creating a spot on the floor. Sparks goes in for his shower while Lupe, her high-heel mules clicking, hurries to wipe up the puddle.

Richard called this morning to say the revolution might be already in progress, that the letter from Maggie hasn't come. He did add that the monthly letter often doesn't come on time, for reasons varying from washed-out bridges to Maggie's disinclination to write. Richard said there's a good chance that for whatever reason, floods, war, or just a general hitch in the system, Sparks's letter to Maggie telling her that he and Olly are coming has not reached her.

Sparks turns on the shower, set at the exact temperature he likes. Lupe has instructions to set the dial back to this position. It's a new showerhead and every time Sparks uses it, he feels a thrill, the satisfaction of having something that works well. Why aren't small pleasures enough, he wonders, as he lathers up with a special black soap he buys for the shower. Why can't he be content with a swim on a cool, dry morning when the air smells of eucalyptus and the mountains are clear in the distance?

There was another near miss. Two jumbo jets nearly col

lided over Minneapolis. Sparks hates to read in the paper about a near miss when he is about to fly. He'd rather it was a crash, a substantial crash. Then he knows it's over with. These near misses are just foreplay, harbingers, preludes to the big one which could be his.

He only has to fly the first leg alone and then Olly joins him in New York. Why doesn't he take the direct flight to Paris, the girl at the travel agency asked him, and meet his friend there for the flight to D'jarkoume? He'd just like to do it this way, and don't tell him how much longer he'll be in the air or how much more it will cost. Just write him the ticket the way he asked. Sparks is not flying any goddamn Great Circle polar route alone to Paris.

Sparks rubs himself dry with a big towel, then cleans and clips his toenails. He's taking special care today, preparing the lamb for slaughter, which is no way to think. If a fragment of ice on a wing can make a craft totter and crash on takeoff, couldn't negative thoughts do the same?

Boots are not comfortable to wear in a plane, but he will feel more secure in them, will have a better chance of making an emergency exit in time. He tucks his shirt into his jeans and fastens his belt. If the plane is going to crash, he would like it in either of two ways: it crashes on takeoff, in which case he might have a fighting chance for survival and maybe then decide that this life is enough for him—the good shower, the morning swims—and that he doesn't have to go to Africa searching for something he hasn't quite defined; or it blows up in midflight over the Atlantic while he is reclining in his seat next to Olly, and their souls will spring free as their bodies explode into an infinite number of unrecognizable bits that mix and swirl around and around, tumbling back into the primordial soup from which they came.

Lupe is hanging freshly ironed shirts in his closet. If he dies, he tells her, she gets all his clothes and his furniture except for the sound equipment. She yells at him in Spanish. Is that any way to talk? He'll make her scorch his shirts, talking like that. The mountains are doing it to him. He looked at them too long and they made him crazy. It's an evil day.

Yolanda is up on the ladder looking for *In the Path of Despond*, a book of poems by Elaine Furst no one ever asks for, but which she keeps in the area she and Roger call the Heights because she thinks it's wonderful and they ought to have it, just in case. "Here it is!" She is blowing off the dust as Gordon comes in. It is pouring outside and water is streaming off his orange plastic poncho. It is an awkward moment, as she hasn't seen Gordon since the unfortunate incident in the office at the back of the store.

"I didn't think you'd be here," Gordon says. "I wanted to make sure you have everything you need." He pulls a rumpled paper out of his pocket. "I made a list. I thought we could go out together, looking for things—"

"Oh Gordon. Oh, I feel terrible. You shouldn't have—"

"Nylon rope. Did you think of nylon rope?"

"My— Sparks is taking care of those things."

"Mosquito repellent. You need a concentrate—"

"See, Sparks talked to someone who's been there and—"

"Band-Aids. It's a good idea if you take your own syringes. I know a doctor who—"

"Syringes?"

"In case you need a shot of something. You know, of course, AIDS is rampant and they don't bother to use new hypodermic—"

"Well, I don't—"

"String, snakebite kit—"

"Gordon—"

"Tang."

"Gordon—!"

"All right. If you're not interested I'll go home. It's just that I wouldn't forgive myself if you were out there and found yourself in dire need of one of these items and I didn't warn you."

Roger, who's been watching this exchange, comes over now to shake Gordon's hand, give him a pat on the shoulder. He doesn't think Gordon has seen the new cafe on the second floor, has he? Roger has been meaning to ask him to give a reading. Maybe Yolanda will take him up to look it over. They could have a cappuccino. Gordon would be doing Roger a favor, getting Yolanda out of the way. She's so excited that she's been absolutely no good to anyone all day.

Even Roger is coming under the general feeling of benevolence Yolanda is experiencing for everything connected with what she thinks of as her old life, her life before she embarks on the journey that will change everything. How sweet Roger's being, how brotherly and concerned. Yolanda leads the way upstairs. There is already a sprinkling of customers although it's not quite eleven.

"It's very nice up here," Gordon says.

"Thanks. The paisley cloths and having the books piled around, old books anyone can pick up and read, were my idea, but it doesn't have the effect I had in mind. Maybe the space is too big. I was thinking about a cozier atmosphere."

They take a table by the window. Yolanda watches yellow taxis swishing by on the shiny black street and feels like a foreign traveler already, and she hasn't even left her store.

"I've been studying my maps and the forest you're going to isn't far from the border with Waza-Balu, so theoretically you could escape across the border if you had to, but then you'd be in Waza-Balu without a visa and they could throw you in jail."

"I guess we won't do that."

"It would be pretty difficult, anyway. I mean, it's only a

quarter of an inch on the map, but in real life, it's all jungle. But it's something to keep in mind."

"Thanks, Gordon."

"I hope you come back."

"Of course I will." Without thinking, Yolanda puts her hand on Gordon's. His is cleaner than hers, which got a little grimy from going through the Heights earlier.

Gordon stares at their hands for a moment as if wondering how it happened. She expects him to pull his hand away, but he doesn't. He turns it so that hers falls into his and then he holds it lightly. A young man brings the cappuccinos. They draw their hands back hastily.

"When you return," Gordon says finally, "I think we should try something new."

"Like what?"

"I'm going to work very hard while you're gone, try to get the first draft done."

"Wonderful!" Should she tell him about the foam on his upper lip?

"And then I can begin to concentrate on breaking through to the physical side."

"Of what?" Yolanda ostentatiously pats her own upper lip with a napkin.

"You know, that barrier two people have to cross to—um—I hate the word intimate. I won't use it. It makes me think of ladies' underwear. Step-ins. Did your grandmother wear step-ins?"

"I'm surprised you would know what kind of underwear your grandmother wore."

"I wonder how I know that."

Yolanda reaches across and wipes Gordon's upper lip.

Waking in the predawn, seeing the outline of a sleeping form, Maggie thinks it's Marion, not in the present but back when they lived in Pasadena and slept side by side in Hollywood beds. Then as now Maggie would wake several times in the night and look over at the other bed.

Pasadena was after George, before Phil. Maggie preferred the times when Marion wasn't with a man, although Maggie got along with most of them, because at least for a while, life was calm and orderly. Their schedule revolved around Maggie and Marion, no man to worry about, his comings and goings, his moods. There were cozy nights in the Pasadena apartment, a remodeled garage with gravel driveway and side door entrance. They'd play Clue for hours and everything Maggie said surprised and delighted Marion, as if Maggie were a wonderful new friend. For a while they would be almost giddy at not having to accommodate themselves to a man.

But even in Pasadena, even at the age of nine, Maggie must have known that the Eden they had created there was temporary, otherwise she wouldn't have kept waking, just to check that Marion was still there, sleeping through the night.

This hiatus in the struggle to dehumanize Hilda is only temporary, but what a relief it is to let up on her, to allow her to be her peculiar half-human, half-ape self. Maggie hadn't realized before how hard it was to be always pushing, scolding, cajoling, how much it was hurting to withhold her love.

Hilda has earned this vacation. She is pregnant. When she gives birth in the wild, it will be Maggie's vindication to all the skeptics and doubters, to all who said Hilda was too hopelessly spoiled to make it. It will be the beginning of the next generation of this band of chimps.

Maggie puts a hand on Hilda's shoulder. Hilda grunts and grabs Maggie's arm, clutching it to her warm leathery chest, already fleshier. She's hardly stopped eating since Maggie took her in. Get up, you lazy loafer. Maggie extricates her arm and Hilda ambles to the toilet, looking broader from behind than she was even yesterday.

The water is running in the bathroom, where Hilda is at her morning tasks: tooth brushing, hair combing, face washing. She'll be at it for fifteen minutes wasting water like crazy. At least it gives Maggie time to go to the storeroom without having to fight Hilda off. She unlocks the door and plays her flashlight over the supplies. The food the girls brought—the peanuts, oranges, cabbages, bananas—is gone. The once fat sack of manioc meal—Maggie lifts it out of the metal chest and shakes it—is nearly empty.

Her surplus of staples is dwindling fast. What seemed like a lifetime supply of sardine cans is down to seven. She still has a canned ham, a luxury Didier brought the last time he came, twelve cans of evaporated milk, eight of soup, a jar of Bovril, about two pounds of rice and an inch of sugar in a tin canister. They can last about a week on this and by then Didier, or Emanuel, or Emanuel's little wife and sisters should have come with fresh supplies.

Maggie takes the sack of meal and a can of evaporated milk. In the clearing, bats as big as crows are swooping in to roost in the surrounding trees. The kerosene stove throws a ghostly blue light on the mildewed wall. Maggie tosses the last of the manioc into the boiling water, skimming off weevils and larvae that rise to the surface. She should probably leave them in, for the protein.

Last night she dreamed that the little wife of Emanuel came back with her sisters, carrying baskets of oranges, cabbages, eggs. It seemed like an omen but perhaps was only a wish. Why haven't they come again? They must know she needs them, and she thought she had treated them well. At least they'd seemed to be enjoying themselves, giggling, eating most of the bread they'd brought. (Don't think of bread, the fresh loaves of French bread.) Maggie had sat still for them while they braided her hair into tiny plaits. How gentle they were! (How weak and gentle humans are compared with chimps, and yet it's the frail and tender primates who have stolen the world away from their tougher cousins. It's because we lie. We're better liars.) The girls had cooed in surprise when Maggie passed them some money. She'd heard them chattering happily in their funny jumpy language as they went walking down the road.

Color is returning to the clearing. The bats are fewer. A bright green pigeon swoops down to peck at crumbs on the porch. Maggie stirs the manioc.

The clearing, with its closely mowed grass and red crisscrossing paths leading nowhere but to the sites of former buildings, has undergone a metamorphosis. The grass is disappearing, being replaced with ever widening patches of red earth. All the trees on the edge have been stripped of their leaves and small branches. It looks as if some terrible disease has struck, but it's the chimps. They're devouring everything, down to termites and driver ants.

At first Maggie couldn't figure it out, the howling and banging on her door, the desperate pacing, G.P. rushing after Katie if she strayed into the forest. Maggie thought she had ruined the whole project by taking Hilda in, that they all wanted to be taken in and returned to captivity. She had one bad morning after they badgered her through breakfast, when she poked the gun through the grid and began firing, luckily not hitting anyone. What if she had gotten Katie, or Poppy? Taken out someone's eye, for God's sake!

That afternoon, she heard for the first time what the others had been hearing—the drumming and cries of wild chimps in the forest. They've come back and this time they seem to have settled in. She hears them daily now.

The wild chimps are forcing her own chimps back on human ways, forcing them into the clearing where the wild chimps won't come. They sleep in Emanuel's house. She's almost certain of it because they come from that direction every morning. It wouldn't be hard to break in, as it's only a mud hut with a tin roof. They must be making a mess of it; they're not housebroken like Hilda. Too bad for Emanuel, but it serves him right in a way, for leaving her like this, without supplies, with cracked or broken ribs.

Tears come. Maggie dashes them away and stirs the manioc. She isn't a weeper. It's G.P. who did this to her, broke more than ribs, fractured her character, cracked her courage. They're not tears of self-pity, but of frustration and anger.

How could Emanuel have abandoned her when he knew what kind of shape she was in? You'd think he'd have more loyalty after what she's done for him, practically raised him after his father died of alcoholism. Maybe loyalty is a Western concept, not African. Even Didier last time seemed to think Maggie owed *him* something, that their sexual relationship put her under some obligation to him.

Hilda comes out of the bathroom, her hair wet and the tracks of the comb still in it. You're so vain, Maggie tells her, but secretly admires the way her hair looks, so shiny and full, less patchy. It's the pregnancy, she supposes, that and Maggie's shampoo.

"No one here. Eat now please hurry up." Hilda means none of the chimps are out in the clearing yet. She sits at the table with her bowl and spoon. Maggie hastens to get food on before the others come to disturb their breakfast.

Even though Hilda fusses with her napkin and spoon, she finishes before Maggie and keeps inspecting Maggie's bowl to see if she's done. As soon as Maggie takes her last spoonful, Hilda jerks the bowl away to the sink to wash it.

The sun is high enough now to draw ghostly mists from the forest. Hilda, sitting near the grid, keeping watch, gets up suddenly and scuttles back into the bedroom. It's the group with G.P. in the lead, G.P. in a quiet mood, but walking with that new swagger he affects. His hair, which used to lie flat, is partly raised, making him seem bigger and rougher. Maggie tries to see him as she did before, as the clown with the ill-fitting wig and the close-set eyes, but she can't. He looks dangerous now, cruel, crafty.

Even Danny, a child still with his white tail, half the size of G.P., trailing at his heels, scares her. His small pinched face looks weaselly and fanatical.

G.P. leaps to the porch, bangs on the grid. Maggie involuntarily jumps backward, then curses herself for her weakness. "If you're so almighty powerful, go out and get some food, damn it. I can't feed you. I'm almost out myself—" A sob breaks her voice and she turns her face away.

Why this plague of wild chimps now, after all these years? She blames Richard because she assumes they are his chimps, the ones he was watching in the west, and because he always said they would come back to the area, that the station was actually within their territory and they had only temporarily abandoned it.

Perhaps they sense that Maggie is at bay, unable to go into the forest. Maybe, because of the drought, food is scarce in their home territory, or—Maggie goes through the possible reasons several times a day—poachers have invaded their homeland, hunting for live infant chimps to sell on the black market; or farmers have illegally burned some of the forest in the west and have planted banana trees, coffee bushes, pineapples. It could be that a band of rebels has established a base there, forcing the chimps east—maybe that motley group she saw in the forest, joined by others . . .

War is what she keeps coming back to, in her dark moments, and there are plenty of those lately. Because war would explain everything: why Emanuel isn't here, why Didier hasn't returned, and why the chimps are invading her territory. It infuriates her that some messy little tribal war could be jeopardizing her entire project, after all these years of sacrifice, when it was finally on the verge of success. It's not fair that innocents who have no part in the conflict, who take no side, should have their lives destroyed by it. Tears again. Fuck it. Maybe she shouldn't try to control them. Maybe she should just bawl her eyes out and get it over with.

G.P. barks at Katie, who is helping the little ones up on the porch.

"Oh shut up, you. There's enough room for everyone— besides, there's no food so you might as well haul yourself off and get breakfast somewhere else."

Katie cowers and backs away from G.P., even though Maggie is standing near. Since the day at the river, the chimps don't trust Maggie anymore to protect them from G.P. It's really for the best, because it's necessary for them to transfer allegiance to a chimp leader. She only wishes G.P. were more of a leader and less of a bully.

Katie is sidling up to G.P. She touches his arm. Maggie holds her breath. G.P. is watching Maggie and doesn't seem to mind Katie's touch. Encouraged, she begins to go through the hair on his forearm. Suddenly G.P. barks and shoves her. Katie flies backward off the porch and scampers away, whimpering, holding her elbow. She sits on the bare earth and watches G.P. Poppy and Biff run to her and they huddle there. He's a brute, a heartless brute, Maggie thinks. The little ones look thin, don't they? Or is it that she sees so much of Hilda, who's putting on weight, that Katie and the little ones seem frail in comparison?

They stay that way for some time, all of them, even Maggie, like figures in a diorama. Only Hilda is moving. Maggie hears her in the next room, turning pages of a magazine.

The drumming breaks the spell, the hollow voice of the bao-hi-soho tree, the one they use because the deep buttresses give the biggest sound. The hooting begins with the drummer, no doubt, the big male, with other voices joining in a chorus that gets louder and closer until Maggie thinks they must be just beyond the clearing. She grabs the gun.

Katie, still sitting with the little ones, vibrates as if a wind has entered her body and joins her voice to the others, calling to her mates in the wild.

G.P. charges off the porch. Katie escapes up a tree, screaming. Cries from the forest echo Katie's. G.P. stops. They are close, perhaps only yards away. Maggie scans the trees with binoculars, sees nothing, but that doesn't mean they aren't there. Katie's head is turned away. Is she watching them? Maggie's heart rattles in her bruised chest and she aches just from holding the binoculars. If one of the wild chimps made a dash for Katie, would Maggie be able to protect her in time?

They're quiet now, feasting on figs, no doubt. Maggie knows the tree. Figs that would feed her own bunch for days. Katie, keeping an eye on G.P., climbs down slowly and settles in the narrow slice of shade left by the bare trunk. G.P. and Danny slink away, to Emanuel's house maybe, to escape the sun.

Maggie sleeps sitting at the table and wakes with a headache. It's Hilda, pulling her arm. She's hungry and wants to eat.

"Be quiet, can't you?" Hilda is jumping and hooting as Maggie unlocks the storeroom. Maggie brings out two cans of sardines and one of string beans. She locks the door behind her and shoos Hilda out from underfoot, back to the day room where she can open the cans and put food on plates.

Katie and the little ones have crept up on the porch and are silently watching. Small hands push through the grid, palms upraised. They look thin. And Maggie would hate to force them into the forest for food, when all around they are being menaced by the wild chimps. Maggie squats down with her plate and carefully places a sardine in each upturned hand.

Instantly G.P. is on the porch scattering the little ones. He must have been crouched at the end, waiting. He reads her mind now—worse, he anticipates what she's going to think, what she's going to do.

She howls and screams and hurls her chair after him. It clatters against the grid. Pain grips her chest. She sinks to the floor, gathers up her skirt and wads it into her mouth. She bites it, trembling, while tears flood down her face.

12

There are sunsets in the puddles on the runway: stripes of fuchsia, crimson, orange against the black; magic carpets of sky scattered on the tarmac. "Sparks!" Yolanda wants him to lean over and look out the window, but a fat man in a business suit, Indian, she thinks, is squeezing between them. Yolanda asked for a window and Sparks the aisle, hoping the middle would stay free.

Sparks doesn't hear her. While the Indian settles himself, Sparks stares ahead in a trance. He hugged her at the airport and didn't let go, clinging, his shirt wrinkled, circles of sweat under his arms. She should have taken the middle seat—it might comfort him to hold her hand—but if she asked the fat man in the suit to change places with her now, she would embarrass Sparks. He told her the flight had been terrible through the Midwest where there were storms. He insisted that he hadn't been frightened, merely concerned.

Sparks always avoided flying when he could, Yolanda remembers, but was he ever this nervous, nearly catatonic? It could be that Yolanda was always too occupied with Roy to notice Sparks. Not that Roy was afraid of flying, but he always needed something, a drink, a blanket, a book. He never thought about reading until he was strapped into his seat and then he would panic because he hadn't brought anything. After giving up her novel to him a few times, Yolanda began carrying a selection of books in her old green college bookbag. Roy called it Olly's Flying Book Show. That's what gave him the idea for the bookstore.

The flying book show landed on upper Broadway and took root. It was to be home base, where Roy would come to rest when he crossed the great divide into thirty. Back then a few years seemed like an immense reach of time. Now she and Roger coolly plan the next five years as if they are talking about tomorrow. Back then, thirty was the drop-off age. In the distant future of after thirty, fans of the Light would presumably be too old to go to rock concerts at Madison Square Garden. The most the Light could hope for would be that enough of the faithful would remain to fill the lounge at the Sierra in Las Vegas for one week a year.

"Maybe I'll die or open a bookstore," Roy once wrote in a song. "Will you sit by the door, baby, and count out the change?"

Roy expected to die. He said his life would kill him. Either someone would slip him bad drugs, or one of the planes the group chartered would go down. Or, Roy's greatest fear, someone in the audience would kill him. This was why Roy wore inconspicuous clothes onstage and stayed in the back behind his keyboards. Yolanda used to scan the crowds for possible assassins and point them out to the security guards so they could keep an eye on them during the performance. "How many paranoid marksmen in the audience tonight, Ol?" he'd ask, only half joking.

Maybe when Roy was about to go from being a member of the Light to performing on his own, he almost hoped he wouldn't make it and would end up in the bookstore with Yolanda. If he was afraid before, what kind of terror must he feel now when he has to walk out alone before thousands? Who is scanning the crowd for assassins these days?

Yolanda leans forward to peer around the man in the middle. Sparks is fixated on the attendant who is demonstrating the oxygen mask. She keeps glancing at him and looking away, uncomfortable at having someone watching her pantomime.

A book, Sparks? Yolanda has a bagful, all on Africa. But he doesn't hear. He sees only the EXIT sign over the wing. Yolanda gets out her reading glasses and starts in on a collection of short stories. She's in the middle of the second one when she notices they've taken off.

The plane climbs steeply, bursting through Tintoretto clouds of pink and gold. Her entrails tug earthward and a slender scrap of gray cloud whirls past, the sheath of her soul, a dull cloak which she's burst like a snake its skin. It floats away, leaving her shiny new and slightly tender, shimmering with possibility.

The plane lurches right. Sparks grips the armrests. The sun, below the horizon, sends a last dying shaft of light through the crazily tilting window, gilding Olly a peculiar golden color. Olly is smiling, which Sparks finds irritating. He's being unreasonable, he knows. It's typical of Olly to be enjoying the takeoff, the most perilous moment besides landing. She's not brave, just doesn't know. It's her strength, this ability to censor out what can harm her. Maggie used to complain that she could never confront Olly, that it was like punching fog. But who would want to confront Olly? Everyone loved her.

Everyone loved Olly. And Sparks won't mind, if this plane ever decides to straighten out and fly instead of careening all over the place, if somewhere above the great gray waters of the Atlantic the terrorist bomb blows the plane to smithereens and his and Olly's souls are linked, chastely intertwined in an ethereal ectoplasmic wreath that spins eternally through the stratosphere.

"Whatever happened to Sparks?" They say it, he knows

they do, when Roy's video comes on, or his single plays on the radio. Maybe someone who knows more than most answers, "He plays backup. You can hear him doing those same licks he used to do on the old Abiding Light albums." Then someone argues that it's electronically reproduced, that a synthesizer is doing his guitar. Ghost licks.

He's turning into a phantom. Wouldn't it be better to go out in a ball of fire rather than a slow fade-out? "Sparks? He was blown up in that terrorist bomb . . ."

The plane sinks. Christ. Sparks tries to squeeze out negative thoughts, tries to concentrate on soaring, flying, living.

"How about a drink?" Olly asks. The cart clinks and rattles toward them, loaded with limes and ice, gently popping fizz water. "Yeah, maybe a beer." No glass. He doesn't need a glass. That a can of beer should exist up here in this alien environment, that he should be able to open his throat and drink it down and at the same time be risking annihilation, is one of the anomalies of our times.

The man in the middle—how did he get there? Sparks can't remember anyone taking that seat, and yet the man exists, more than exists. He is spilling past his seat, is leaving for the back of the plane where, he says, there is more room for expansion. Does Olly think he is a Sikh? Sikhs wear turbans, she says. For the first time Sparks notices that Olly is gotten up in a safari vest, crisp and new, and some matching skirt or pants, one of those in-between things.

"What's the name of that thing you have on?"

"This?"

"Yeah."

"Culotte."

"Ah, culotte."

"Do you like it?"

"It makes you look like you're going on safari, an African safari."

"Is it all right? Or is it too much? I got kind of carried away at the last minute and went flying through Banana Republic flashing my American Express card. I'm excited."

Yolanda is going to tell Sparks about how she feels the presence of Roy, that they are in synch with him, but she doesn't because she's afraid it will sound foolish.

Sparks signals for another beer. "Olly, would you mind pulling the shade? All that black out there, all that nothing . . ." He gestures toward the window.

She indulges him, although she enjoys looking out trying to decipher the dark. How odd that Sparks is afraid of the flight and yet unconcerned about what will happen when they land in D'jarkoume. Maybe that scientist he's been talking to hasn't been as alarming as Gordon. Yolanda suspects that Gordon's imagination has colored his research and what he fears is not D'jarkoume, but something within himself. Which is why he didn't succeed in talking her out of the trip. In fact it's as if his fears are propelling her in the opposite direction, toward whatever terrifies him.

Gordon said it today, only hours ago, although it could have been years. A departure stretches time so that once you are on your way, whatever happened before might have occurred in another life. They were leaving the Banana Republic, hours ago, or a lifetime ago, sharing her umbrella even though he was covered head to foot in his bright orange poncho, hurrying through the streets back to her place where she would pack to leave. His arm was lightly, tentatively around her waist.

"I know this will annoy you," he said, "but may I please say it one last time?"

"Don't go."

"Well, yes, basically, but I think you should know that I feel responsible." The arm around the waist tightened slightly.

"Gordon—"

"I think you wouldn't be going if it weren't for me."

She laughed; his arm dropped and he waited a moment so

that she and the umbrella went ahead. When he caught up, he was outside the umbrella, his shoulders drawn up. She'd hurt his feelings, but she hadn't laughed because she thought it was absurd, but because it struck her as being oddly true. They walked the rest of the way in silence.

"See you. Call when you get back." He veered off at her door.

"Wait." She lifted her arms for an embrace. His lips were cold from the rain.

"I'll be fine. Don't worry," she said.

He patted her, then let go. "You don't know."

She watched him cross the street, his feet turned out like a duck's. Twice he stepped in puddles. Then she went in and closed the door.

The plane has stopped swooping and diving over New York and is now vibrating in place, or at least that's what it feels like, although the pilot comes on and tells them they are flying at x number of feet at x miles per hour over Nova Scotia, not that the pilot can see Nova Scotia any more than they can, but that's what the instruments say and he's taking their word for it. And the passengers are passively accepting trays of colorful mucilaginous food. It's not nourishment as much as diversion to keep them from thinking about the terrorist bomb in the luggage compartment which will send them showering down in fragments all over Nova Scotia.

Olly gets yellow food and Sparks gets brown. Olly leaves most of hers and pulls out something in a plastic container. "It's mung bean casserole. Want some?"

Sparks thinks his brown food looks better, even though Olly warns him it's full of preservatives.

A week ago, Sparks went down to the REI outlet and bought some mosquito netting and insect repellent, a high-tech, high-price water purifier, and several packages of freeze-dried dinners, the kind backpackers carry. He took them out of their original packages and put them in sturdy screw-top plastic containers. Then he took apart his .45 and wrapped each part in plastic. The slide is hidden in the beef Stroganoff, the frame in the chicken curry, the ammunition in the rice pilaf.

Sparks asked Richard what he thought about taking a weapon and Richard said it was a bad idea, that you never knew if the customs officials would wave you through or take apart your luggage. It was safer to expect the worst. Also, there were other checks, interior roadblocks. Sparks didn't tell Richard that he always carried a gun; he just wanted to know how well he should hide it.

"Want some wine with your whatever it is, Olly?"

"No thanks, Sparks. Alcohol makes me break out in hives."

"All alcohol, Olly?"

"I'm allergic."

"Christ, that's terrible. You didn't used to be."

"It's a recent development." She gives him the brave Olly smile she uses to cover up pain, one he remembers well. It occurs to him that it might not be a good thing for Olly to see Roy again, Roy and Maggie . . .

"What about Olly?" Sparks asked Maggie. Their room faced the harbor so the light came in from two sources, the sky and the water, above and below, that colorless light you get in Scandinavia. It turned Maggie's skin translucently pale. She was undressing, insolently, in front of the window and in front of him, pulling off the dress she had been wearing with Roy, so just in case there was any doubt Sparks could see she was wearing nothing underneath. She rummaged in her open suitcase on the floor. When she bent over he could see the furry pudendum between her buttocks.

"What about Olly?" She plopped naked on an armchair by the window and reached for a cigarette. "Olly doesn't sleep with Roy anymore, only when he's between women." But those are outsiders, Sparks argued. They never last long. Maggie was one of the family, a sister to Olly practically. Hadn't Maggie said—? Sister, friend, OK, Maggie felt bad about it but what could she do? It was Olly's fault too, wasn't it? Olly saw it coming and she left. If she really cared, she'd have stayed and defended her territory.

"Maybe not, I mean, maybe she didn't know. I didn't, until now."

Maggie had a look. Sparks called it her "no shit" expression. It was as if she were looking at you with her soul, or, less mystically, it was the same as in a movie when an actor steps out of character and looks directly at the camera. We're always playing some part or other, but Maggie had that ability to suddenly stop the action and look at you that way.

She didn't actually say anything, just stubbed out her cigarette in the ashtray, and he said, "Don't sit like that. You'll leave a spot on the chair."

"You're such a little housekeeper," she laughed.

"And you are a pig."

"Come here."

They began in the chair but ended up on the hard itchy rug. Afterward he asked her who was better and she said neither, they were different . . .

"Do you want mine?" Olly asks, meaning her pink jiggly dessert. He has eaten all of his.

"No. I don't even know why I ate mine. It's gluey and sweet. If you see the girl with the coffee, grab her."

Maybe if they have decaf, says Olly, but only if it's made from water-decaffeinated beans. Real coffee will make him jittery, just as he's beginning to relax.

The plane shudders across some rough air. Sparks feels the pink dessert again in his mouth.

———

Maggie has been up all night, reviewing what brought her here to this point, and she has come up with a large, ringing contradiction. She came to Africa to free Hilda and instead she has crawled into the cage with her.

Something she learned long, long ago was not to show weakness. Somehow the lesson slipped her mind (at about the time G.P. whomped her in the mud) and yesterday, when she sat chewing her skirt in frustration, the lesson was brought home to her once again.

By the blue light of the kerosene lantern, she is cutting up the precious canned ham. The sardines are already in a bowl. The rice is simmering on the stove in the sugar and evaporated milk. A banquet.

When the chimps come this morning, there will be food set outside for them. G.P., of course, will scare everyone off and wolf it down for himself. But there's too much here for one chimpanzee. When he's had his fill, Maggie will shoo him off with the gun and let the others eat. Then they will set off, all of them, into enemy territory.

Maggie has packed a few comforts for herself, a hammock, a change of clothes, matches. She will stay with them, in the forest, at least until the baby is born.

Is she mad? It's a question she's asked herself all night. It seems logical, a natural extension of her commitment. In a way, she has felt it coming for a long time, since the drought, when the water ran out and she thought, This is it. She didn't come, didn't bring Hilda here, to sit in a cage waiting for people she doesn't trust—Didier, Emanuel, Mfui—to take pity on her and bring her food. She didn't come all this way to wait around for one side or another of a tribal war to decide she was on the wrong side and gun her down.

Hilda claps her hands when she sees the food. This time Maggie doesn't try to shush her hooting. Let the others come running.

G.P. is first. The rest hang back. God, how miserably thin they look. How could she let them go this long?

G.P. sees the ham, all cut into chunks set out on a plate for him. Maggie expects him to devour it with one gulp. Instead he stops. "Hoo?" He looks at Maggie. For the first time since the incident their eyes meet, and Maggie is startled at the intelligence there.

"Yes, it's for you, you greedy lummox. Go ahead. Eat."

G.P. squats down and begins picking up the chunks of ham. She doesn't know if he's ever tasted meat, but he seems to like it, chews it and swallows it down with determination. Slowly, the others are creeping up near him, Katie, Biff, Poppy, Danny. A little thread of saliva escapes from Katie's mouth. She moans.

G.P. looks up, sees them all coming close to him. Maggie takes up her gun. Katie, smacking her lips, holds her hand out to G.P. Maggie freezes. Even Hilda has stopped clanking her spoon against her bowl and is watching.

G.P. picks up a piece of ham and puts it into Katie's hand. The others press in and with royal largess, G.P. gives each one a chunk of meat.

13

Maggie props her gun against the bao-hi-soho tree and squats to beat the upraised root until her palms sting. The sound is weak. It won't carry far. G.P. stares at her. The hair rises at the back of his neck. She grabs the gun and steps aside, but he's coming for the tree, not her. He rocks back and forth on the rim of the high root, then races around the trunk, beating the roots like a set of drums, sending the message that they are coming through far into the forest. Maggie's chimps are reclaiming their territory.

"Ooo-ee, go to it, man, do it to them. We'll show 'em!" Richard's chimps can't hold them prisoner anymore. Maggie and her chimps are moving out. Because they're united. They've reached an understanding, she and G.P.

Hilda is with them. She stays close to Maggie, whimpering, fearful, as bad as she was in the very beginning. She won't climb after figs when the others swarm up a tree. Maggie can't climb either. She and Hilda have to pick up the ones that fall to the ground.

Another time, Maggie would have forced Hilda up but she's afraid Hilda might fall and injure the unborn child. She's indulgent with Hilda, reluctant to destroy the harmony they found living together again.

But it's more than that. Maggie watches G.P. walking the branch on two feet, using the knuckles of one hand to steady himself, the other hand to carry figs to a comfortable eating place. Before, Maggie monitored their progress from outside, through the eyes of people like Richard who would judge Maggie a failure if her chimps didn't thrive. It got to be the chimps against her and neither one could win. But since G.P. proved himself a leader, she has joined them. They are no longer adversaries.

The fig sends her saliva glands into spasms, but she forces herself to eat. Forest food. She'll get used to it.

The terminal at D'jar is a futuristic palace of reinforced concrete. Yolanda was expecting something more ramshackle, more third world. But it would figure, Sparks said, because after the coup, the government changed the airport from the old capital, Koume, on the coast, to the new capital, D'jar. The few passengers who straggled off the flight with Sparks and Yolanda didn't do justice to the wide gleaming spaces that had been built to accommodate them.

They had to go around to at least five booths, having documents checked and rechecked, probably to keep the many employees busy, give everyone a chance. Sparks kept whispering "fascists" and "Gestapo" under his breath, but he doesn't speak the language. If he understood French, he would know that everyone was very polite and correct, certainly better than that woman at the UN mission, who must have learned her manners in New York City.

Sparks was especially jittery when the customs inspector began going through their bags. Sparks wouldn't have been foolish enough to carry dope in with him, would he? Marijuana, cocaine? The Light was always so careful when they went on tour never to carry anything like that, because of course they were always searched. Yolanda slipped the inspector a twenty-dollar bill inside her passport, just in case. The inspector zipped up their bags with a smile.

"Want me to carry that, Olly?"

"I have it, thanks, Sparks." It's a duffle with a long strap, which Yolanda slings diagonally across her chest. Her carry-on is over one shoulder. Sparks opens the door and Yolanda gulps at the pungent gritty air.

Instantly, they are in a swarm of ragged boys grabbing for their bags. "Les blancs sont à moi! Les blancs sont à moi!" one cries. "The whites are mine."

Yolanda does feel white, like a pale helpless grub at the moment when its sheltering log is overturned, no match for the fierce dark boys who've come up fighting every day for their bread. No match, but she tries, clinging to her duffle bag as if to a life raft, bobbing in a sea of boys, watching Sparks being carried away in the tide.

"Laisse-les. Laisse-les. Laisse les blancs tranquils!" Someone is calling to them to leave the whites alone, a tall man in starched khakis, coming toward her now. The boys fall back to let him through. He comes quickly but with easy long steps, smiling, either in friendship or amusement at their plight.

"Please." He reaches for the duffle and Yolanda surrenders it without question. He is Didier, a friend of Maggie's. He knows their names, shakes their hands, and leads them through the disappointed boys to his car, an immaculate light-colored Mercedes jeep.

"This is fantastic, this is really great. What were they doing, trying to steal our bags?" Sparks is saying, but Yolanda can tell by Didier's expression that he doesn't understand, that he exhausted his store of English on the introduction. Yolanda translates and Didier answers that the boys were trying to direct them to a cab, that they get a commission from the drivers.

Didier is going to drive them to Maggie's. He takes supplies out to her about once a month. The trip lasts two days because of the roads, which aren't as developed as the roads in the United States. They will start early tomorrow, around eight, if that's all right.

Yolanda is surprised to see so many people walking along the side of the road, women with bundles on their heads, more women than men. The women are small and seem very feminine with their long wrapped skirts. Many have babies tied to their backs. Are we close to the city? she asks Didier. We are in it, he says.

He swings around a corner and up a broad boulevard lined with state-of-the-art street lights and behind them, low mudbrick buildings. "Allée du Président." Except for an army jeep going the other way, theirs seems to be the only vehicle on the road.

"Hôtel du Président." Didier pulls up in front of a spanking clean, brightly lit entrance.

A short squat bellhop takes charge of their luggage. Didier leads them into a lobby so new that it could have been furnished yesterday with its leather sofas, African tapestries on the walls, canned music, deep air conditioning, in time for one of those international conferences, on world hunger perhaps. Sparks pictures diplomatic haunches draped in the finest broadcloth finding comfort on the smooth leather seats. But no one is sitting on the chairs and sofas. Sparks sees no one in the lobby except for Olly, Didier, the bellhop, and two tall men in suits behind a long shiny black counter. Olly, on tiptoe, seems to be arguing with them. Her face is pink. She keeps running her fingers through her hair.

The problem is, she tells Sparks finally, they got the reservation wrong. Instead of two rooms, there is only a double prepared for them. In all this huge empty hotel there aren't two single rooms? Sparks finds this hard to believe, but after all, it doesn't matter, does it? If they share a room? Olly's cheeks flare up again. Well, she'd rather not. She's trying to persuade them to prepare a room for her.

Célibataire is the word they use in French to mean "single." It may have the same meaning, but there's a whole other connotation, Yolanda thinks. Single implies freedom, sexual adventurism, the potential for finding a partner. *Célibataire* sounds monkish and final, as if one has withdrawn forever, renounced sexuality. Sparks wouldn't mind sharing a double room with her. He probably wouldn't even mind sharing some sex with her.

When Yolanda packed for the trip, laying her new khaki clothes out on the bed, her supplies of wheat-free, yeast-free food, she went to the drawer and fished out the negligee she'd hidden there at Christmas. She smoothed the wrinkles and packed it in the duffle, along with her diaphragm in its pearlized case.

For Roy? She never asked herself who it was for, she simply packed it. "Olly Olly in come free . . . come free." What did that mean?

They can have separate rooms, says the man with the mellow voice, the impeccable fingernails, but it will take time to prepare them. Perhaps they would like to wait in the bar?

A jazz tape is being played in the bar—sophisticated, urban, it's Bob James and David Sanborn. Sparks recognizes it. Not what he expected in Africa, but then he wasn't anticipating a lacquered and mirrored bar either. Didier's hugging and back-slapping two guys at the bar, speaking some African language with them. They are talking about what Sparks would talk about to his buddies in Lubbock if he met them in a bar: "How's it going?" "Not so good. Goddamn truck broke an axle." "The Ford? No kidding . . ." Or they could be saying: "You found them." "It was easy." "You want us to take care of them here?" "No, wait until tomorrow. I'll drive them out into the bush and you can make it look accidental." They laugh, all of them, including the bartender.

"Didier, can we buy you a beer?" Sparks asks. Didier accepts before Olly can translate.

"So, Olly tells me you're going to take us to Maggie tomorrow. You . . . drive . . ." Sparks makes driving motions.

Didier bends close to Olly and begins a long earnest conversation. Olly's neck reddens.

"Sparks, Didier is explaining that he'd like to be paid for driving us—"

"But that's his job, taking supplies, isn't it?"

"He says he wants to drive us, that he likes us, but in all fairness, he should be paid extra because of the risks involved."

"He said that? There are risks? What kind, did he say?"

"He says the people, the peasants, have been inflamed by a song on the radio—an old song that has no meaning anymore, but it has stirred up old feuds and anyone who has made something of his life could be endangered."

That's Roy's song, of course. He's talking about Roy's song. It's happening. The pieces are falling just the way Richard said they would. Sparks gets another beer and tries to bargain with Didier, but it's difficult using Olly as a translator because she looks apologetic. At least Sparks gets Didier to agree on half paid when they get there and the other half when they get back. Olly pours more beer into her glass. Didn't she say she was allergic to alcohol? Maybe beer is OK.

Didier turns to say goodbye to his buddies. They laugh and slap him on the back. In his mind, Sparks is already tearing apart the packages of freeze-dried food to get to his .45.

"What's that?" Olly comes out of the bathroom wearing a negligee, her arms folded across her breasts. They are sharing a room after all.

When they were finally shown to their separate rooms, after beers with Didier and dinner in the dining room (where they were the only ones except for a French-speaking family, doughy blonds, with a large dog who sat under the table), Olly's was all the way down a long deserted hall. A dirty shirt was hanging in the bathroom, a half-empty bottle of cognac was on the desk, and the bed was rumpled.

"Can I stay with you?" she asked. She was afraid that whoever was using the room before might return and she lacked the energy for another hassle with the men at the desk.

"This is the frame of a .45," Sparks says.

They went through customs with a gun? Outside of Texas, women generally have a hard time understanding why a man would need to carry a gun. Olly knows Sparks always traveled with one. But that was back then, when they were a rock group, when there was some reason at least—

And this isn't a reason, traveling in a country in the middle of a revolution? Didn't she hear what Didier said? Christ, Olly, wake up. She's got to understand that Didier is a Moro. He's tall, taller than Sparks, and did she catch the gold Rolex on his wrist? He's supposed to be a driver—a driver with a Rolex? And Roy is against the Moro. His song is of the Ilido tribe. Sparks knows this sounds very unreal to her, but now they are inside the country. Its reality has become their own, doesn't she see? Didier could be, probably is, their enemy.

Yolanda wonders if Sparks has taken to using cocaine in recent years. She doesn't remember him being so paranoid. This gun business is upsetting, and now he's turning lamps upside down, crawling under the desk, looking for electronic listening devices. He says it just occurred to him that the reason it took them so long to get the rooms ready was not incompetence, as he first assumed, but that they had to rig up the bugging devices.

Yolanda is still betting on incompetence. These people live

in mud huts. A modern hotel like this is foreign to them. How could they bug a room when they can't even get the in-house telephone to work properly? Even after Sparks has unscrewed the bases of the lamps, dismantled the ceiling fixture, he is still not convinced. Come to bed, Sparks. Come to bed.

It's hopeless trying to find it, Sparks thinks. They make those things so small now that it could be on the water glass, in the corner of the mirror, which holds Olly's reflection as she sits on the bed, her knees clasped to her chest. She's wearing something strange, a negligee that doesn't look like her. With her skinny neck coming out of all that black fluff, she looks like a buzzard or something. He'll come to bed. Why doesn't she just go to sleep and he'll be there later.

It's been a while since Maggie's slept in the hammock. She used to when they were starting their foraging trips, just Hilda, G.P., and Katie then. She would show them how to nest by the food source, the way chimps do in nature. As soon as it was dark they would try to sneak into the hammock with her and end up tipping everyone out on the ground.

If the hammock had held them she might have been tempted to let them stay. Chimps, except for mothers and babies, sleep in solitary nests, but humans in the natural state huddle together in small bands for safety. She felt painfully alone and exposed in her fragile hammock, listening while nocturnal animals rustled on all sides, hearing the cough of the leopard, the whisper of snake belly against tree bark, the slow progress of the pangolin climbing its own curling tail, the rattle of the bushbuck browsing.

Primates, except for a few forms such as the bush baby and the loris, are helpless in the dark, blind and confused, prone to panic. The imagination fills in for what the eyes can't see. Chimps hate dark as much as humans. Once G.P. stole her flashlight and wouldn't give it back until the batteries wore out. She has her flashlight with her and has to force herself not to shine it at every stirring sound.

The absurd thing is, she's sleeping within sight of her own house. As soon as the sun began slanting in through the leaves, G.P. trudged off for the station like some faithful Joe heading home after work, and the others followed him. Maggie hooted for them to follow her deeper into the forest, but she was bucking habit. They have grown used to sleeping in Emanuel's house.

She followed them there, waved her gun, shrieked, bared her teeth, but nothing would move them. They hid behind what remained of Emanuel's furniture, screaming back at her. Hilda wanted to return to Maggie's house but Maggie wouldn't unlock the door. Instead, she strung her hammock on the edge of the clearing. Hilda must have gone to sleep with the others in Emanuel's house.

It hurt to see the way the chimps have wrecked Emanuel's house. Maggie seldom looked inside it, but when she did she was always touched by how clean and neat he kept it, a boy on his own without any parents.

Tomorrow she will take them deep into the middle of wild chimpanzee territory. They will be too frightened to leave her and come all the way back for the night.

14

Seen from the sixth-story balcony outside their room, the water breaks up into dapples of light and the swimmer appears levitated above his shadow, which glides along the bottom of the pool. Sparks doing laps is a sight that could break your heart for the precision with which he lifts his arms and lets them fall, the smoothness with which he moves. (She, on the other hand, must struggle and splash merely to keep herself afloat. The chlorine gets up her nose and burns inside her head. Roy told her once that she looked like a bat in the water.)

Sparks in the swimming pool is an emblem of power—the way he commands his environment, the way he commands the privilege to be the only one in the sparkling water while outside the tall whitewashed walls around the hotel are thousands of hot dusty bodies that would swarm in and obliterate the aquamarine rectangle with their desperately bobbing shapes, if given the chance.

Seen from another perspective, Sparks looks like a rare amphibian held captive in a small enclosed space, unable to make contact or function in the world outside the high white walls.

They tried. They were up early, packed, waiting for Didier. When he hadn't come by noon, they asked around the hotel but no one knew him. Last night it seemed Didier was friends with the entire staff, but it's hard to tell in a strange culture. In her confusion, Yolanda stupidly forgot to get Didier's phone number, or even his last name. Perhaps it wouldn't have done much good anyway. Sparks wasn't able to reach any of the numbers he'd gotten from that scientist friend of Maggie's.

Maybe they shouldn't have argued so with Didier about the price they would pay him for driving them, Yolanda said (meaning Sparks shouldn't have argued so—she was willing to pay what he asked). "Do you think we insulted him?"

They didn't need Didier. They could rent a car and drive themselves, Sparks said. He had a map of D'jarkoume which he'd bought in Los Angeles in a store that specialized in travel books and maps of far-off places. D'jarkoume was only slightly larger than New Mexico, after all. How long could it take? Six hours at the most. There was a Hertz office in the lobby but no one was in it. The butcher in town rented cars, the man at the reception desk told them finally.

As soon as they passed through the gates of the hotel grounds it was the same as when they left the terminal last night: the clamoring, the pleading. This time it was boys who wanted to shine their shoes, sell them elephant-hair bracelets, ivory trinkets. One young woman, her face radiant at seeing them, crawled across the road on her hands and knees, her crippled calves and feet waving in the air like twisted sticks. She wore her shoes, rubber thongs, on her hands. "Give her something, Sparks," Yolanda cried because she hadn't changed her money and didn't have anything with her, but he wouldn't because he was afraid they'd be inundated with beggars if he did. They were anyway. A pretty little girl, with silky curly hair so she must have been half something else, held Yolanda's hand all the way into town, softly pleading. But Sparks wouldn't budge. He's not himself here. He's wary, watchful, so that even a small child frightens him.

The open market was a maze of wooden booths, some with flimsy tin roofs, some with awnings, selling everything from oranges and okra to rubber boots and bright bolts of cloth. They didn't dare stop to look or a boy would come rushing out to thrust something into their hands and ask for their best price. To Yolanda, it all seemed cheerful and lively, not what you'd expect in a country on the verge of revolution. Sparks pointed to several very tall men in warm-up suits standing here and there, apparently watching the scene. They seemed harmless enough to Yolanda. After all, they weren't armed. Don't be so sure, he said.

The butcher, whose shop in one of the permanent buildings was crowded with customers, was about five feet tall, an Ilido, Yolanda assumed. When she asked if he had cars to lease, he took his apron off, handed it to an assistant, and showed them into his office, where he changed to a cotton sports jacket and ceremoniously shook their hands.

He assumed they wanted to go to Koume, to one of the resorts on the coast. No, to Dobo, Yolanda said, to the national forest. Oh, his voice was soft, then he was very sorry but he couldn't lease a car for that purpose. If they wanted to travel to Dobo, they should arrange with the officials for official transportation, or they could go on a *camion*, a truck, but renting a car for that purpose would be impossible. It's really better not to go there at all, he said. The people are *sauvage*, the forest is not interesting, just green. You can't see animals because it is too thick. You can't see anything.

What did he mean by saying that the people in Dobo were wild? What kind of trucks went to Dobo? Sparks had all kinds of questions he wanted to ask the butcher that Yolanda wouldn't translate for him. Sparks doesn't understand that there is not only a language barrier, it's cultural as well. How much can you question a small man who runs a butcher shop without making him uncomfortable? Although they might have a literal translation for a word, they can't know what it means in this culture. What is the meaning of *sauvage* or *camion*?

A camion, as it turned out, was one of the small buses waiting outside the market. Sparks had Yolanda go around and ask if any were traveling to Dobo. They were instantly surrounded by boys who claimed they knew the bus that was going direct to Dobo. It seemed half the vehicles in the market were going to Dobo, leaving immediately, or whenever she and Sparks were ready. Sparks was all set to run back for the luggage but Yolanda said it was suspicious, all those buses going to Dobo, when it was supposed to be a tiny town on the edge of the national forest. She'd like to ask back at the hotel. Sparks said he hated not speaking the language.

The man at the hotel desk said that the camions were not for tourists, that it could take days to reach Dobo by camion because they stop for passengers and don't move until they are full. Eventually, they would probably get to Dobo, but they would end up spending nights in little villages with no accommodations. He said he might know people who would be willing to drive them. He'd ask around.

Sparks said that there was no reason to think the man at the desk was telling the truth, that he was a Moro after all. He went up to the room to check his revolver, which he had locked in his hand luggage, and went down to the pool for a swim.

Sparks continues doing laps with the regularity of a mechanical man. What connection is there between Yolanda and this swimming machine except that they were both blown to this incomprehensible corner of the world by the same whim. They came because of a song? The scrap of a song?

This is what comes of having too much money and not enough commitments. You rattle around too easily. You end up places you have no business being in. Mother was lucky she never traveled. Yolanda imagines her alone, off in some foreign country, overcome with the terror of being displaced, feeling like a button that has popped off a shirt and rolled into the dark under the bed.

Now Yolanda understands why Gordon doesn't travel. It isn't fear of icebergs and revolutions. It's the horror of being without the comforting web of routine and responsibilities which secures you to the rest of the world.

Sparks comes out of the water in one enviable motion. Yolanda turns away, back to the room they share. She makes the bed because the hotel staff is not likely to do it (she didn't see anyone in the hall this morning with clean linens). When she finishes she feels somewhat better. She has claimed one piece of this foreign place, if it is only the space of a bed.

"Olly? What are you doing?" Sparks has come in, damp, cool. He has a towel around his waist. He holds her chin and looks at her face as if he's never seen tears before.

It's only a sense of dislocation and maybe some jet lag, she wants to say, but instead she moves into his cool arms and blots her cheeks against his chest.

He undresses her slowly, therapeutically. He knows how to make her feel better. He's done it many times. No wonder the women come to him to have their sorrows caressed away. She holds him, holds him tight, and he knows just what to do.

When it is over, the breeze comes in through the window and dries the sweat on their bodies. The room, which before looked unfamiliar, somewhere she had drifted into by accident, has been transformed into their place, their own secret home.

———

Maggie and her group have been traveling all morning, making good time—that's one way of looking at it—since the wild chimps have cleared out everything worth stopping for. They left piles of shells under Maggie's favorite nut tree. Her stomach twisted when she thought of the tender waxy nutmeats. G.P. went clear to the top until Maggie feared he would break a branch and fall, but came down sulky and empty-handed. The rest of them wasted precious minutes sifting through the shells for pieces that had been overlooked. They found a few figs of the kind they had yesterday, sour little fruits. Maggie forced herself to eat some even though they gave her cramps and diarrhea.

Now they are leaving what they consider their territory, their home range, and entering that of the enemy. This terrain is not new to Maggie. She followed Richard over it plenty of times, but then she was a disinterested human observer. Now she is leading an invading party of chimps.

The trees on this side of the unmarked border look darker, the vines snakier. The very molecules in the air seem to be pressing closer, resisting Maggie's advance. Hilda curls her fingers around Maggie's. Katie and the little ones are at her heels. G.P. and Danny are out of sight but keeping close. Maggie hears them drumming periodically. She drums back, or hoots. From her compass readings she can tell that they are circling her group, just as males in the wild will sometimes circle a troop of females and young.

She wishes she could tell Richard this, how G.P. is taking on a leader's responsibilities, but she can't because Richard isn't on their side. He's on the side of the enemy, the wild chimpanzees. He would not want to see this. He wouldn't want to know what Maggie is prepared to do to protect her own.

Richard asked her to marry him once. Was it here they camped? Or farther north? It's hard to tell because things change so fast. What had been a massive fallen trunk could be a stand of young trees by now. They did talk about getting married, however. It had seemed possible when they were camping here together, but when Maggie got back to the station Hilda had that skin fungus, and there was the problem of her not eating. Finally, Richard had to go back for his classes at the university and he left without bringing up marriage again. Just as well, because as it turned out, they're not on the same side.

A big tree has fallen, allowing some sunlight to leak through and ferns have sprung up to take advantage. If you peel the stem, there's a spongy lemon-tasting core. Even Hilda doesn't need to be coaxed to start in on them.

It was in clearings like this that Maggie and Richard would wait, hoping to hear the call of a chimp. When they heard one, they would take a compass reading and tear in after it. This time, Maggie hears a voice, not G.P.'s or Danny's, and she wants to run and hide. The hair creeps on the back of her neck. Her lips pull back. Hilda runs to her. Katie stands on two legs. She hoots in answer.

"Katie! Shhh!" Is she a traitor, little Katie, or does she remember the voice?

"Shhh!"

Maggie takes a compass reading on the calls. They're coming from the same direction as G.P. and Danny, or at least from where she last heard their drumming. They can easily skulk away if they want to, circle back. There's no need to challenge the strange male. He may be traveling with others. Maggie tries to communicate all this to G.P., human to chimp, through thought waves. She believes that chimps can communicate like this, that humans used to but that they lost the power, most of them.

"Katie, shhh!"

She can't even communicate with Katie, who is right in front of her. The problem is, Katie knows what Maggie wants but she doesn't agree. She thinks it's in her interest to let this strange male know where she is.

Katie looks expectantly over the ferns. Hilda is clinging to Maggie. Poppy and Biff have scaled a rough tree and are huddled high in a fork. The afternoon hangs like a blanket around them. They wait, quiet and motionless, suspended in the humid body of the forest.

The stillness cracks open into bellowing, crashing, screaming. Katie and Hilda flee in different directions. Only Maggie stands on the booming earth, gripping her gun. G.P. thunders into the clearing, pursued by another. Seeing Maggie, G.P. takes courage and dives at the other one.

"G.P.! Out of the way!" She can't fire with the two of them tangled up together. At last G.P. breaks and comes charging toward Maggie. Maggie fires. The wild chimp falls. He looks up at Maggie, seeing her for the first time. Maggie knows who he is, from years ago. He's the one Richard called Boris. She recognizes his mangled ear. G.P. lunges at him, but Boris rolls up and scuttles off on three legs.

They hoot after him, everyone, Maggie too. They sing their victory song. G.P. is magnificent, his eyes blazing, his coat frizzed around him. He hugs Danny, moves toward Hilda and Maggie. Hilda screams and runs but Maggie stands still, her gun at her side while he wraps his long arms around her hips and hugs her to his chest. It is brief. He lopes off, but Maggie has felt his powerful heart.

15

Didier showed up this morning at the hotel exactly twenty-four hours late. Sparks wanted an explanation, but Yolanda couldn't get one out of Didier, other than vague mention of complications and trouble with the *fonctionnaires*, whoever they might be. Yolanda found it hard to work up a case of righteous indignation when she was actually grateful to Didier for giving her that day.

Is this what Roy planned for her and Sparks? Jealousy was never one of Roy's faults. He used to encourage Yolanda to take on new lovers, said the sexual revolution was passing her by. He'd even suggest possible candidates, from the group, from the fans who came backstage. But Yolanda couldn't go with the sexual revolution. She was stubbornly stuck back in another time. Her dream was that Roy would return, and when he did she didn't want to be involved with someone else.

"*Maggie days*" . . . "*Sparks fly up*" . . . "*Olly Olly in come free.*" Roy, in his mysterious way, has brought Sparks and Yolanda together, may even have delayed Didier just for this purpose. And what is the rest of his plan if this is the way it begins?

Yolanda is not making sense. She knows this. When she

surrendered her body to Roy's plan, she opened her mind to thoughts she'd never had before. It's Africa too, the heat, the dust, the interminable road that doesn't even look like a road much of the time, just a track of dust.

"Olly, you all right back there?" Sparks in a dusty stetson, a bandanna tied outlaw fashion over his face, aviator sunglasses, reaches for her hand.

"I'm fine." She pats him.

"Want to switch? Ride up front for a while?"

"No, no, I'm perfectly fine." Sparks would never fit back here. There's barely room enough for her with all the supplies Didier is taking for Maggie. She shifts to avoid a box that's banging against her hipbone, tucks the canvas around the edge to keep out dust, and settles back among the boxes.

She dreams she is walking along the road, the dust like powder between her toes. She has left behind her khaki pants, which the man at Banana Republic assured her would be perfect for Africa and which looked so disappointingly sexless in the mirror this morning, along with the matching khaki shirt with the pockets everywhere (what are those pockets for? The salesman never explained). She traded her khaki clothes for a length of African cloth, which she tied around her hips, a bright blouse, and a tall basket full of—Didier, what are they carrying on their heads? Maize meal, he says, bringing it home from the mill, or clothes that they've washed in the river—a basket of freshly washed clothes.

She stops to watch the jeep passing with *blancs* inside and scowls at the mountains of dust billowing after. When the *blancs* are gone, she turns onto one of those narrow tracks that disappear so tantalizingly into the underbrush. She climbs steadily, her hips swaying gently under the load balanced on her head. She sets the basket down outside a mud hut with a roof made of raffia palm. She moves across the packed-earth yard, scattering chickens around her ankles, to look out past her own vegetable garden to the neat cultivated squares in the valley below, and beyond that to the forest hazy blue in the distance.

Coming back she passes under a mango tree with leaves shiny, not dusty like the trees by the road. When she goes inside she can't see at first, it is so dark after the equatorial sun, but gradually she becomes aware of someone sitting, waiting. Sparks? Roy? But when his hand reaches out from the shadow, it has the slender shape of Didier's.

Olly looks like she's nodded off again, although it's hard to tell, under the safari hat, the glasses and bandanna. Before, Sparks thought she'd fainted, she looked so uncomfortable squeezed in among the boxes, but she's sleeping in all the dust and noise and heat, the jouncing around. Olly's tough in a funny way.

When you make love to her, you can feel the blood going through her veins and even, it seems, the electricity pulsing across her nerve endings. There is no protective layer, just the thinnest stretch of skin between her and the outside, so fragile that you can see why men would be afraid to touch her, and yet she doesn't break. He looks at her, awkwardly tucked among the packages and he knows that she will live a long time. Olly will live to be a hundred years old, for Christ's sake, and she will always be this way.

Didier is not wearing a bandanna. His face and neck have turned from ebony to dust red. He downshifts to go over a section where the road has completely washed away. It looks like a dry riverbed.

"Why don't they fix the roads?" Sparks yells.

"No money." Didier spits out the open window.

He speaks English fine, has been answering most of Sparks's questions. Of course they've been using hands a lot and keeping it simple, but his English is better than he lets on.

He tells Sparks the crops planted along the road (sugar cane, coffee, tea, cocoa) and who owns the land (the government because small private farming is not economical).

"So who owned the land before the government decided it wasn't economical? The Ilido?"

Didier doesn't understand the question.

"You know, Didier, the two tribes, Moro, Ilido—"

"There are no tribes in D'jarkoume. All one people." He slams the brakes to avoid crashing into a pothole.

"Oh come on, Didier. It's pretty obvious, isn't it, that all the high government officials are tall and all the people carrying bananas on their heads are short."

Suddenly the road commands Didier's complete attention and he isn't able to continue the conversation. There's probably a micro bugging device in the steering column.

"Didier, hey, who are these characters in warm-up suits?" They've had several roadblocks already on this trip, but this is the first time they've been stopped by the men in warm-up suits. The device they're using to stop traffic is a fold-out strip of metal spikes. Can these strips be purchased at any hardware store or are they strictly government issue? "So who are these guys? Secret police?"

"The *fonctionnaires*." Didier stops the car and jumps out. Hugs and backslapping all around. Sparks brings his arm down to hide the holster under his shirt. The fonctionnaires come around. For what? To shake hands. Relax. They want to shake hands. They want to shake Olly's hand. She's awake now. There's a minibus rattling up behind. One of the fonctionnaires folds up the road block to let them pass while the other stops the minibus.

"What are they looking for?" The passengers of the minibus are being made to get out and line up alongside the road. "Olly, would you ask Didier if they're looking for anything special?"

Olly extricates herself from her space and leans forward to talk to Didier. Didier answers rapidly in French.

"Sparks, Didier says that while he doesn't mind all our questions, he thinks we should know that it is considered rude here to have too much curiosity."

Sparks sees himself reflected in Olly's sunglasses. They're two masked raiders, outlaws, coming after whatever secrets they can uncover. It isn't surprising that Didier doesn't want to confide in them. He's a Moro after all, government agent probably, but then what is he doing running supplies to Maggie? Unless he's not Maggie's friend, and the outlaws are being outmaneuvered . . . Sparks rests his arm on the reassuring lump of his .45.

The best hotel in Ouagoubua, the Hôtel Riviera, has a lakefront view but no screens. When you open the window, the burned-marshmallow stink of the sugar refinery wafts in along with, presumably, small malaria-infected mosquitoes. Sparks locks the door and puts his gun on the bedside table. He and Olly slather themselves with wintergreen-scented insect repellent.

Olly does his back. "Look what you did to me," he says.

Olly smiles. "But I only touched your back . . . No, wait." She hands him the bottle. "Do me first."

When Sparks wakes, he and Olly are lying with their heads at the foot of the bed. The sheets are clammy with sweat, sperm, and other effluents of love.

There is no art to how he makes love to Olly, just mindless want and need, not the way he usually goes about it. This rush to get into her, to use her body and make it his own and at the same time to surrender himself to her, is not his style. He has apologized to Olly but she doesn't know what he's talking about, has had only one lover before Sparks, and that was long ago.

When Sparks first met Roy and Olly they reminded him of a couple of high school nerds, the pair who never dated, never went to parties, and suddenly senior year they are seen walking down the hall together. One day you catch him with his hand on her ass while she opens her locker, and you know—they're doing it! The nerds, without going to make-out parties in eighth grade, without trading pointers in the locker room on techniques of back-seat courtship, without participating at all in the collective coming of age, have discovered sex on their own.

Sparks used to imagine Roy and Olly making love like two innocent nerds, ineptly but passionately. And this is how Sparks finds himself with Olly, like he's never done it before in his life. Beginner's love.

Sparks untangles himself from Olly, gently so as not to wake her. He finds the sheet on the floor and covers her. At the window he can see the moon. Across the lake where in the daylight he remembers only sugarcane fields are many fires, campfires. He hears that sound which started while they were having dinner. He thought it was wind chimes but the waiter told Olly it was frogs. Joined to the frogs now are drums and voices singing faintly from across the water.

He stands a long time, breathing the burned-marshmallow smoke of the sugar refinery. *"Frangipani daze . . . night chiming frogs . . ."*

He is coming close, to Roy or to whatever Roy is summoning him to. Maybe even the delay in D'jar was part of the journey. Sparks had to find Olly first. He had to align himself along the coordinates of her narrow body before he could travel the road to Roy.

"Sparks fly up . . ." The reflected moon winks in the black water. If he were on the other side he would see the sparks shooting up from their fires. He would hear their song. But all he gets is the vibration of drums, murmuring voices. He

shivers in the light breeze, slaps a mosquito on his chest. *"Olly Olly in come free . . ."*

He crawls back into Olly's wintergreen embrace.

Something has disturbed her, pried at her sleep, scattered her dreams. The moon. It has bored through a space in the forest roof to spy down on Maggie in her paradise.

Paradise is a curtain, a wall of figs. Maggie can smell them rotting on the ground. Hilda likes the fermented ones best. She gathered them up and stuffed them into her mouth, staggered around happily, and passed out against a tree.

Maggie thought she remembered vines of figs in this area, but never this many. It was like a vision when she came upon them, glistening orangish pink against the black green. She could see where wild chimps had started in on them, had perhaps fled only moments ago.

Maggie and her group came upon the figs in late afternoon, just as the shadows were deepening. They hooted, clamored. Maggie was afraid that the wild chimps would come back, maybe bringing others with them. But no one came. Word must have gotten around, the way it does from chimp to chimp, that the strange band had a human with them, a human with a gun.

Maggie's chimps fell to, slurping, farting, filling their bellies tight and round. When it was almost dark, they crawled off to make their nests close by. Maggie strung up her hammock here, under this tree which, for some reason, fails to block out the sky completely.

While she was tying her hammock to the tree, she had a sensation of harmony, as if she were stringing not a hammock but a musical instrument, a long taut string that vibrated in tune with all around her, her chimps, her forest. And the curtain of figs seemed like a sign to her that no longer would she have to fight the chimps, the forest, that she had found the right direction at last and they were all moving effortlessly together, as one.

It was a feeling without words. She did not bring it up into those regions of the mind that would want to explain it. Rather, she held it close to her heart and crawled into her hammock with it, very carefully, afraid to turn too sharply lest she lose it forever.

And now comes this silver eye piercing her dreams, disintegrating her feeling, forcing her to analyze it, which only drives it farther away. She swims after it, but it shatters from the force of her stroke, the intensity of her need.

Like that moon she swam after one time—where was it? New Hampshire, a lake with an Indian name, a cottage Roy rented, or someone lent him, a place with hemlocks growing close all around so it was always mossy and damp. The moon one night was on the water and no one would come out to see. Roy and Sparks were working on a song. Olly had bread in the oven that hadn't risen in time to bake for dinner.

Maggie went to the dock alone to honor the moon, took off her clothes, and dived out to where the moon lay floating like a disk on the water. Only of course it moved farther out as she swam after it, swam and swam, as if by catching the moon she could find her way out of the stagnant place she had drifted into.

Waiting for Roy—that was all she did that summer. She would brush against him in the hall, plot to be left alone in the cottage with him. She wanted everything from Roy and he gave her nothing—worse, he took away what little she had.

And now thoughts of him are riding down to her on moonlight. She presses the heels of her hands against her eyes. She knows what will come now, although she tries to stop it. But the harder she tries, the more she makes the next part inevitable. It's all wound like a tape in her mind and once she admits the first part, she must see it through to the end, to the song, the one song Roy did for her, the ballad of the hollow woman who searched for love to fill her. The wind far above soughs in tune with its rocking, mocking chorus. "Don't lay that one on me, girl. Oh baby, baby, don't lay that one on me."

"That song's for you, Maggie," he says, his face a moon above her. "It's your song."

16

Yolanda and Sparks are already at the table having wonderfully fresh croissants and café au lait when Didier comes in. His boots are gleaming. Yolanda wonders how he managed to keep them looking that way through the dusty ride yesterday, or has he been out for a shoeshine already this morning before the rain? His face, when she gets to it (she's a little shy; the fantasies of yesterday continued more or less through the night), looks drawn. Perhaps her dreams kept him awake.

"Bonjour, Eland." Her name, when Didier says it, comes out "eland," which is a kind of antelope, she thinks. He takes his coffee black and eats only one piece of baguette with some confiture, no butter. They will go to the market, he says, to buy fruits and vegetables. This is the last big town before the station. Will the road be as bad today as it was yesterday? Sparks asks. Worse, Didier says, without waiting for Yolanda to translate.

There are more of those tall characters in the warm-up suits walking through the market, two of them, sticking close together. Sparks notices that no one looks directly at them; the eyes wait until they pass and then slowly follow them with routine hostility. Even Didier gives these unofficial officials just a nod, the briefest flick of his elegant head, to acknowledge but not commit.

Didier picks his way in his shiny boots across rotting cabbage, slippery mud. It rained hard during breakfast but the sun is out now, making the wet thatch roofs steam. Two naked babies play in a filthy puddle. The women giggle as they hold lengths of cloth around Olly for a screen. She is trading in her safari khakis. Soon Olly is revealed, wrapped in red and yellow African cloth with a high matching turban.

"Don't laugh," she says, so Sparks holds her close, burying his nose in the sweetly rotting cloth of her headdress while the women, girls really most of them, giggle and cluck their approval.

Didier is telling Yolanda that he would like to marry Maggie. Yolanda is sitting in the front seat because Sparks insisted. He is sleeping now. He didn't get much rest last night, said there was music that kept him up. Yolanda, lost in voluptuous dreams, didn't hear a thing.

Didier can't understand why neither Yolanda nor Maggie is married. In D'jarkoume, rich women have many suitors. She and Maggie aren't rich, Yolanda says. If you can afford the air fare to America, you must be rich, says Didier. It's all relative, Yolanda supposes, although if Didier can afford a gold Rolex watch, he should be able to fly to the U.S. if he chooses.

Abruptly, they are in a downpour. Didier and Yolanda roll up their windows. The air inside turns steamy and smells like incense burning or flowers rotting. It's her clothes, Yolanda realizes, her new African clothes that are giving off this rich ambiguous odor.

She leans back and closes her eyes. Didier tells her that he would like to marry Maggie, but they would have to live in the U.S., he would insist on that, and she would have to give up her animals. He refuses to live with animals.

Squatting in the tentlike shelter of the roots of the Gbohohé, the one they call the pygmy tree, Maggie and Katie are cracking open kontoué-be nuts and feeding them to Poppy, Biff, and Hilda. Hilda accepts the nutmeats with a languid gesture, more regal than ever in her pregnant state. She's looking out at the rain—wondering why they don't go home where it is dry? She doesn't say.

It has been raining off and on all day. In between downpours there has been feeding. Not much traveling. Not a sound from Richard's chimps.

Maggie hoots, then listens. No answering call from G.P. He and Danny have been missing since early afternoon. It's all right. Sometimes she has gone days without seeing them, but still, in enemy territory, they should stay closer, at least signal to her from time to time.

Katie stops her nut cracking to listen as well, turning her face, with its perpetually worried expression, from side to side, searching, although in this dense part of the forest she can't see more than ten feet in any direction. Hilda, smacking her lips, begins taking bits and pieces out of Maggie's hair. It's to calm her, Maggie knows, but she could also use a little grooming. She didn't bring a comb or brush; there wasn't room in her pack; she already regrets not having them.

She settles back, leaning against a root, to yield to the ministrations of Hilda's strong fingers.

"Phew!" A stench fills their pygmy chamber. Maggie crawls out and scrapes a large dead ant from her pants, a cadaver ant. It gives off an odor of rotting flesh when squashed. A sluice of rain water falls at Maggie's feet and she hears the beating of hornbill wings overhead.

"Hoo?" Hilda questions from inside the root shelter. How can Maggie explain that the stink of the cadaver ant, the rush of wings overhead, and the memory of a stark white moon have thrown her into a panic?

She doesn't have to explain. Her face says it. They come out from the tree, whimpering, grinning, and press their bodies close around her. The rain falls and soaks them through but no one moves.

Where could she have gone? Does she do this often, disappear into the bush with her animals? Bush, *la broussaille*, is the word Yolanda and Didier are using, a word that conjures up a Mediterranean tangle of brambles and tall grasses and seems laughably inadequate to describe the inky dense wilderness that Maggie has gone into with her chimpanzees. Does Didier think Maggie's been kidnapped? Killed? Yolanda knows she's only making Didier more nervous with her questions, but she has to know if Maggie is in danger, if there is a way they can help her.

Didier says that Maggie is often out during the day, which is why he has a key to the house, but he admits that several signs disturb him. Maggie's boy, the person who helps her, is missing as well. The clearing is all red mud. There isn't a blade of grass and it used to be green. The surrounding trees are stripped of foliage and bark. The room where Maggie keeps her food is empty.

"I wonder if we should go to the authorities, if there's someone we should talk to . . ." Yolanda, Sparks, and Didier are sitting in Maggie's battered mission oak chairs, staring out at the rain through the sturdy wire grid that is Maggie's fourth wall.

"Olly, remember, we're not in the States." Sparks rolls his eyes toward Didier, meaning, she knows, that he might be a spy, if Maggie is involved in a revolution . . .

Didier keeps looking at his watch. He wants to go back, before dark, before rain washes out the road.

Sparks pulls Yolanda aside. "Let's let him go, Olly."

"But how will we get out?"

"Have him come back for us in five days."

In spite of herself, Yolanda has a vision of their bullet-riddled corpses lying on the floor. She remembers the war window she did for The Constant Reader, Dorothy in her gas mask, and Roger saying that Yolanda lived vicariously through Dorothy. But why should Yolanda want to plunge herself into a war? Why would anyone? You certainly wouldn't find Roger out here in the bush, surrounded by rebels, keeping company with a spy.

"We're not going to find out anything with Didier around," Sparks says. "He's a Moro. We've come this far—"

"We don't know. We don't know anything, Sparks. We're making things up, about revolution, about Didier—"

"Hey." Sparks puts his arm around her. She feels the hard lump of his gun against her ribs. "Sometimes you have to act on intuition. Last night, I didn't tell you, but last night I was standing at the window and I saw fires on the other side of the lake. I heard singing and those frogs that sound like wind chimes, and I smelled burnt sugar from the refinery. It all came together, just like Roy's song, the one with our names in it. We're so close. We're inches away. I feel it. You don't want to turn back now, do you, when we've come all this way, come this close?"

Sparks is talking about trusting instincts. Yolanda's are telling her to run, to flee. The message is being received principally by the backs of her knees—run, hide. But she'll stay, because of the excitement and warmth of Sparks's voice, because she feels that Maggie needs them, and because she too senses that Roy is nearby, approaching even now.

Sparks pays Didier the money he promised, as well as some

extra for the nights Didier will presumably spend at the hotel in Ouagoubua. After five days Didier is to come back for them. Will he return? If he does, what will he find? Yolanda watches Didier spring into his jeep. His tires shoot back blobs of mud; she can hear the gears shifting after the jeep has disappeared into the black green shadows.

It's already dark in Maggie's kitchen. Now that Didier is gone, Yolanda lights the kerosene lantern and begins making supper. Sparks removes his loose outer shirt, revealing his gun in its holster. It's ugly. She doesn't like to see it on him, but Sparks won't take it off. He's going into the jungle. There must be a path. Maggie does it all the time, Didier said.

There are a number of paths, fairly well worn, leading out from the clearing. Sparks chooses the one directly opposite Maggie's house. Although he didn't say so to Olly, it seems obvious that the surroundings have been denuded of vegetation to make it difficult for the enemy to sneak up on the house. This place could easily be a rebel headquarters. Sparks can see tents set up around the house. He could be walking on a rebel highway.

As leaders of the Light, Roy and Sparks flirted with social issues. They wrote a couple of ambiguously worded antiwar songs and did a few benefit concerts, but neither one burned his draft card. They didn't have to. Roy flunked the physical because of an erratic heart. Sparks had already done service with the National Guard.

Roy was too cool, too self-contained, too skeptical, to throw himself into a cause, any cause. If he is involved in this thing, it will be in a detached way. He could even be in the thick of it, but he will have a helicopter ready to lift him out if it gets too hairy.

Maggie is another story. Roy once said Maggie was a fanatic looking for a cause. Now that Sparks has seen where Maggie lives, the isolation of it, the Spartan conditions, the full force of what she has done hits him. He is almost afraid of the intensity of conviction this place bears witness to. It's like visiting the den of an anchorite. Has Maggie achieved sainthood? If so, what god is she serving?

In the space of a few steps, Sparks finds himself surrounded by jungle. The path that seemed so defined at the outset has frayed into several traces, hints of trails. He keeps looking back, fixing landmarks in his mind, but it is difficult because he can't see far and every tree and plant is strange. He expected more noise in the jungle, more activity. He knows that a tropical rain forest teems with life, but this forest is keeping silent, watching him from high branches or obscure hollows.

When Sparks sees the eyes looking at him, he isn't surprised. They only confirm the feeling he had of being observed. The eyes are reddish brown in a black face. The hair, shaggy black, looks almost combed and parted low on the forehead. The head is set into broad, bushy shoulders. Sparks can tell by the way the animal is sizing him up that it is one of Maggie's, no timid forest creature. He tries to remember what he knows about Maggie's chimps, which one this could be, but he never paid attention to their names, their characteristics.

This eyeballing standoff is making the chimp nervous. He rocks from side to side and draws his breath in and out in a hooting scream.

When it moves it's fast, a sideward gallop. Before Sparks has time to brace himself, he's down. His hand is caught in the beast's mouth. Sparks doesn't feel it, but he sees his hand trapped by the creature's fang. The eyes of the beast, above Sparks, register astonishment in the instant before the fireball blasts them apart.

Sparks looks at the gun in his hand. He can't remember pulling it from his holster. The right hand rescued the left, the body protected itself. No need to go through channels of command all the way to the upper cortex. It was routed through directly, an automatic response.

Sparks kneels beside the body. The whiteness of bone and brain tissue draws to itself whatever light the forest provides and blood gathers in a thick wet shadow around it. Hands very like a human's, with flat fingernails, lie limp and passive.

It is a male. The one Maggie brought here is female? Hilda, yes, that's right. This is one of the others.

Sparks gets behind the beast, planning to drag it back with him, for burial maybe, or identification, but an intense, urgent signal of pain from his left hand stops him, fills his mind, presses against his eyeballs, rings against his eardrums. He staggers back the way he came, to the muddy clearing where Yolanda is holding a lantern over her head as if she would light up the entire jungle for him.

17

An entomologist would go crazy here. Every one is different. Yolanda picks something out of her plate that looks like a two-inch flying dragon.

"All these bugs," she says. "Maggie must eat dinner before it gets dark, but then the night is so long, and there's nothing to read except for some mildewed *Vogue* magazines. How does she get *Vogue*, of all things?"

"Her mother sends it to her," Sparks says. "I have one in my bag. She asked me to give it to her."

"*Vogue*? Out here?"

Sparks shrugs.

"I wish I'd thought. I could have brought her piles of things to read." She wonders what kinds of books Maggie would want, if Maggie reads at all any more. She thinks of the two unmade beds in the other room, one of them with coarse black hairs on the pillow. What state of mind has Maggie come to that she spends twelve hours of equatorial night with a chimp for a sleeping partner?

Didier said that Maggie sometimes spends the night in the bush. She does that when the chimpanzees get too far away to come home for the night. But one of her animals did come back, so Maggie can't be that far off.

Bugs hit the glass lantern and fall to the table. There's a wind somewhere in the trees but hardly a breath passes into the room. Yolanda thinks of the dead chimpanzee lying out there. Should they have brought it home? Buried it? Sparks was in no shape to go back for it.

Shadows have settled into the hollows of Sparks's cheeks, his eyes. His hand rests on the table. Yolanda bandaged it the best she could but she's afraid it needs stitches. He should see a doctor right away. She considered walking to town for help. It would have taken hours, in the dark. Sparks was against it. Besides, she didn't think he should be left alone. Sparks picks an insect off his plate and pushes his supper away. He's going to sleep, he says.

In the morning Sparks's hand is hard and red, swollen and hot. A fever came over him in the night. How could Yolanda have slept through and not heard his groans?

She heats water to boiling in a kettle, washes the wound, puts on antiseptic and fresh bandages. In the medicines Didier brought, Yolanda finds an antibiotic, which she makes Sparks take with orange juice, forcing it between his chattering teeth. She puts cold cloths on his forehead, his wrists. She takes one of his limbs at a time out from under the cover and bathes it with cold water. His body, so hard and muscled a day ago, is limp, as if the tendons are losing hold of the bones. He begs her to put the wet cloth over his eyes and to let him alone. After she's lowered his temperature a bit, gotten him to drink the juice, and brought him a bottle to relieve himself in (his urine is dark and thick, strong-smelling), she leaves him in peace.

Yolanda brews up some camomile tea for Sparks later, when it has cooled. She pours herself some and, cup in hand, makes a slow tour of the clearing. It's peculiar, this area of barren red earth in the middle of tropical jungle. Ringing it is the girdle of broken and dying trees, stripped of leaves and bark. Whatever affliction the clearing suffers from is spreading outward. Other buildings once shared the space—she sees their foundations—but now there are only termite bells, as tall as she is, standing like ruined sand castles left here by giant children, or eruptions of the earth's crust, pustules. Some drama is being played out here, some catastrophe. Even Maggie's house, with everything put away in locked chests, looks as if it is subject to periodic raids.

At the other end of the clearing, down a small hill, there's a house Yolanda didn't see when they came in yesterday. It is simple, schematic: mud brick, tin roof, two squares cut out for windows, one rectangle for a door. If there were a mango tree and chickens, this could be the house in Yolanda's dream.

The smell from the open door makes her pull back. Soft but unmistakable comes the sound of footsteps within. Bare feet. She holds her cup against her breastbone and approaches again, this time to see a shape inside, a form, something waiting in the foulness. It grins, a white scar stitched into the darkness, and screams.

The cup drops from her hand and rolls toward the house. The long skirt clings to her legs when she runs, and trips her. She lands flat on Maggie's porch and scrambles in the door. She sits at the table sweating, holding both hands over her thudding heart.

In the poor light of the forest just before dark it could be mistaken for a fallen branch or even an odd massing of shadows. It happens sometimes—the shadows are so thick they seem to be solid objects, logs, stumps. But she knows. All she needs to see is the angle of the torso to know.

She knew when it happened. The locals say that the odor of the cadaver ant presages death. A superstition, but what of it if you feel it is true?

She knew when they woke this morning that it was no use waiting for G.P. to come back. But still she called and hooted. They stopped dozens of time to listen for G.P., his voice, his drumming.

Maggie kept them walking through the rain, couldn't bear to sit still and let her thoughts catch up to her. They rested only once, under a kontoué-be nut tree. While the others were cracking and eating nuts, Maggie searched around and came upon a neat pile of shells. She sifted through them, as if they could tell her something. What message could they relay, little cups, some of them holding a raindrop or two? Only that a chimpanzee had passed by sometime before the last rain, a small, contained fact, only that, nothing more. She wishes she'd kept one.

It was quick, that much to be thankful for. The bullet tore his forehead away. The ants have already carted off his brain, leaving the white skull glowing in the dusk. The close-set eyes, the look of understanding they held the day she gave him food, are gone, blasted to bits.

That bunch of amateur guerrillas is to blame, with their stolen weapons, firing at anything that moves. They've taken over the station; G.P. came back and found them; they shot his head off and went back to laugh about it. Emanuel did it. He always hated G.P. All he needed was a gun. Cowards, all of them. Killing innocent animals.

The others huddle behind, grinning, squeaking, clinging to each other. They're afraid to come look. Maggie isn't afraid. She's boiling with rage. She's sweating with it. She glistens with it, trembles with it as she clutches her gun.

It's raining when Maggie breaks through to the clearing. She rips off her shirt and wraps it around the gun to keep it dry and races for the house. The others are there before her and they want to come in. She fights them off with the butt of her gun, even Hilda, and clangs the door shut behind her.

Yolanda is in with Sparks, forcing more antibiotics on him,

more juice. His fever broke in the afternoon but now he's shivering again and there are no fresh blankets to put over him. Yolanda undid her long lappa and turban to make two narrow sheets. She found a sweatshirt to put over him while she dried the blankets, but the blankets won't dry. They seem to be absorbing even more moisture. She would change his bandage but he won't let her touch his hand. He allowed her to sponge his forehead for a while to get the fever down and then clutched the cloth to his eyes and told her to leave him alone.

She is at the window watching the rain. Even the rain seems harder and wilder in Africa. The creatures charging past don't register until they are already at the door, banging and screaming. The woman is somewhat slower. Yolanda has time to see the hair plastered against her face, the bare breasts flapping, to hear her animal cries.

Maggie. It can't be anyone else, although Yolanda would be hard pressed to find the Maggie she remembers in the wild woman out in the rain. Has Maggie lost her mind? The strain of living alone? The tidiness of the house, the strict organization argues for a sane mind. Then she found her animal dead in the forest and the shock of it—can people go mad from shock? Only in Gothic novels, she thinks.

"What the—" Maggie, in a shirt now, although hastily and crookedly buttoned, is standing at the door pointing a gun at her. The shirt, even buttoned wrong, is a reassuring sign.

"Maggie? It's Olly."

That they should come like this, dropping into her life through a hole in the sky, a hole in time, that they should not only invade her world but in one small motion reduce it to shreds, is almost more than she can take in. Sparks, the Texas redneck. She used to hate it that he carried a gun. She was afraid of his gun. That he should have carried it with him all this time, brought it across the ocean to blow away everything she's done . . . The moon did it, drew them here, the hideous moon that found Maggie out in her secret Eden, that stirred up her thoughts and sent old memories bobbing to the surface.

Olly, the same Olly but older and skinnier, pinched together by time, is trying to dry Maggie with a towel, get her some tea, a drink. Olly, as always, offering small comforts while lifting not a finger to prevent the great catastrophes. Maggie brushes her off and is amazed at how weak and frail those white hairless arms are. Olly staggers back, holds where Maggie touched her, her gray eyes wide. Maggie must be calm. She makes her voice gentle.

"Olly, I'll dry off. I'll have a shower and something to eat. Don't worry. I'm OK. But first we have to bury him." Bury who? Olly asks.

Maggie takes a tarp from one of the locked chests. They can drag his body on it. Wear gloves, she tells Olly, because there will be ants all over him that can crawl up your arms and bite you. They take flashlights.

The chimps must be hiding in Emanuel's house. Only Hilda comes to watch them pass. Don't look at her, Maggie says. Don't ever stare at them. It makes them nervous.

Yolanda's arms and legs are trembling when they finish. They worked in the dark, through the rain. The remains of the chimpanzee, wrapped in the tarp, went in heavily. They shoveled mud back on top. Stones are scarce around here, but they found one near Maggie's house that Maggie said G.P. once dragged from God knows where to hurl at her when she was in her house, behind the grid.

At first Maggie worked without speaking, except for grunting from the effort, or giving Yolanda terse instructions, but as they dug in the clearing by Maggie's house, she began to talk. She didn't ask questions, didn't seem to care how or why

Yolanda and Sparks had come. She was reminiscing about G.P., how he came to them from a Belgian circus, what a clown he was at first, how he challenged Maggie, almost killed her, raped Hilda, and finally how he and Maggie had worked out a kind of truce, a partnership. Maggie spoke of him in such human terms that Yolanda nearly asked if he spoke French or English.

Yolanda holds the light as Maggie smooths the grave with the back of the shovel.

After a while, when she sees that Maggie is smoothing non-existent lumps, she asks if they can go back. She's worried about Sparks.

18

Is Sparks going to die?

Maggie doesn't think the wound on his hand is causing the fever. The antibiotics would be bringing it down by now. It could be anything. There are scores of tropical fevers, many fatal. Olly's talking about getting him to a hospital, but she doesn't know what hospitals here are like. The vet in D'jar might be able to help him, but if Maggie were Sparks she'd rather take her chances on dying than endure the jolting ride to D'jar, especially if he has breakbone fever, which feels like it sounds.

He's sleeping quietly now. Maggie could tell by the way Olly handled his body that they'd had sex together.

"How long have you and Sparks been lovers?" Maggie asks. The tip of Olly's nose reddens, or rather in the glow of the lantern it purples and purple splotches come out on her neck. Maggie was too blunt. She's lost the skill of human discourse. She could blame the Scotch Didier brought. She's not used to alcohol.

"Only since coming here, I mean to D'jarkoume." Olly's lips twitch.

"Oh dammit Olly, let's not cry." Maggie blows her nose on

a paper napkin, then feels wildly wasteful. Olly has to understand that there's no room here for tears or sentiment. Merely staying alive is difficult, takes concentration. Tears and the feelings that go with them are luxuries, like paper napkins.

Olly takes the napkin away from her face. What should they do? How can they save his life?

Maggie picks up the Scotch. Would she like some more? Yes, please. She pours a healthy shot into each of their cups. They don't add water this time. It ruins the taste.

Maggie holds the whiskey in her mouth, then lets it burn down her throat, leaving a smoky taste behind. In spite of herself she's enjoying being home, being clean, having a hot meal. Olly stopped eating a while ago. Maggie saw her watching as she ate and ate until there was no more.

What were they talking about? Oh yes, Sparks. If Olly wants she can walk to Dobo tomorrow. There are some people who might be able to send a truck for Sparks. But Maggie thinks he's just as well off here as anywhere. Olly's eyes go liquid again.

"Olly, why the hell did he come? Why did you?"

Olly goes into the bedroom and comes out with a Walkman, which she gives to Maggie. Listen, she says. It's a song from Roy's new album.

Roy in her ears. An up tune, sounds African, even vaguely familiar. Maggie switches it off before it's over. This is why they came to see her? This song?

"It comes from here. It's kind of the national anthem for the tribe—the Ilido."

Roy! God damn! Roy is the one, even now, even here, pulling strings in her life, breaking through the clouds, boring through the forest canopy to spy her out and destroy everything she's built.

"Our names are in the song, did you hear? Maggie, Sparks, and Olly, at the end. Sparks found one of your letters mailed to Roy, to his office, and we thought you and Roy must be involved in what was going on here, and it seemed, with our names in the song, that we should be here too." Olly's voice fades.

Olly's earnest naiveté brings Maggie back to earth. Roy involved with the rebels, Roy calling a reunion, here of all places. Maggie turns off the lantern before every bug in the forest comes in. She pours some more Scotch.

It's because Olly and Sparks were far away that they thought there was a pattern. Certain events seemed to be connected by cause and effect. Now they are close and they, or at least Olly, can see that the connections between Roy and Maggie, Sparks and Olly, do not exist. Maggie has nothing to do with Roy or with the unrest his song has stirred up.

They drink in silence. Maggie sees the moon, the way it was last night and the way G.P.'s skull glowed white against the dark forest floor. Olly sniffs and surreptitiously wipes a tear. What Maggie can't understand, she says, is how Olly and Sparks would come halfway around the world, risk their lives because their names were in Roy's song. Don't they have anything else? If they're so cut off from Roy that they couldn't even call him up and ask him why their goddamn names were in his goddamn song, why would they drop everything for—

Olly takes a flashlight, says she's going to look in on Sparks.

Maggie was too harsh. She didn't know what she was saying until it was said. But it's true. Olly and Sparks have been wandering around like lost souls waiting for Roy to come back and—and what? Give them a reason to live.

Maggie sees Roy's big head, his red-rimmed eyes watching. He watched. He waited to see what you were offering him. Writing music, he'd play a melody on the piano and wait for Sparks or Eddie to turn it into something more. What did he give any of them really except permission to show him what they could do? It was his Buddha-like passivity that made him powerful, his willingness to take.

Olly comes back and sets the flashlight, still glowing, on the table.

"How is he?"

"The same." Olly's voice quavers.

A swirl of phototropic insects gets caught up in the flashlight beam.

"I guess I did it too," Maggie says. "I put in my years hanging out with Roy. If he smiled at me my day was made. He didn't even smile, did he? He'd just look interested. That was enough, if you got his attention. But we kept on giving. Maybe we were held in thrall by what he took from us. It was our own light that was captivating us, reflecting off of him."

She cuts the flashlight beam and the bugs wander away, dazed and disappointed.

Yolanda is sweating, burning up in her cot. She's caught Sparks's fever, she thinks, then realizes it's only the alcohol burning off. She's been dreaming of Maggie and the life she has here. She's been replaying their conversation, what Maggie said to her, what she said to Maggie.

She sits up to clear her brain and sees Sparks staring at a shadow on the ceiling or at something she can't see, out of eyes sunk so deep into their sockets they look black. His beard pushes up in heavy bristles and his skin melts down against his skull. His wonderful silver hair is dark and wet, matted in clumps.

She takes her flashlight, hurries past Maggie in her hammock hung in the day room, prepares cold wet cloths for his forehead, his neck, wrists, places where the blood runs close to the surface. He doesn't move or groan or even blink when she lays them on. Before she finishes with the last, the first is already hot. Another trip out for water. This time she brings a basinful so she can rinse the cloths as she kneels beside him.

Although she works with urgency, she feels it is futile, that Sparks isn't suffering from an illness that can be helped by cold cloths. It's something else, a third thing in the room, the shadow on the ceiling that is pulling Sparks away, that he is burning through his skin to get to.

She spreads ointment on his lips and feels the hot breath seeping out.

"Don't die."

She sits on his cot and pulls his head onto her lap. She pronounces his name: "Samuel Parker King." She's never called him that. No one does. He doesn't stir, doesn't blink. She says it over and over, twisting the syllables into a rope, a lifeline to pull him back to her.

She stretches out beside him and chants his name until it loses meaning, becomes a mantra. She is still breathing and dreaming his name long after she falls asleep.

The room is light. Sparks is no longer staring at the thing on the ceiling. His eyes are closed. He is sleeping. His fever is down. Maybe Maggie was right and it would be better not to move him, but if his fever comes back in the night as fevers sometimes do, what then?

A racket outside draws Yolanda to the window. Maggie is feeding her chimpanzees. She moves among them, not as their keeper but as one of them, speaking their language, touching them, being touched by them. Her expression is serene, saintly. It's a dream, isn't it, to be one with the animals, to speak their language, a holy myth, Saint Francis, the Garden of Eden. This is what Maggie has found. No wonder she can't understand what drew Sparks and Yolanda here.

Maggie faces dangers every day, real physical dangers to

herself and her chimps, but she isn't terrified because she can deal with the dangers. She doesn't know the fear that strikes when you find yourself with a day off, wandering down a street you have no reason to be on, and you know that it doesn't matter where you are on this day. Whether you stay in bed all day or stand in a cold sweat on the corner of Prince Street and Greene, it won't matter.

Yolanda heard her name on Roy's record and she came running. She didn't actually expect to see Roy here, in the flesh. It was the idea of Roy that called her, the remembrance of the way it used to feel to be with him, to be in the group.

Before, Yolanda couldn't imagine how Maggie would give up all comforts to live out here, but now she understands that Maggie gave up the least important things, and that Yolanda is the one who has been living in privation. She's been afraid to love, afraid even to eat most foods, afraid to venture beyond the boundaries she set for herself, which were growing ever closer. And still she couldn't shut out the terror of being invisible, of walking through life like a ghost.

19

"How is he?" Maggie calls as Yolanda passes through the day room.

"Better, I think."

The chimpanzees all turn and look at Yolanda. This time, in the house, protected by the grid, Yolanda dares to look back. They bound up to the porch and press their faces against the bars, like curious children at the zoo, only Yolanda is the one on display. They reach their hands through and Yolanda is moved to see how human those little hands are. Better not touch them, Maggie counsels. They have very strong grips.

Yolanda wants to get out to play with them. They look harmless enough, but Maggie says there is one hiding nearby who can't be trusted, who is spooked by G.P.'s death and who might do anything. The bigger one, the only one with a dark face, is looking at Yolanda intently. She has a triangular high forehead and deep-set eyes as well as—it seems odd to think of her this way because she is, after all, a chimpanzee—a patrician air, a delicacy the others lack. Is this Hilda? Yes, Maggie says, this is Hilda.

Hilda, standing easily on two legs, is making intricate patterns with her hands. Yolanda remembers with a thrill that Hilda knows sign language.

"Maggie, look! Is she talking to me? Is she trying to tell me something?"

"She's talking, all right." Maggie reaches down to pick up one of the small chimps.

"What's she saying?"

"Not much. She wants to be your friend. She likes you."

Hilda keeps looking at Yolanda and emphatically signaling the same thing over and over. It gives Yolanda an odd feeling, as if the chimp is trying to tell her something more urgent, more important than a mere wish to be her friend.

"Does she talk much?"

"All the time."

"What kind of things does she say?"

"Mostly she complains."

Hilda cocks her head, listening for something.

"What's she saying now?"

"She says Mfui's coming in his truck."

Now Yolanda hears it too, a truck that needs a muffler, she'd say, making painful progress through the jungle.

"It's Emanuel, my assistant," Maggie shouts. "I didn't even know he could drive."

The truck rattles into the yard. The chimpanzees are hooting and jumping around.

The driver is very young, although it's hard to tell because the interior of the cab is dark. He looks more like a soldier than an assistant. His hat gives this impression—a peaked cotton hat, the kind American GI's would wear—also his expression, which is angry, cold, not what one would expect from an assistant.

He gets out on the driver's side, which is facing Maggie, away from Yolanda. She can just see the back of his cap through the windows. He's short, shorter than Maggie. Maggie's face flashes fear, and then an icy control. Yolanda feels the fear, wants to act, but she doesn't know why or what she should do. Even the chimpanzees, seconds ago so eager to see this assistant, are squeaking and backing away.

When the assistant and Maggie come around the truck Yolanda sees what has caused the abrupt change. It is a thick, dun-colored weapon, some kind of automatic rifle, she thinks, which this assistant—Emanuel—is holding on Maggie as she walks carefully back to the house.

Emanuel is wearing a faded Bud Lite T-shirt, khaki shorts held up with nylon rope, rubber sandals, and his GI cap. Yolanda finds this haphazard costume more upsetting than a full uniform would be. It means that this boy with his murderous weapon will not be following any rules, that anything might tip the balance and cause him to send bullets whizzing around the room.

Her vision of the bleeding, riddled bodies on the floor of the house seems prophetic to her now. Why didn't she heed it? Sparks.

Yolanda must have looked toward the bedroom because Emanuel is going toward it now, demanding something of Maggie. He's speaking French. It takes Yolanda a while to recognize it because the rhythm is African. It's a wonder Maggie doesn't speak better French, after all these years. She and Emanuel barely communicate.

Yolanda explains to Emanuel that there is a very sick man in the next room. Of course Emanuel has to see. Yolanda can understand that. He herds the women into the darkened bedroom. The room smells close, unhealthy, the odor of sickness. Sparks has kicked off his covers and lies unconscious on his bed, gaunt and pale. Emanuel draws back a little.

May I touch him? Yolanda asks softly. He nods. Sparks's forehead is cool but his lips are scaly and his eyelids crusted over. Yolanda longs to put a wet cloth to those eyes, but instead she draws back, mimicking Emanuel's response. He's very, very ill, she tells Emanuel. Can't Emanuel drive him to a hospital?

Emanuel grunts, motions them out of the sickroom. He makes them sit in chairs with their backs to the bedroom door while he sits on the table, his gun balanced on his knee. What does it take to fire one of those things? Could it go off accidentally? The chimps are anxious, clinging to the grid. One of them hoos and Emanuel trains the weapon on them.

Leave them alone, Maggie says.

Suddenly this taciturn boy begins an impassioned speech, about how the chimpanzees defiled his house, destroyed it forever, and how she let them do it.

Maggie argues that she was ill, that if he had stayed and taken care of his house, of her, the chimps never would have gotten in. He can have this house, if he likes. Maggie's house. She's going away soon. He can have the key. What does she mean by that, Yolanda wonders. Does Maggie intend to go back with Sparks and Yolanda?

Emanuel is not mollified by Maggie's offer. He has a long list of grievances against Maggie. She treats her animals like humans and treats Emanuel like an animal. She lets her animals desecrate his house. When he was a child, she had him treated by an animal doctor. Maggie retorts that he was the best doctor available, that he did a good job.

Yolanda is trying to make out what this is all about, why Maggie's disgruntled assistant is holding them captive with a gun. Maggie, after the initial surprise of seeing the gun, seems more angry than frightened. She is trying to explain to Emanuel what will happen to him if he kills her or the chimpanzees, telling him that they have many powerful friends in America.

Emanuel says that so many people are going to be murdered that a few chimpanzees and two white women aren't going to matter that much. Apparently he's forgotten Sparks.

But why should you kill me? Maggie asks him. She isn't involved in his war.

Because you fuck with the enemy, he says.

Didier. He means Didier. Of course. A Moro. Yolanda had completely forgotten the uprising, the revolution that she and Sparks came here to observe, participate in, the uprising that Roy began.

Was this Roy's plan? Did he lure them here to be caught up in the coils of this thing he had started? Is this what Roy envisioned, their bodies on the floor? "Olly Olly in come free"—did that mean death? Yolanda, you're going crazy. Stop. Breathe. She forces herself to listen to Maggie, who is taking a pacifying tone.

What Emanuel has to understand, Maggie is saying, is that she is a woman with certain needs. After all, Emanuel was a boy, and Didier was a man. Perhaps Maggie had thought of Emanuel as a boy for too long. It's only natural. He's like a son to her, or a nephew, but certainly he is a man, a strong virile man . . .

Maggie, as she talks, pushes out her breasts slightly, re-crosses her legs. Her courage takes Yolanda's breath away. Maggie is a fighter, a warrior.

It seems to be working on Emanuel, in spite of himself. His eyes are lingering on Maggie's body. Maggie pushes herself forward in the chair.

Outside, unobserved by Emanuel, a new chimp has entered the clearing, a small one with a nervously twitching head. When he sees Yolanda, he starts, then scampers off. Emanuel is absently stroking his weapon. Yolanda wishes she knew more about those things, how they go off.

A rivulet of perspiration rolls down Emanuel's cheek. It is hot, even here in the shaded house. Is it midday already? How much time has passed? Yolanda looks at her watch, and Emanuel nonchalantly asks what time it is. Eleven almost. The others will be here soon, Emanuel says. Other men with more weapons? And what will become of them then?

If they are killed, will the news get out, will anyone ever know? Will Roy read it somewhere and will he wonder at how his old friends got caught up in his revolution?

Roy didn't plan this. He didn't have any plan in his mind at all. Yolanda sees this now, so clearly that she wonders how she could have let herself be deluded. She knows how Roy works, how he'll use anything at hand to make a song. He heard an African song somewhere, in a dark little club on the outskirts of Paris where the expatriates hang out, and he picked it up. He hired those very musicians to play their song and then he put his own words to it. He used African images, he used names of old friends, stirred them up until he was happy with the effect he produced, without a thought in mind that there would be consequences.

How could he have planned or even imagined this, Maggie fighting for her life, for all their lives, with the tricks she learned long ago when she made her way through the various members of the group on her slow deliberate journey toward Roy?

Maggie's voice is low, almost a purr. She leans forward, by gesture inviting Emanuel to look into her cleavage, which he does.

The little chimp has reappeared, this time lugging something, a stone, the one Maggie laid on G.P.'s grave. He totters, unseen by Emanuel, close to the house and heaves the rock at the grid.

Emanuel whirls around and fires. The chimps scream. Bullets sing and ricochet off the walls. Yolanda slides flat to the floor. When she looks up, Maggie has Emanuel pinned under a chair. Yolanda jumps up and grabs the gun and points it at Emanuel, although she has no idea how to work it, if it has ammunition left, or even if she would shoot if she knew how.

She stands back from Emanuel, holding the gun which is still moist from his hands, while Maggie, outside, is clutching a limp bleeding body to her chest.

"Kill him, Olly! Kill that bastard! Kill him!"

For some time there have been new voices in the house. Minutes, hours, days? Sparks can't tell because the fever folded the arrow of time back onto itself and tied it in a knot, leaving him confused about what came first and what came after.

One voice is Maggie's, he's almost certain—Maggie's voice, roughened by abuse, by too much screaming, or by debilitating fevers. Anyway, it's lost some in the upper register.

The other is young, male, black, African, speaking an African language, or is it French? Sparks can't tell.

Maggie's voice, Maggie's and Olly's. Sparks strains to hear Roy fitting a word, a sound, into the interstices of the conversation, but there are only these three voices.

Chairs move, a solid, prosaic sound. Chimpanzees scream. Chimpanzees, real or imagined, have been screaming through all his dreams and awakenings. They are the chorus he keeps coming back to.

Another sign, an excellent sign that the fever is losing its grip, is that he is beginning to figure out sequence. The sounds out front, the chimp screams, the rising voices are present and actual. The battle with the beast was also real, but it took place before the onset of fever.

The chimps have stopped but the voices go on, the same voices. The male is African, speaking French. Not Didier, his precise, almost prissy French, but with a rolling accent, angry, accusatory. Maggie answers, shrill, nervous. Olly's voice is calmer but it's deliberate, the calm you might assume when approaching a wild horse.

Carefully, Sparks opens his eyes. The shutters have been pulled and only a stripe of light lies on the wall. His body stretches away from him. He has no clothes on. The skin shines where his knees poke close to the surface.

He feels dizzy, bending down to get a T-shirt and a pair of shorts out of his bag, but he does it and dresses himself one-handed. In his bag, wrapped in a pair of undershorts, probably put there by Olly, he finds his gun.

The gun is heavier, much. Until now Sparks had found it a comfortable weight, a reassuring presence in its holster, in his hand. But the gun had never killed before. Now it has taken on the weight of a death and it is all Sparks can do to hold it in one hand.

That's crazy, that's fever thinking. The gun feels heavier because Sparks is weaker. The fever just ate him up.

Sparks leans against the side of the door. His wrist aches from holding the gun. He tries to hear what is being said. It's Maggie, speaking French so Sparks can only understand snatches of what she's saying. Even though he doesn't know the words, he can sense the care Maggie is taking to say the right words. It's as if there is a large object in the room balanced on one point. The slightest movement could topple it. He doesn't want to be the force that sends it over, or if he is, he wants to be sure that it falls the right way.

There's a thud, followed by a pause while the house, the clearing, the forest, draw a breath. Then a gun rips it all open.

"Olly! Olly!" Sparks cries—no, it's Maggie.

Olly is OK. Olly's holding an automatic, has a black man under a chair. The door is open and Maggie is in the yard, pacing with a mess oozing blood from her arms. Chimps are gathered like goblins around her legs, clutching for the bleeding thing, while Maggie howls for more killing.

———

"You know how to use these things?" Sparks pushes the Walkman across the table to the kid and motions for him to put on the headset, which he does.

Sparks has been sitting at the table with his revolver and the automatic rifle laid out beside him, keeping watch over the kid, who by turns is scared out of his mind, then cocky and defiant. Maggie and Olly are burying the dead chimp. The kid's friends are supposed to be arriving any minute, heavily armed, and Sparks is to hold them at bay, a pretty tall order for a sick man with one hand. What Sparks is trying to figure out is how he got on the wrong side of the war.

He's holding his gun on a short guy in ragged pants, who has to be an Ilido. Sparks wasn't able to ask Maggie any questions because Maggie was too grief-stricken to do anything but moan and rail against this poor character across the table from Sparks. But it seems to Sparks that there's been a failure of communication, that they are really all on the same side. Finally he saw the Walkman he had smuggled in along with Roy's tape. It had been sitting on the table the whole time but Sparks's brain was a little slow after the fever.

The kid listens, suspicious, then confused, and then he smiles. He starts singing and moving to the music. All right.

Maggie looks good when she gets the blood washed off, tall, sexy in a remote sort of way. Her face has been chiseled down. There's a quality to it that wasn't there before. Sparks studies her in the lantern glow, wondering what about her has changed.

They are having another buggy dinner. Maggie's house doesn't have screens because the chimpanzees would just rip them out, she says. Besides, they are expensive. How about mosquitoes, Sparks asks. Can't you get malaria? Several kinds, Maggie says, and there are other insect-borne diseases. Sparks probably had one. Maggie's used to living with tropical diseases. Luckily she's generally healthy. She's careful to purify the water. That's the main thing, the water.

Now that she's calmed down, she admits that executing Emanuel would have been the wrong thing to do. His small band of compatriots came looking for him, armed with everything from machetes to parade rifles. By that time, Sparks and Emanuel were buddies. Sparks donated the Walkman and tape to the cause. They think the song is just the beginning of what Roy's going to do for them. They had Olly write a letter to give to Roy, telling him they need guns and medical supplies. Sparks promised to deliver it, but he tried to prepare them for disappointment.

Roy is not here in the jungle with the Ilido. Maggie insists that he was never in D'jarkoume, doubts that he ever will be. His song entered the country on radio waves, which were picked up, briefly, before the government came through and confiscated everyone's radio. Most of Emanuel's friends hadn't even heard the record. Just the rumor that it was being played and causing unrest was enough to encourage them to take up arms.

Olly says Roy probably heard the song in a club in Paris, liked it, and paid the musicians to duplicate it for his album. She says it's so clear that Roy would do it like that. How could they have imagined Roy here, how could they have presumed that he wanted them here with him? She said she feels like she's waking up from a dream.

Dreams don't leave you with a stiff, throbbing hand, don't leave you weak and wasted, don't leave chimpanzee graves in the yard.

Emanuel is arranging for a truck to pick up Olly and Sparks tomorrow to take them as far as Ouagoubua where they will either meet Didier (Maggie doubts he is waiting there for them) or be able to arrange a ride to D'jar.

"Maggie, come with us." Olly reaches across for Maggie's

hand. Emanuel could have killed Maggie today if Olly and Sparks hadn't been there, she says. Olly doesn't know much about the politics of this country, but it seems to her that Maggie is bound to be the loser, the one caught in the middle. Can't she hire some village people to come in and feed the chimps if they need it? Maggie can always come back when the situation calms down.

Maggie studies her hand as it lies in Olly's and pulls it slowly back. It's not possible, she says. She is the only one who can care for her chimps. Katie, Poppy, and Biff are still juveniles. It will be years before they are able to fend for themselves. Hilda is pregnant—

"But if someone from the village looks after them—" Olly argues.

"It's not just that," Maggie says in a low tone. "There is no way I could explain it to Hilda. If I left, she wouldn't understand. She'd die. It might be from disease, or an accident, but she'd die, within six months. I know it, and I just couldn't live with that on my conscience."

"I thought the whole idea of this project was to get Hilda living on her own, like a regular chimpanzee. Isn't that the idea? Rehabilitation? What you're saying is that you're never going to leave her."

A smile twitches at the corners of Maggie's mouth, as if Sparks has just guessed her secret. That's the way it is for now, she says. Things change, all the time.

Sparks wishes he could think of a way to help Maggie, maybe get her and Hilda out. As it is, he came all this way to wreck things for her. He tries to apologize, to explain how it happened with her chimp, but she waves him off.

"Olly told me the whole thing. I don't blame you. It's Roy. He killed G.P. and today he killed Danny. We could all be dead, Hilda, Katie, all of us. Fucking irresponsible—" She dashes tears off her face, rejecting Olly's offer of a napkin.

No one knows what to say. They listen to bugs bumping

heavily against the lamp, to frogs chiming in the dark. Maggie picks up what looks like a flying worm off her plate. "The locals roast these and eat them." Her voice is shaky. "Anyone want to try?"

"Who that?"
   "Sparks."
   "Sparks? Fire man. Sparks nice man?"
   "Yes."
   "Sparks, nice man, fire man, take me home. Get me out. Hurry quick."
   "She's talking to me, isn't she?" Sparks is on the porch having coffee while Maggie feeds the chimps. There's no reason why he can't mingle with the chimps, now that Danny is gone. Hilda waddles up to Sparks and puts a hand on his arm. To Sparks's credit, he doesn't flinch. She's giving him the meaningful stare, the very one that captured Maggie years ago, the little witch. And Olly. Hilda was working Olly over yesterday to take her home. It's because Sparks and Olly are the only white people Hilda has seen here since the coup. She assumes they come from her old home, the land of TV, crayons, coloring books, and hot cocoa.
   "What's she saying?"
   "She likes you."
   "That's all? It looked like a whole speech."
   "That's basically it, with variations."
   "She really is special, isn't she?"
   Sparks, cleaned up after a night's sleep, looks none the worse for his fever, or for that matter, for the years that have passed since Maggie last saw him. Removed as she's been in time and space from Sparks, Maggie can see more clearly what attracted people to him. It had something to do with the way he carried his head, his chest. And his voice, of course, which

if anything has acquired more warmth and resonance with maturity. He could be irresistible, Sparks could. Hilda certainly has a crush on him.

Maggie goes in to pour herself a cup of coffee and joins Sparks on the porch. "How are your parents?"

"Great. You know, older, but doing great."

"And Jeanie?" Maggie is pleased that she's able to recall the name of Sparks's older sister. In fact, she remembers all their names.

"Wonderful. She's a grandmother now."

"Who? Not Todd? That little kid in the cowboy hat?"

"That little kid's twenty-six. Still kind of young, but he has a good job down there, doing something with computers . . ."

It doesn't seem possible that these lives, the lives of Sparks's sisters and nephews, whisked by while Maggie was occupied elsewhere. Loulou, Sparks's youngest sister, a teenager when Maggie met her in Lubbock, is married, has three children. Sparks catches Maggie up on all of them, including the children who have come into existence without her knowledge.

"You know what I just remembered? We named our children that week, Christmas week, in Lubbock."

"Oh yeah." Sparks chuckles.

"What were their names? Sarah—Biblical names."

"That's what you wanted. I was arguing for Fuzzy and Gus."

Hilda looks up. She's not used to seeing Maggie laugh with another human being.

"They would be teenagers now."

"Old enough to wreck the family car."

"In Lubbock."

"Lubbock, Texas."

Hilda, sitting on her haunches, is still watching, as if this conversation has something to do with her. Maggie is thinking about standing next to Sparks in the open window of a hotel room overlooking a harbor, sailboats and houseboats moored at the edge, light dancing on the waves. A marching band passed for no reason that she knew; it must have been some Scandinavian holiday. Maggie and Sparks were close enough to almost read the music, but no one noticed them until a young drummer in the back looked up and saw them naked there. His mouth shaped into an O.

"Remember the drummer in Stockholm?"

Sparks laughs. "He kept on marching and his eyes were popping out of his head."

"That was a crazy time. I wonder what I was doing then, or why? Why?"

"Trying to get back to Lubbock?"

" . . . "

Sparks shrugs. "Just an idea. If you don't know, who am I to—"

"No. It sounds true."

Sparks nods and swallows his coffee.

"Anyway, it didn't work," she says.

"No."

20

The plane pops into the sky, leaps off the runway as if the ground is too hot for the wheels. It spirals over D'jar, from this height just a raw red spot rubbed out of the green jungle fur.

Sparks, to his chagrin, giggles. He's still fragile since the fever, might laugh or cry or jump in fright at the smallest thing.

He and Olly worked all day at getting out of D'jarkoume. There were rumors that the airport might be shut down. Documents were examined over and over again. Luggage was inspected. (Lucky thing Sparks ditched his .45. It's already rusting, the dismantled parts of it, along the road to the airport.)

When they reached the Hôtel du Président last night, the big plate glass windows were boarded up. There was no porter, and the bar was closed. This morning there was a guard with a rifle down by the pool.

Olly somehow persuaded a doctor to come to the hotel to look at Sparks's hand. It's healing all right, he said, but it will never be the same. It will be able to do all the ordinary things a left hand does but it will never be as sensitive, as agile. The doctor, a short stocky man with a melodic bass voice, shook his head when he heard that Sparks played guitar. He was a musician himself and had the deepest sympathy.

When Sparks was in his fever, he thought Roy had set it all up, the trip to D'jarkoume, the encounter with the ape, because Roy had always envied him, his looks, his voice, his way with women, and above all, his ability to play. (Roy gave up guitar when he met Sparks, actually gave it up and took to the keyboard, said he couldn't compete.) He thought Roy wasn't satisfied that he had proved he could go on without Sparks, and that Sparks was nothing, an uncredited sideman, without him. Roy had to take Sparks's hand as well, chop it off to destroy the magic and render Sparks powerless.

Now Sparks is sane or nearly. The fever has passed, leaving him with only a temporary emotional looseness, a vulnerability if you will, and Sparks now sees that he made a mistake going to Africa. It was a desperate move, a reckless bid to retrieve the irretrievable.

It's as if the feverish delirium was just a culmination of the deluded state Sparks was in ever since he ran across the letter from Maggie. How could he think that a reference to sparks in a song was a message to him? He had read so much into that fucking song of Roy's that Maggie had to tell him over and over that Roy had never been to D'jarkoume.

"But there's that one town, with the sugar refinery—he seemed to be describing it exactly. I mean, how could he know?" he asked Maggie after dinner when they were around the table talking in the dark.

"Maybe he does know," Maggie said. "That's funny. When Olly told me the name of his album, *Night Journey*, it reminded me of something the people out here believe. They think you can travel at night, leave your body sleeping and actually go somewhere, in spirit. You can say they're primitive people, and that's the way they explain dreams, but even Didier, even the educated ones believe it. So maybe Roy night-walked here. Maybe he does know, not consciously, but somewhere—I don't know—" She stopped. Something stirred in the dark, outside.

Sparks doesn't like to think of Maggie alone with nothing but a BB gun for protection. She's too conspicuous, too obvious a target. It would be easy for either side to take her hostage, to kill her and blame the other side. But Maggie doesn't see it, says she survived the last time.

"Sparks . . ." Olly is standing over him with a blanket. How did she know he was cold? He was shivering, she says.

The bar cart rattles down the aisle. "How about a beer, Sparks?"

He's afraid a beer would bring on his fever again. He feels it still lurking in his body, waiting for him to let his guard down. Olly gets a white wine. He has a Coke.

"Let's toast Maggie," says Olly. She clinks her plastic glass against his. Her eyes are shining. Her skin is glowing, from the sun, or the excitement. Africa was good for Olly. Whatever her own quest was, it worked, at least short-term. She left her special food, her wheat-free pancake mix, her gluten-free crackers unopened in a neat pile for the cleaning staff at the hotel. She ate everything in sight while they were in Africa and never had a rash. She breathed in about a pound of African dust and never sneezed.

Sparks would say something to her about it, but he's afraid it wasn't Africa that cured her, it was him, or sex, and that topic has become taboo between them.

The first night out of Dobo, they went back to the Hôtel Riviera and Sparks immediately fell into a long dreamless sleep, no frogs, no drums. He was out cold before Olly got into bed and she was up washing at the sink by the time he woke.

But in D'jar, in the same room at the Hôtel du Président,

Sparks assumed it would be the same. In fact, he wanted her. Olly's little half-starved breasts aroused him as much as the full and perfect (and sometimes not so perfect) breasts he had watched tanning beside his pool in LA. He wanted to explore the soft parts of Olly again, hidden away beneath the blades of her hipbones.

This time everything was different. He reached across the bed and found, not warm bare skin, but a cotton T-shirt. Still, the breast came to a point, instantly. Olly caught her breath and stiffened. She flinched when he moved toward her abdomen.

"What's the matter?" If it had been anyone else, any other woman, he would have asked that. Sparks does not have trouble talking to women. He's famous for being the kind of man women can talk to, so why didn't he ask Olly? Because he suspected he knew the answer.

Last time they were in the hotel room, they were headed toward adventure. Who knew what they would find, what would become of them? There was a freedom, a letting go of past lives. Now they were going back. It would be easy for Sparks in the few days they had left to enjoy himself with Olly again. The easiest thing in the world. He was even amused by how much he desired it.

But Olly's hesitation, that little catch of breath, the twitch when he reached for her, made him realize what it meant for Olly. He'd asked her how many lovers she'd had since Roy, and she'd told him he was the first. It thrilled him then, as if he'd walked into a room Roy had just left, or had found a door leading back in time. He forgot what it would mean to Olly. He had chosen to ignore the responsibility he was undertaking by becoming Olly's lover.

Olly living in his house, Olly figuring in his life: it was hard to imagine. He couldn't place her there. His was a house that took a woman in, welcomed her, but only for a few days, two weeks max, and then it became apparent that there was no closet for her clothes, no shelf for her cosmetics. It was a spacious house, but there was only room for a solitary man.

He could see Olly in the Bronco, visiting Lubbock. Traveling up to Steamboat to see Eddie and Wanda would be fine, but Olly in his house, part of his daily life, he couldn't see.

So he didn't say anything then. He did not say, "What's the matter?" and they slept chastely through the night. Today a certain formality exists between them, a wall of politeness.

Olly has taken out a book and put on her reading glasses. She feels him looking at her and smiles a brave smile. She's letting him off the hook, the one—who was that girl whose hair matched the cabinets? June—that June didn't want to let him off, the one he's avoided so neatly for so long. He's known for it, and also for having no hooks of his own. He's a good friend and he leaves no marks. They come to him when their marriages break up. They stay and then they leave, healed, ready to go on, if they like, to more hooks.

"Olly, is it OK if I crash over there in the middle section instead of staying up for dinner?"

"Of course."

"You don't mind?"

"No. Get some sleep. You should."

Yolanda has dinner alone, sitting by the window as Africa slips away beneath her. She thinks of Maggie down there trying to negotiate a solitary path through a field where everything is polarizing. She couldn't do anything for Maggie except take some letters back for her.

Yolanda gives her tray to the attendant and makes a bed on the three seats. She sleeps some, dreaming of Sparks, and wakes with such a yearning heart that she's afraid to move for fear it might break. The plane starts jumping around when they cross the Pyrenees. The seatbelt sign lights up. Yolanda prudently buckles hers; Sparks sleeps on. The stewardess wakes him. He sits up, puts the belt on, and immediately falls back to sleep. He used to be afraid to fly. Yolanda wonders if he even remembers.

The morning they left the station, Yolanda was packing her things as well as Sparks's. She came out to see Sparks and Maggie on the porch. Sparks's bandaged arm was slung awkwardly across Maggie's back, his head bowed over hers. When real people kiss it never looks like it does in the movies. Even Sparks and Maggie, who should be able to pull it off with grace if anyone could, looked maladroit, with their arms in the wrong places. Yolanda retreated to the bedroom, closed the door softly, and stood hugging her ribs, staring at the bags open on the cot, afraid to move, afraid Sparks might have seen her watching for what seemed like a scandalously long time, but really it took her that long to figure out what they were doing.

"Your only sin Yolanda is your pride." Mother used to say that to her. When Roy had his affairs with other women, Yolanda would be hurt but she still had her pride because she knew those women didn't count, really. They were interchangeable. Only Yolanda truly belonged in that charmed inner circle. But when she learned about Maggie and Roy, she was powerless. She had to withdraw out of the circle which was no longer a haven. She made a world of her own where she could hide and wait for Roy to come back.

"*Olly Olly in come free.*" Yolanda blushes. She can feel hives coming up on her neck. It's so clear, so obvious. Sparks and Maggie must have known but didn't say for fear of hurting her. The words are transparent. How could she not have seen until now? It's simply Roy's way of saying goodbye, one last time. It should have been enough that he didn't call for years, that he sold back his share of the store. Any one of those signals should have been enough. "*Olly Olly in come free.*" Of course.

The plane is pitching and rolling. If she gets up now to go to the washroom the attendant will stop her and send her back to her seat. Yolanda pulls the blanket over her head. How often has she wept in her adult life? Wept. Occasional tears don't count. Once, not when her mother died, but when the doctor talked to her about how her mother's condition would progress. But the doctor's sympathy sent Yolanda over the edge.

It's that way again. There's no stopping it. It's as if there's a grief train which rumbles along the bottom of every human mind; you forget it's there until something happens and you see its iron engine approaching and you know you are going to get on and ride it down to wherever it takes you. Yolanda is boarding the great smoky train, letting sorrow steam through her, not just her own but everyone's: Maggie's, the girl who walked on her knees with her twisted calves in the air, the child with silky curls who held her hand in the marketplace. Maybe people pass in the aisle and see her blanket shaking, hear the sobbing engine underneath, but no one stops to disturb her ride.

Once you're on the train you can't stop it, you can't get off. You ride until it drops you at last, drawing shaky breaths beside the tracks.

The plane falls into an air pocket and Yolanda laughs out loud at the feeling of all her organs being left in the air as her body plunges. At the jolt, her heart splinters into a thousand shining pieces that race tingling through her veins.

In the dim light of the cabin she can make out the hump of Sparks's shoulder. She moves to the aisle so she can watch the way his hair falls forward, the way his mouth curls in repose. She feels no anger or resentment, none. Only tenderness and, oddly, guilt, as if she's used Sparks for something.

An orange, dislodged no doubt by the turbulence, rolls down the aisle. She reaches out to capture it. Sparks heaves in his sleep. She digs her nail into the orange and peels it, watching his face, memorizing the slant of his cheekbone for later, for when she's an old woman reviewing her life.

21

Mist from the swimming pool mingles with fog rolling in from the ocean. Unusual for it to come this far inland. Sparks watches as it swallows the lights in the valley.

Lupe went home hours ago. She looked in a few times to scold him for not getting dressed but she liked it when he turned on the conga drums, and she did a little shimmy with her shoulders. She wanted to come in to dust, said he hadn't let her in that room for weeks, but there are too many wires. She might trip and knock out the whole rhythm section.

Sparks sheds his pajamas poolside and plunges in. The ritual morning swim—these days he hardly gets it in before midnight. Social life doesn't exist. Calls have dropped precipitously since he turned on the answering machine and forgot to play it back. When he's finished he'll explain to everyone that he's been away. What did Maggie call it? Night-walking, soul-tripping.

He was a social butterfly for about six weeks until his hand healed, out every night, telling his story. No one else, they said, would go to Africa and get tangled up in a revolution, come down with fever (what was it? dengue? paratyphoid?), get into mortal combat with a chimpanzee.

Then he wasn't happy with the story anymore. It had gotten

too smooth. He was losing the parts he was leaving out, like the night in the town with the long name when he heard the frogs and the drums. Even Olly's sharp bones when she arched her pelvis up. He was losing the parts that didn't fit the story they wanted to hear.

So he stopped going out and telling it. He went back to music, put all this equipment in, and began fooling around with it.

Eddie got him started. Wanda gave Sparks Eddie's Macintosh Plus computer and keyboard. Eddie would have wanted him to have it, she said. There wasn't a will, of course, because Eddie didn't intend to die, never imagined that the cocaine was silently ripping up his heart. He died in his sleep, never knew what hit him.

Sparks paid some kids to haul the stuff down from Colorado. When he set it up, he found some floppy disks with Eddie's electric bass on them and some of his own stuff too, things he will never be able to do again.

His guitars are packed away in a closet. The nine keyboards, the computer terminal, and tangle of wires are less picturesque than a Gibson on a stand, but it's the computer that turns him on. The ape did him a favor. It freed his music from the tyranny of his too-clever hands. Now he does drums, piano, flutes, his own guitar, and Eddie's bass. For this piece he has a special effect that sounds like insect wings and night frogs calling.

OK, it's not a number-one album. It will be background music for people who drink wine and sit in hot tubs, but it will be more interesting than most. A sliding African rhythm. Will it play over there?

Richard wants him to send a tape when it's done. Sparks went up to see him when he first came back from Africa, the hand still wrapped in bandages, the mind still back there somehow, as if the fever had weakened his ability to take in new stimuli and he was still processing what had come before.

He wanted to see that idol again. Richard blew the dust off it and handed it to him but Sparks couldn't touch it. Richard said a fever might do that, a fever and a fight with a male chimpanzee.

This time it wasn't raining. It was a clear dry autumn day. Come back with me, Richard said, if you have time, and I'll cook us a steak and you can see that I actually do have a view.

You have a little paradise up here, Sparks told him.

How had he found Maggie? Was she changed? Did she seem rational, in good health? Richard handed Sparks a glass of Chianti. They sat watching the sun go down while the charcoal burned to the proper state for grilling. It was good wine, with some of the abrasiveness you expect in Chianti, but mellow, rich, complex.

"Does she realize what her situation is," Richard asked, "with the alpha-male gone, with the peasants carrying around guns, for Christ's sake? And with that other chimp killed too, the lab chimp, she's going to lose a lot of her support. Maggie was getting heavy contributions from a primate research facility in Maryland. I don't think she knew it, but she was. They wanted her to prove that lab chimps could be rehabilitated. Now with the lab chimp gone and the locals going around shooting—Maggie's got to know that it's over." Richard turned the steak and the flame leaped up. "Or is she too far gone, that's what I wonder."

"Oh no, she's rational, I think. She was upset, of course, with both chimps killed like that . . ." Sparks saw the blood-streaked figure screaming for Emanuel's death, pacing in front of the house hugging the bloody corpse to her breast. He chose not to tell Richard that, nor of her strange smile when he accused her of planning never to leave Hilda.

Richard said he'd been hoping when Maggie saw Sparks she would decide to come back home with him.

"You didn't tell me that when I left," Sparks said.

"No, well, it was a small hope."

Should Sparks have tried harder to get Maggie to leave with them? Maybe he should have said something that morning when he and Maggie were having coffee. Sparks is good at rescuing women. "You saved my life, Sparks." Many have said that to him. But he didn't save Maggie, not in Sweden and not in D'jarkoume.

In their hotel room in Stockholm Maggie sent him a message he chose to ignore. And the kiss, the kiss on her jungle porch, was that a message too? The kiss disturbed him, made his wounded hand pound. He searched her face for signs but her expression was calm. There was none of the expectation he used to read there. For the first time in the history of Sparks and Maggie, he knew there was nothing Maggie wanted from him.

It came to Sparks as he was talking to Richard why he hadn't taken Maggie's hand, as Olly had done, and urged her to come with him.

"You know how she's changed," he said to Richard. "She's got this look to her that's otherworldly, like a nun, or one of those people who get hooked into a religion, any kind of religion in which there's a truth—you know, a way—and anything that falls outside of it doesn't count. They don't consider it."

Richard lifted his glass. The dying sun caught the Chianti and ignited it to a ruby glow. That's what he was afraid of, he said.

On the way back down the coast, Sparks stopped off in Ojai to give Marion back her shoe box of letters, as well as a new one Maggie had dashed off as they were leaving. He found Marion in the back yard, where she'd been sunning herself. She greeted him at the gate, Scotties yapping around her legs. Marion, barefoot and in a bikini, her hair pulled into a ponytail with wisps hanging out, confused Sparks once again. How old was this woman? She kissed him on the cheek and he felt her warm skin against his, smelled her perfume, something sweet and musky he wasn't familiar with although he knew all the popular ones.

Marion sat in the lawn chair and opened Maggie's letter immediately, motioning Sparks to sit by her feet. She laughed at one part. Sparks wondered what Maggie could have chosen to tell her mother that would make her laugh.

"God, I'd give anything to go see her, and those adorable chimpanzees," she said. She put a cigarette to her lips and handed Sparks her lighter.

"She's devoted to them." Sparks lit her cigarette.

For the first time, Marion noticed Sparks's hand. He had to tell her the story, how the chimp had attacked, how he'd been forced to kill it.

"She didn't say anything about it in the letter . . ."

"I guess she wasn't ready to write about it."

A crease came into the center of Marion's forehead. "She doesn't . . . she doesn't tell me anything, Sparks. You know that. She's always been that way. Secrets." She squinted, drew on her cigarette. "I was kind of hoping she'd come back with you." Another one who had wanted Sparks to rescue Maggie but hadn't told him. Maybe if they expected him to do it they should have given him instructions on how to go about it.

"We tried. But she's committed, you know, to those chimpanzees. She can't see any other way to do it but stay there with them."

Marion flicked her ashes on the ground. "She's an idealist. I used to say to her, 'Honey, God didn't make the world to be perfect.' But she could never accept it. I was never perfect enough for her, I know that." She took a drag. "You know, I was hurt when she left, when years passed and she never came back. I felt like she was punishing me, you know, for not being—" She waved her cigarette in the air. "But now I think I understand what she's doing. She's trying to go back to the beginning. She's trying to go back to Eden, before Eden, and create her own perfect world." She formed a circle with her hands and the one with the cigarette in it left a shaky blue arc that hovered between them in the still air of late afternoon.

Marion seemed to want him to leave before Jack came home. Sparks didn't stop for dinner, but bought a couple of candy bars at a gas station. The sun was going down. There was a phone booth off to one side and Sparks had the idea to call Olly, which he hadn't done since he'd gotten back from Africa, not even when he heard about Eddie.

Their parting at the airport had been awkward. Sparks had originally booked on the same flight as Olly, going through New York and then connecting to a flight to LA. He was able to change it for a plane direct from Paris to Los Angeles. Olly agreed it made sense. Olly's connection was a little tight so there wasn't time to linger over goodbyes. As she was in line to board, Sparks reached for her tentatively, maybe to kiss her on the cheek. The wall of politeness crumbled and they were locked, mouths, hearts, groins together, and then she was running through the door and he was left standing in front of the flight desk, the object of curious but sympathetic stares. He almost felt he should run after her, as if that was what they expected him to do.

"Hi, Olly. How's it going?" The booth smelled of gasoline. There were oily rainbows in a puddle nearby.

He smiled to hear her voice. They talked about his hand and he held it up as if she could see how it was healing. He told her about Marion and the Scotties, and what Richard had said. As they talked twilight turned to dusk. The lights came up. The puddle went from opalescent to lacquered black, like the Bronco standing beside it. "I should have taken you up there with me to see Richard," Sparks found himself saying. "As the epilogue to our trip."

There was a pause and then Olly said there was a new number she should give him, in case he wanted to call. She was moving.

Oh, where? To a bigger place?

Yes, it was actually the home of a friend of hers, a friend she'd had for a while, but since the trip to Africa, the friendship had developed into something different and . . .

She put it so delicately that it took a while for it to sink in.

"You give up too easy, Olly." He put the phone back in the cradle and leaned against the glass booth, feeling stupid because he was angry with Olly, not only because she'd let him go, no hooks, but because she'd let Roy go too, as if she'd once had the power to keep all of them together. Maybe she had.

The speed of his stroke picks up. He beats out a couple of more laps, thinking of nothing in particular. When this tape is finished he'll probably take it to New York and he can see Olly and this guy she's living with and it will be fine. He's happy for her and he's glad he helped her. Olly says he did. She says he and Africa changed her life.

Sparks leaps from the pool, landing on both feet. He worked to get this trick back after the fever. He leaves puddles on the dusty floor when he goes to play the stuff he did today. He turns it up loud, gets a beer, and sinks into the Jacuzzi, jets off so he can hear the music.

"Do you want to go back?" they always asked, after he'd told his story. Not in the immediate future, he would say, in fact, he wouldn't recommend a trip to anyone just now. Christ, they nearly shut down the airport when he was there. "But in a way I can always go back," he said once. "It's like it's in my bones, or maybe it always was and I had to go there to find it." That went over well. He never said how real Africa wasn't at all like he'd thought, that he could not comprehend it, only enough pieces of it to know it was beyond his understanding.

He and Olly went there on a search, questing after a chi-
mera, Roy, who had never gone there and never would. Yet
they accomplished something on a small scale, the personal
scale. So maybe—this idea just comes to him; he might suggest
it to Olly sometime—maybe they went there not to find Roy
but to lose him. And maybe this is what they accomplished.

Sparks lifts his beer in his scarred hand to drink a toast to
Roy. Here is where the frogs and drums come in.

22

SEPTEMBER
VOLUME VII, NO. 8

FRIENDS OF HILDA

First, an apology. The last time you heard from me (if indeed you received the letter) we were waiting to see if Hilda was pregnant. Now, in her second month, she is really beginning to show, has a distinct waddle to her walk and eats all the time. Unfortunately she is also clumsier than ever. After years of trying to force her to climb trees I find myself urging her to keep out of them. I wish I could send you a photo of our blooming mother-to-be but we are completely out of film and don't expect to have any in the near future. If things go well we'll have film in time to take our baby pictures in June.

G.P. and Danny died last month within days of each other. They were shot and

killed. Mercifully neither suffered. G.P.'s
death was accidental. A visitor was walking in
the forest near the station. G.P. attacked and
the visitor was forced to defend himself. At
the time I was a day's walk from the station
and had no idea that unauthorized visitors
had arrived. He was a friend who had come
with good intentions, but I must emphasize
that we cannot accommodate visitors
here at the station. This is a place in which
humans do not belong. They can only do us
harm.

Danny was accidentally shot by a local the
next day.

Even after a month, we can't get used to
them not being with us. I keep seeing G.P.'s
stocky form in the shadows, or Danny
scuttling across the clearing, and when I look
it's just the play of light on a dust devil. Our
group is so much duller without them. We're
missing our highs, our lows.

Now without males, except for little Biff,
we've had to give up our dream of becoming
a self-sufficient band of chimpanzees. We
have gone back to the original plan of
integrating our group with the wild
chimpanzees in the area. Because I don't
want to risk Hilda's unborn child in this
enterprise, which could turn violent, we will
wait until the baby is born and both mother
and child are strong and active.

You may be aware of political problems
here that are preventing me from getting
messages out. I hope that this letter at least

makes it through, because I would like to
thank all of you Friends of Hilda for your
generous donations and more than that, for
your faith and encouragement over the years.
Without your help Hilda might now be sitting
in a cage in a laboratory instead of walking
free through the forest. In many ways Project
Hilda has not gone as planned. There have
been disappointments, tragedies. But at least
we have accomplished this, you and I: we
have taken chimpanzees who were wronged
by men, stolen from their natural
environments for the purpose of research or
entertainment, and we have restored them, if
only briefly, to what was theirs by right.

If for any reason we disappear, I urge you
to keep on being on the side of chimpanzees.
We are their closest relative and their greatest
enemy. Only we can save them. And please
know, that whatever happens from here on in
to Hilda, Katie, Biff, Poppy, the new baby,
and to me, it has been worth it. Project Hilda
is a success.

With warmest regards,
Maggie Russell

Yolanda looks at the date. Nearly a year ago. It's odd, coming
now, with no explanation. It was mailed from that place in
Oregon, the anthropologist or whoever he is, whom Sparks
knows.

A month ago there were articles about D'jarkoume in the
New York Times, the first Yolanda ever remembers reading
about it in the newspaper, although it must have been in before

and she never noticed, probably because D'jarkoume didn't have significance for her then. This was a front page story about how peasants in the west, Maggie's area, attacked some Moro officials and how the army took it out on the villagers, killing at random. Yolanda called Sparks, who called Richard. No one had heard from Maggie since Sparks and Yolanda visited her. Had anyone tried to reach her? Not very hard, apparently.

Gordon takes the lamb out of the oven. "What's that," he asks, pointing with his chin to the letter in Yolanda's hand. Yolanda tells him but she knows he's concerned not for Maggie but for Yolanda. He worries over anything that enters her, whether it's food and drink or information, worries that it will affect the baby.

Yolanda places her hand on the slight rise of her belly. Maggie's chimpanzee's baby would be born by now, if the chimpanzee survived, if Maggie did. It's disturbing to think Yolanda and Sparks were the last of Maggie's friends to see her. They should have brought Maggie home with them, should have insisted.

"Sit down," Gordon says. "I have everything ready. Go sit at the table."

In the dining room the table is set. Candles are lit and the light reflects in the glass of Mother's breakfront. Yolanda had much of the furniture moved down from Geneva after she and Gordon were married. Her brothers' wives were glad to get rid of it and it looks even better here than it did at home.

"Gordon, is this some special day I've forgotten? What's the occasion?"

He sets the leg of lamb in front of her to carve. He's hopeless at carving. "Don't you remember? One year ago today you came back from Africa."

One year ago today. It isn't possible that only a year ago the cab dropped her off in front of her house and she lugged her bags upstairs to an apartment that no longer felt like hers. Her bags, still red and dusty from the roads of D'jarkoume, sat in the middle of the floor exuding a sweet sad rot smell. She showered and changed to fresh clothes, left her bags stewing in their own exhalations, and walked to the store.

Dorothy was elegantly attired in a plaid dress with white collar, although the theme, *Back to School*, wouldn't win any awards for originality. Yolanda smiled to see *Mombatu* prominently displayed in the foreground.

Inside, the air-conditioned store seemed bustling, clean, and rich. How wealthy we all are, Yolanda thought, standing in the middle of a store that she knew was hers but in which she didn't quite belong. Someone said, "She's back!" and she found herself surrounded, everyone talking to her, everyone reaching for her as if to bring her home, to help her complete the final steps of her journey. And then Gordon came through and hugged her to him so that her nose jammed against his neck. He smelled of soap.

Yolanda puts her left hand beside her plate so she can see the wedding band on her finger. She finds she doesn't think of any of them anymore, Roy, Sparks, Maggie. They are all so extraordinary, in what they've chosen to do, in the ways their lives have gone, and she is ordinary. Completely. The way she sees it now, she was headed for this ordinary life when she was seduced into a different world. Yes, charmed away, dazzled, and it took her all this time to find her way back to this blessed and ordinary life.

Yolanda stops herself, feeling guilty for gloating over all she has when Maggie is possibly in mortal danger, suffering, in pain.

She takes the letter out of her pocket and reads it again. It sounds like a valedictory. Of course, if Maggie were in danger she wouldn't be able to tell about it. It wouldn't have gone through the censors. Only someone who had been there would know the hidden message in the simple statement that she's run out of film. Yolanda remembers there was plenty of film in the supplies they took her. It must have been confiscated, by the army, or the rebels.

Yolanda stares at the candle flame, thinking she can conjure up the image of Maggie. She sees Maggie the way she was on the morning they left her, standing in the clearing with her chimpanzees. The big one, Hilda, ran after the truck. She was signaling furiously with her hands. What message did she have for them?

Yolanda feels something finlike flutter inside her.

"Gordon! Gordon, come here! I think I felt it!"

Gordon rushes in, wiping his hands on his shorts. He bends over her.

"No, not there, here. Do you feel it?"

"Wait! Maybe. Yes. Yes!"

The candles sputter unwatched, throwing their shadows against the wall.

Maggie takes the BB gun and very carefully pokes the barrel up against the tarp that she's strung up over the hammock. Water spills over the side. The baby is still sleeping, nestled against her breast. Once he's up and moving, he could jiggle the ropes and send all the water that accumulated overnight crashing down on top of them.

It is light enough now so that Maggie can distinguish his pink face, his fine black hair. She even sees his eyeballs moving under his lids, dreaming. His lips begin to twitch. He'll be awake, looking for his bottle soon. Luckily Maggie was able to get away with plenty of powdered baby formula, which she keeps locked in the metal chest, hidden among the roots of her pygmy tree. Even so, G.P. Jr. is going to have to learn how to eat solid foods much sooner than he would if he were truly a natural-born chimp.

If Maggie had still been writing to the Friends of Hilda, and if she had still been in contact with Anita and Richard, she would have been upset with Hilda when she rejected her newborn infant. But now Maggie is freed from the judgment of people who aren't here and therefore can't understand. Hilda was taken from her mother when she was an infant. She has no recollection of how a chimpanzee mother acts. Naturally, she was horrified by the tiny thing that clung to her chest and wanted to suckle. She tried to bite it and tear it off her body.

Maggie had anticipated Hilda's reaction and had some formula and bottles ready, just in case. The baby's thriving with Maggie as his mother, and he plays with Katie and the little ones during the day, so he knows he's a chimp.

In a way it's to their advantage that Hilda chose not to nurse her baby, because she's come into estrus. With a baby at her breast, it could have taken her four years before she had her red swelling again.

They've done well, Maggie and her chimps, better than she hoped the day she watched Olly and Sparks go off in Mfui's truck. The peace between her and Emanuel lasted longer than she expected. The rebels left her alone long enough for her to drag all her chests into the forest, to hide away a good store of supplies, medicine, and food, and to set up barrels in various places for collecting rainwater. The rebels didn't take over the station until after G.P. Jr. was born. By then, Maggie was already living part time in the forest.

She moved west with her band, careful to keep out of the way of Richard's chimps. For the past several weeks there have been helicopters flying low overhead. She's heard guns from time to time, but she's managed to keep out of sight.

This is the closest they've ventured to the station in a month. Maggie had to come back for more formula and rice for herself. The forest food was giving her diarrhea again, making her so weak she could hardly walk, but she's feeling better after some rice, some tea.

Two days ago, Maggie left the others feeding on figs and, taking only the baby with her, went back to the station.

"This is where your father died," she whispered when they passed the place. He looked up at her with round close-set eyes as if he understood. She smoothed his hair back from his bony forehead. He looks just like G.P., seems to have inherited hardly anything from Hilda, although his fingers and toes are like hers.

Maggie stood well back among the trees, in a place she knew where she could observe the station and not be seen. She needn't have bothered. No one could see or hear her now.

She thought she recognized Emanuel but she couldn't be sure. She began to go to them, thinking she might be able to help, but the sight of the first one, the smell, was enough to tell her that it happened too long ago to be able to save anyone now.

They did a thorough job, burned her house, Emanuel's too. She turned away, shielding the baby from the sight, gagging on the smell. She can still taste it somewhere back in her throat.

Bright eyes upon her. She jumps up, swings out of the hammock. He'll tear her to pieces if she doesn't get his bottle immediately. The others are calling to her from their nests. They'll be climbing down, hoping for a handout.

Here's Hilda, coming for a hug. Her bright red bottom is shamelessly sending off signals: "Female in heat. Come and get it." Richard's chimps are nearby. Maggie heard them drumming yesterday.

Maggie finds some dry kindling that she had saved in the shelter of the pygmy tree and makes her morning fire for tea and rice. After breakfast they go back to the spot where they found more figs yesterday.

Maggie, who's abstaining from figs just now, sits on a log and lets the baby dangle from her foot, climb her leg. She tickles his round milk belly and finally rocks him to sleep in the crook of her arm.

She thinks of Emanuel and the others, their bloated bodies on the red earth. Were these deaths because of Roy, his song? Or was it inevitable that sometime— Cause and effect. When is it actual and when is it a trick we play with our minds because we need to connect things?

Sparks and Olly would never have come if Sparks hadn't seen Maggie's "Friends of Hilda" letter. These letters were messages that Maggie sent out, messages that said she was here, that gave her a location on this earth, that other people could read and respond to. Even if Maggie didn't intend to, she sent a signal to Olly and Sparks and they came. To save her? They did save her from Emanuel and the rebels, although she might have been able to pull that off on her own. And they killed G.P. Maggie no longer sends messages to humans.

She lays the sleeping infant in the hammock, out of the way of whatever might ensue. Because it will happen today, she feels. The thing she isn't certain of is whether or not Hilda will be able to do what must be done. She wishes she could protect Hilda, that there was a way of living in harmony with the wild chimps without mating with them. But for chimps, one is either friend or mortal enemy. There is no neutrality.

Maggie strokes Hilda's head. She takes out pieces of leaves, sticks, a flea which she crushes between her thumb and forefinger. This is Hilda's graduation day, the day she learns that she is a chimpanzee. It will go unreported to the Friends of Hilda because it's not being done for the approval of human friends. It is being done out of necessity.

Hilda looks at Maggie with those preternaturally intelligent eyes that seem to understand. Or is it merely the effect of her triangular forehead? Can Hilda comprehend how everything has changed? Does she know that before Maggie was powerful because she had many allies—allies Hilda never saw—and that now Maggie is alone and a lone human is a fragile thing?

If Maggie can live just long enough to see Hilda make the bridge between her own group and the wild chimps, she will have accomplished her life goal. How many can say they've fulfilled their purpose in life, even those who die in their beds at ninety?

A tear slides down Maggie's nose. She catches it with her tongue. "Poor Hilda. We raised you to be a human and then came with the bad news that you were a chimp, didn't we girl?"

Hilda grunts and moves so that Maggie can get the other side of her.

Hilda fell in love with Sparks. When he left in Mfui's truck she ran after him, signing: "I love you Sparks. Fire man. Save me. Take me home."

The hair on the back of Hilda's neck rises. She sits up, then stands, staring. Maggie moves back and crouches behind a fallen tree. It takes her a while to see what Hilda has seen, the figure approaching through the trees. Hilda is watchful but calm. Does she see, does she finally understand that this is the shape of her lover, her ally? He doesn't look like Sparks or Emanuel or Didier. He walks on all fours and takes the forest floor with grace despite his slight limp. When he stops he blends with the shadows until one could almost think he isn't there and that it doesn't have to happen today after all, but then he moves again, approaching until he is standing in the clearing. He has a mangled ear. Boris.

A NOTE ON THE TYPE

The text of this book was set in a typeface called Times Roman, designed by Stanley Morison (1889–1967) for *The Times* (London) and first introduced by that newspaper in 1932.

Among typographers and designers of the twentieth century, Stanley Morison was a strong forming influence—as a typographical advisor to The Monotype Corporation, as a director of two distinguished English publishing houses, and as a writer of sensibility, erudition, and keen practical sense.

Composed by PennSet Inc., Bloomsburg, Pennsylvania

Printed and bound by The Haddon Craftsmen, Inc., Scranton, Pennsylvania

Designed by Valarie Jean Astor